UNDELIVERABLE

UNDELIVERABLE

Rebecca Demarest

WRITERLY BLISS
Boston

For my mother
and my father
who made it possible
for me to get this far.

For Mili;
Thanks for your support,
You are the best!
Hugs,

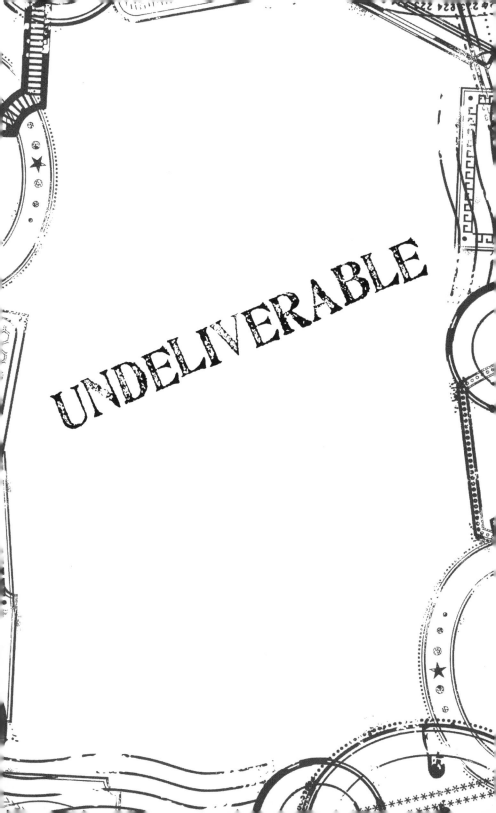

UNDELIVERABLE

CONTENTS

A BRIEF HISTORY OF THE MAIL RECOVERY CENTER

For over 100 years, this office was called the Lost Letters Office, but then some bureaucrat got this idea in their heads about needing to be more professional and we became the Mail Recovery Center. More hopeful sounding, I suppose. But for all their marketing and planning, we are what we are. A repository for the lost.

~ *Gertrude Biun,* Property Office Manual

Benny was their miracle child. Jeannie and Ben had given up trying to conceive; no form of hormone regimens, temperature taking, or cycle tracking had done any good. They didn't have the money for in vitro fertilization, so that wasn't an option. He was sure she was over stressing herself trying to keep up with all her social obligations while running the antique store, but she insisted it was the chemicals he was using in his refurbishment workshop. The blame game got so bad that they agreed to stop trying.

And then, Jeannie missed her period.

"It might just be late," she warned him. It had been late before with all the hormone treatments she had tried. So Ben bought three different kinds of home pregnancy tests, insisting she try all of them before he gathered her into his arms, hollering and spinning. She was pregnant.

In the evenings, while Ben rubbed her swollen feet, they made lists of things they wanted to make sure to do with their son. The Grand Canyon was a must, so they could show him where they had gotten lost on the trail and Ben had first jokingly proposed that they get married, just in case they were never found. Then there was the boardwalk arcade where he had proposed in earnest, pretending to buy the engagement ring with tickets won at skee-ball.

Of course, they didn't always agree on what was appropriate. Ben wanted their son to see Star Wars and Indiana Jones as soon as he was old enough to talk. Jeannie insisted it would give him nightmares. She wanted him to play the "safe" sports like soccer or baseball while Ben proposed football and rugby. Every time they started arguing, Jeannie would defer to one of her new gurus of child developmental learning, and Ben would agree to put off the conversation until it was relevant.

They baby-proofed the house and workshop and talked about getting a dog because shouldn't every young boy have a dog? Ben started planning sex talks and how to teach his son to pee standing up. His father had just said, "What are you a pansy? Only pansies pee sitting down!" which had been startlingly effective, if slightly traumatizing.

Ben worried over reviews for baby formula and diapers. He hunted for alternative chemicals to use in his workshop that wouldn't be quite so dangerous if, God forbid, they were ingested. He lay awake at night, listening to Jeannie shift uncomfortably in her sleep and worried that his son wouldn't like him, or that he wouldn't understand his son.

Ben was determined to be as prepared as possible to keep his son safe. He was ready for the various ways a child's development could get knocked off track. There was padding on the corners of all the hardwood furniture and white locks on all the cabinets. He thought he was ready to bring his son home from the hospital.

Nobody warned him that he should prepare for the day when his son would disappear.

THE PROPERTY ROOM

This is the last stop for a lost package. Once it's made it to us in the Property Room, there's almost no hope of finding its original owners again, and it just waits to be sold off. But every once in awhile, the readers miss something, and we get to make someone very happy. Though, if they'd packaged it correctly in the first place, it wouldn't be here, now would it?

~ *Gertrude Biun,* Property Office Manual

Ben wandered through the maze of industrial shelving deep in the heart of the United States Postal Service's Mail Recovery Center. Wiping one finger through the dust that coated a shelf of miniatures, porcelain dogs, and Santas, he studied a line of whimsical women of varying ages holding numbers. He picked up number eleven, noting the paper tag attached with a bit of twine.

06-11-21-62 Posted from Boise, Idaho.

A female voice broke through his study. "I always thought those figurines were a crime. My grandmother tried to convince me they were appropriate presents for a young woman. I wanted a BB gun."

Ben set down the figurine too quickly, and it almost toppled before he caught it. The real woman standing at the front of the alcove leaned against a cart filled with gray plastic trays. She was fingering the pile of lace that lay in the top tray, but dropped it and pushed back the over-sized pageboy cap perched on her short strawberry-blonde braids in order to look at him. He felt like he was being weighed and measured by a pixie playing dress up, and he tried to stand up just a little straighter. People constantly commented on how his slouching would cause back problems. He maintained he would stand up to his full height when they stopped making doorways and desks so low.

"Sylvia," she said, and stuck out her hand. "Really, it's Chrissy Sylvia. My grandmother still insists on calling me Chrissy, but my mother wanted to name me Sylvia and it's what I go by."

Her brisk delivery reminded him of his estranged wife—thoughts he shoved away. He blinked a couple of times then gingerly took the slim hand offered him. "Benjamin. Grant. New Property Clerk. Call me Ben." Her grip was warm and surprisingly strong for such a slight girl. Ben dropped her hand a little too quickly and waved at the large warehouse behind him. "I think you're the one they said could help me figure out how all this works."

She was not what he had been expecting based on the description he had been given. The HR rep who had told him to look to Sylvia for help during his first week had said something about a unique personality and he had expected...well, not this. Someone older and less attractive, for sure; not the perky co-ed he was presented with. "Am I supposed to know what to do with all that stuff already? They really didn't tell me much yesterday other than, 'Start tomorrow.'"

"No, that's what I'm here for—part of my job is helping you do yours: keeping track of all the lost bits in the mail and eventually selling them off. And you're thinking, 'If she already knows how to do all this, why do they need me?' Well, I didn't want your job. I aspire to the lofty title of reader, just like my great-great-something grandmother Patti Lyle Collins." She struck a triumphant vaudevillian pose before pouting. "But for now, it's shredding and sorting because they think I don't have the proper restraint for the job." She hopped on the back of the cart, riding it up the warehouse to the bay with 2012 on the front shelf. "Enough kibitzing. Let me show you how to shelve this stuff."

Ben couldn't help but smile at her antics and he was surprised at the realization that he was glad for his new assistant's energy. The last time he had been moved to amusement was the day before Benny's disappearance, when his son had shown him a trick he had learned at school: balancing a spoon by its bowl on his nose. The spoon had stayed for a split second then dropped into Benny's cereal bowl, sending milk and Lucky Charms everywhere. He had laughed until Jeannie came in to see what all the noise was about and then scolded them for making such a mess. The next day he was gone. Ben sobered at the thought of that day and tried to shake it from his mind. He didn't spend enough time thinking about the happy days. Probably because he hadn't had any for the last year.

Shoving his hands in his pockets, he followed the clattering of the trays and found Sylvia thumbing through a book. "I wonder if this is Cyrillic." Without waiting for him to comment, she shrugged and slipped it onto a shelf labeled Foreign Books.

Ben kept his hands in his pockets and bent over the cart to examine the lace Sylvia had been playing with. "Doesn't all of that have to be entered into the computer first?"

"Done and done. Did it this morning. You weren't around yet, and I didn't have all that much shredding to do. So instead of being roped into a Starbucks run for the readers, I told them I had to do entry. Kept them from doing it, so they didn't complain." She picked up the lace and shook it out, revealing a teddy, which she smoothed against her slight figure. Ben felt his ears turning red as he shoved away other, more lustful, thoughts. "Oh, seriously, Ben. It's just a nightgown." She stepped over to a chest of drawers, pulled open the top drawer, and shoved the cloth in.

Ben turned back to the cart to hide his discomfort. He doubted that nightgowns usually had peek-a-boo holes over the nipples. To distract himself, he cleared his throat. "I still can't believe that people lose all this stuff every year." He picked up the now-empty tray and moved it to the bottom shelf of the cart. The next held a dog collar and leash.

"I know! Did you know that in 1899 they had six million pieces of mail go through this office? Eighteen ninety-nine! Do you know how much goes through now? Billions…" She snatched up the doggy accessories and tossed them into a basket. Flipping the trailing lead up to the shelf, she turned to the cart. "There's money in them, the mail that can't be delivered that is. It's part of how our salary gets paid. The other part is auctioning off these treasures." She paused to pet a stuffed penguin on the shelf. "Keeps the price of your stamps down, too."

"But the price of stamps keeps going up." He handed her the next tray, this one with a spiky broach in a violent green.

"Yeah, well, look at some of the crap we're trying to auction." She wrinkled her nose as she set the broach in a velvet-lined drawer of a four-foot-tall jewelry cabinet. "I sure as hell wouldn't pay money for that thing; I don't know who would."

"Plenty of collectors would like it. It was made in the twenties, maybe thirties." It had been an instinctual assessment, and Ben extended his hand to retrieve the empty tray, but Sylvia was examining the broach.

"How do you know?" She glanced up, saw his outstretched hand, and tossed him the tray.

Inwardly, Ben groaned. There were some things he didn't want to talk about, and the ten years spent at Jeannie's side learning how to accurately identify antiques in her family antique store was one of them. "I...well. Alright. The soldering. It's still a lead solder on the clasp, and that's lead-based paint, plus the design is reminiscent of the flapper era. Twenties."

She blew him a half-hearted raspberry while she poked at the clasp. "Fine, Mr. Literal. *Why* do you know that?"

Ben hesitated, but he knew he'd have to answer these questions sooner or later. He hoped if he gave her noncommittal answers, she wouldn't dig too deep since he didn't feel like sharing certain details with a stranger, particularly one he was going to have to work with every day. "Tremont and Sons." When her mouth opened to ask another question, he added, "I worked at an antique shop for ten years."

"Ah." Sylvia tilted her head to the side, curiosity piqued, and then decided to move on from the topic. "It still looks like a firefly on acid," she decided and closed the drawer.

"On that point we agree." Relieved, Ben handed over the next tray with a copy of *Catcher in the Rye*. "English shelf?"

"Naw." She gestured to the shelves below the foreign books, and he noticed different signs for Fiction, Nonfiction, and Rubbish.

"Rubbish?"

"Mrs. Bunion, the last property clerk. She didn't like anything that wasn't 'real.' Fantasy, science fiction, all of it went onto this shelf. Just meant we had to sort it out later for the auction." Sylvia slid the book into a spot between a tattered Jane Austen and an unread copy of *100 Years of Solitude*.

Ben was slightly peeved, since he rather enjoyed the speculative genres, but he was willing to let it go in pursuit of the more interesting name. "Mrs. Bunion?"

"Mrs. Biun really, but she was such an old cranky lady and she was always complaining. Thus, Mrs. Bunion." The empty tray landed back in the cart with a clatter. Ben quirked an eyebrow at her back and wondered what nickname he was going to end up with, before deciding he didn't really care. His only goal was to keep this job as long as it was useful, as long as it didn't get in the way of his search.

Ben pulled the empty trays off the bottom rack of the cart and dropped them onto the empty top shelf. "That can't have been all the items for today, right?"

"Nope, that's just one reader. There are nine other readers, nine other carts, and this cart was really empty today." Sylvia grinned at the faint frown on Ben's face. "C'mon, let's go see what else the readers have for us in the bullpen."

Sylvia maneuvered the cart out of the warehouse and across the industrial hall toward the bullpen. Here, the readers opened, scanned, and directed the inadequately addressed mail. The long, low room buzzed with the ripping of envelopes, the murmur of consultation, and the tick-tack of keyboards. Occasionally the sound of a box opener tearing through tape rent the background hum. As readers finished processing one bin of mail, they got up from their desks and retrieved another of the opaque plastic bins from the next room.

The sorting didn't pause when they came in, and Sylvia approached one of the desks, trading her empty cart for the full one at its side. Then, instead of returning directly to the property storage warehouse, Ben followed Sylvia as she slipped out a door on the opposite side of the bullpen and entered an enormous garage lined with twelve bay doors, two of which were open. At one a truck was unloading sacks of mail, the burly postman simply heaving them into waiting laundry-type carts. At another, a truck was being loaded up with a much smaller load of sorted and re-labeled mail.

"I thought you might like to see the sorting process in action. We have twenty sorters working eight-hour shifts a day in here." Sylvia parked her cart at one long table covered with mail and hopped up to sit on an uncluttered portion, her gray Converse dangling. "These guys figure out what's what with all the mail that comes in. Returnable mail goes on the west wall; forwardable mail goes into the bins on the east wall. Mystery mail that might make it to the right people with a bit of detecting goes on the north wall to wait for the readers' attention. Items found in boxes or loose in the bottom of mail sacks go in gray trays and then get taken into the reader room. And lastly, mail that has no chance of ever reaching the recipient or being returned to the sender goes in those boxes next to the shredder. That includes everything for fictitious figures such as Santa, Jesus, God, Satan, The Perfect Man, The Easter Bunny…"

She trailed off and started flicking through the stack of mail the sorter next to her had accumulated and received a smack on her hand from the swarthy woman. "Sylvia, you leave off. You should know better. Now stop playing at tour guide and git."

Ben took note of how the woman dealt with his chatty assistant. No-nonsense and forthright, even if it didn't seem to dampen Sylvia one bit. He was about to suggest that they go back to their warehouse and leave the nice woman alone, but before he could say something to that effect, Sylvia slipped one of the letters under the tailored vest she was wearing. Ben wondered if he should draw attention to what was probably a blatant violation of the Center's rules, and most likely a few laws, but decided he should wait to see just how many rules he was going to want to bend himself before creating an image of the hard-ass for himself.

"Of course, Marta. I was only curious." Sylvia scowled, then hopped off the table and reclaimed her cart, all while ignoring Ben's pointedly raised eyebrow. "Let's go get these onto the shelves."

They made their way back into the warehouse and Ben was struck by the drastic change from the hectic environment of the bullpen to the calm, quiet dark of the shelves. It was the warehouse that had made him decide to take the job regardless of how much it might contribute to his search. It was the smell of it—musty paper and dust. It brought back his days as a Library Science major at Concord University, where he had met Jeannie, and they had stolen moments in the stacks away from their classmates and professors. He knew they weren't the only students who had used the mostly empty archives for a rendezvous, but it felt delightfully illicit and had added a layer of excitement to their romance. That was before a life of antiques and restorations and fights. Before Benny.

Though, if he was being honest with himself, the warehouse wasn't the only reason he had taken the job. The property clerk position would give him access to advanced search systems that browsed a wide variety of files—everything from mail forwarding requests to DMV and police records—all information that he could use while he continued his search for his son on his own. And so he had said yes, he would accept the position as Property Clerk at the Atlanta facility.

A white and blue binder was waiting on Ben's desk when they got there, square to the front corner. He flipped it open, idly wondering who had dropped it off. It was titled: *A Manual for the Property Room of the United States Postal Service's Mail Recovery Center by Mrs. Biun.* It was massive, indicating that Mrs. Biun had spent more time putting it together than he—or anyone else, for that matter—would bother to spend reading it.

He called out over his shoulder to Sylvia. "Hey, any idea where this came from?"

"Not really, but I'm sure one of the office ladies dropped it by. That's the tome that Bunion wrote, isn't it?"

Ben wrinkled his nose. "If you mean manual, yes. It seems quite extensive."

Sylvia snorted. "You mean excessive."

Even though he was in agreement, he still felt he should stand up for the absent woman. "Come on now, it can't be that bad. If I have questions, did she leave any contact information?"

"No, she moved to a tropical island somewhere." Sylvia pushed the cart into the warehouse and Ben followed, sure he hadn't heard right. He had done the math before accepting the job and there was no way anyone could manage to retire to an island on the provided salary.

"How on earth did she afford that?" They stopped at the shelves and started to sort through the newest pile of offerings.

"I'm pretty sure she was fencing things for the mob." Sylvia made a shushing motion and winked at him before turning back to the cart.

Ben picked up a hunting knife by the tip, examining the hilt, which appeared to be a skull carved out of bone. There was just no accounting for some people's taste. "I didn't know Atlanta had a mob." He placed the knife carefully on a shelf that held contraband such as smoke bombs and fireworks.

"No, the knives go in that drawer over there." The tool chest had labels marking the drawers: tools, knives, kitchenware, and office supplies. "Of course Atlanta has the mob. Every city has the mob." Sylvia leaned on the cart handle and stared at him through wide eyes. "Aren't you even the least bit curious how she did it?"

No, no he wasn't. But he could tell she wasn't going to drop the subject unless he humored her, so he decided to guess. "Fencing the items? I'd expect through the auction." Opening the drawer, he placed the skull knife next to several pocket-knives and a machete.

"Well, duh. But I spent a lot of time thinking about it, and I know exactly how she could have done it. Particularly since she was in charge of the warehouse. She could have all this mob stuff just sitting here, waiting to go to auction till the heat dies down, and then, bam! Auction it off under the table." Sylvia dropped the empty trays back in the cart with satisfaction.

Ben couldn't help trying to poke holes in her logic. "I thought the accountants came in to do the registers for the auction. Wouldn't it be hard to sneak in unaccounted items and get back the money for them?" Ben took the cart this time, leaving Sylvia frowning behind him.

"You're ruining the story, Ben. Sometimes you just have to suspend your disbelief. Anyway, that's how she retired to France."

"I thought you said she retired to an island."

"Yeah, it was somewhere off of France." Ben laughed and she scowled at him, but she couldn't keep it up and shrugged. "Regardless, she didn't leave a number or address." Sylvia slid between him and the cart, jumping on the back and riding it down the hall. "You go open that manual of yours. I'll just go get the next cart."

Ben rolled his eyes as she sailed down the warehouse and returned to his corner where Mrs. Biun's instructions were waiting. Surely the staid mind that had produced such a manual wasn't going to participate in illegal auctions and then retire to some mysterious island off of France. He was pretty sure she was furiously pulling weeds out of the walkway of her little retirement-community bungalow in Florida.

The binder was one of those two-inch affairs with enough paper stuffed in its rings to make it a neat block, the whole of the 300-odd pages handwritten. A neat, trim hand had taken its time accumulating knowledge about the warehouse behind him, the handwriting exactly like his fifth grade teacher's. He imagined they even looked alike: tight buns of white hair gathered at the napes of their necks, wearing cardigans and long skirts.

After a quick flip through the densely written pages, Ben decided that delaying just a little bit longer wouldn't hurt anyone. Instead, he decided to go out to his car and grab the box of office supplies he had brought with him.

He almost got lost coming back in as he tried to navigate the warren of offices. After a few false turns, he made it back to his "office," which consisted of a double-wide cubicle set off from the general warehouse by carpeted partitions. He dropped his box on the desk and sat, slouching with his elbow on the chair arm, fingers braced under his chin. He swiveled back and forth, taking in the pale blue walls with their navy blue detailing and the slightly newer industrial carpeting covering the concrete floor. A desk with an aging computer, some metal shelves, and a file cabinet completed his furnishings. He missed his workshop at the back of Jeannie's store with the smell of wood shavings and sealants, and the sounds of the occasional customer as reminders of less painful times. But it was also full of reminders of what he was missing.

Ben started to unpack his file box, mostly filled with the usual personal accessories for an office taken out of his old desk drawers: some well-used research books on appraisal and antiques, a stash of peanut butter crackers and beef jerky, a mug referencing the old Prisoner TV show. At the bottom of the box, his hand brushed a picture frame.

He paused, running his fingers over the image of a smiling redhead and a young boy, about five, holding hands on the beach and waving. He had completely forgotten that he had thrown it into the box when he was packing up a month ago, and he propped it on the edge of his desk, trying to see if it felt right there. Tracing the line of her hair, and then touching their linked hands, Ben couldn't tell how much of what made his chest tight was anger, sadness, or fear that he would never have an afternoon like that one ever again. After a long moment he tipped it into the bottom drawer where he had put his snacks. All he needed to feel right now was determination, and that picture wasn't going to help him keep his head on straight.

He took a deep breath, trying to put the picture and the accompanying emotions out of his head. He would rather be out on the streets canvassing for possible witnesses, but he needed this job to keep himself afloat while he continued his search. And to keep it, he needed to figure out exactly what this job entailed.

Flipping back to the front of the binder, he adjusted himself in the worn office chair. There was no title page, just a table of contents. It included topics like *Sorting and Auction Preparation*, but his eye was drawn to the heading *Live Animals and Other Contraband*, pg. 209. Curious as to what kind of things Mrs. Bunion might consider contraband, he flipped through the pages until he found the right chapter.

Live animals are prohibited in the United States Post, but some imbeciles insist on sending them anyway. We have had occasion to receive everything from tarantulas to birds, bats, and occasional puppies. When you receive post that contains a living organism, your first task is to make sure it's still alive. If it's dead, contact the Georgia State Government Department of Community Health at (404) 206-6419. They like free samples to dissect in their lab. If the animal is still alive, contact Animal Control at (404) 794-0358. We have a special arrangement with them to hold the animals for ten days before they go to the local shelters for adoption. And for God's sake, take the puppies for a walk so they don't pee all over the office before Animal Control picks them up.

Despite himself, Ben was drawn in by the sardonic attitude of Mrs. Biun. He pulled open the top desk drawer and took out a notepad emblazoned with the USPS logo. Using the fountain pen that was always in his pocket, he started a list of questions. First, just how often did they deal with live animals? Second, what exactly was the arrangement with Animal Control? He turned back to the beginning of the binder, determined to start making his way through more when Sylvia returned with another cart.

"Enjoying Bunion's work?"

Ben got up and followed her into the warehouse proper. "Sure, I guess. She seems like she was a special woman; at least she looked at things in a…well, interesting light. Do you mind finishing the sorting today while I get settled? I might have some questions for you later." Like, just how sane were the rest of the employees? Mrs. Biun and Sylvia were quirky enough. He wondered if the Center drew unusual people to it or if dealing with lost letters made them that way.

Sylvia laughed, open and un-selfconscious. "I'll be in and out of your office every ten minutes with a cart. Just holler."

Ben thanked her and returned to his desk. Before he re-opened the manual, he heard the first strains of a whistled waltz echo, out of tune. Wincing a little bit at the discord, he sat back down and started in on the first chapter of protocol; *The Property Room.*

Your job as property clerk is to ensure that all of the items that get lost in the mail don't end up permanently lost. You are the accountant. Don't lose an item, and don't put an item up for auction that someone might claim later. He wondered how he was supposed to predict whether or not someone wanted an item back or was beyond caring about it. *You will sort the items as they come in and keep track of their entry dates so you know when they are to be auctioned off. Four years is the standard with exceptions for live animals and perishables. See those respective chapters.*

If an item is particularly valuable or personal, at the end of four years, it is moved to the long-term storage bay. It then becomes a judgment call as to when those items are to be auctioned. My rule of thumb was journals after fifty years, jewelry after ten. Some things should never be auctioned. Uncle Shem is one of those. Familiarize yourself with the contents of bay five.

The empty cart clattered through his office, and Ben glanced up to nod at Sylvia before he got up to go explore bay five as instructed. This one was organized differently than the other bays and was much smaller. He started at one side and worked his way slowly over the three walls, noting shelves for journals and diaries, file drawers for photographs, shelves full of paintings, and a safe bolted to the floor. Centered on a shelf on the back wall was a black and gold marbled urn. The bronzed plaque on it read *Beloved Uncle Shem, 1934-1989.* He lifted the lid and gazed in at the pile of ash, closed it, and picked up the tag. *Posted from Storm Lake, Iowa. 89-12-26-78.* He couldn't believe that no one wanted to claim the old man; no one cared enough to find out what happened to him. There was surprisingly little dust on the urn, especially compared to the rest of the objects on the shelves above and below.

The door swung open. "You in here, Ben?"

"Over here. Meeting Uncle Shem." Ben stepped back from the shelf, scrubbing his hands on his pants to rid himself of phantom particles of his new uncle.

Sylvia poked her head around the shelf, grinning. "Isn't he wonderful? The one relative you never have to worry about entertaining. Or disappointing. He's been here a long time."

"Twenty years by the tag. No one ever found his family?"

"Don't know. All I know is no one paid to have him shipped home. Could be they never found his family; could be they didn't want him. Haven't looked up his claim log though." She patted the jar fondly. "He's a good listener, you know? And I'm not the only one who thinks so, either. Jillian, the reader? She comes in and talks to him all the time. She only does it after hours, but I've seen her." She drifted back to her cart. "Any other questions?"

"A couple. How many live animals do you get here?" Ben followed her back around to the 2010 bay.

"Oh, I'd say about one or two a month. My favorite was the bat. He was just the most precious thing ever! A little fruit bat that would hang off your finger or curl up in that little hollow by your collarbone." She indicated the spot with an unconscious caress. "I wanted to keep him, but the animal control guy said that bats carry rabies, and I shouldn't have taken him out of his tank. He just looked so scared I couldn't help myself."

"Are bats common then?" He picked up a jar of preserved peaches and tucked it on the shelf next to several mason jars of vegetables. He prayed she would say no, since he really didn't care for the creatures. They were firmly in the realm of freaky for him.

"Oh no, mostly we get reptiles. They're easy to ship 'cause they get all lethargic. Once we had this six-foot ball python; she was just darling. We called her Cuddles because all she wanted to do was curl up around you. Well, I called her Cuddles. No one else would touch her."

"For good reason, I should say." Ben leaned his elbows on the handlebar of the cart. "Sylvia, just how long do live animals stay with us?"

"Oh, until Animal Control can pick them up. Not long. Maybe a day or two at the most. Though, that hedgehog was with us for almost a week. I just about took him home myself. When Spike wrinkled his nose, it was just the cutest."

Bats, snakes, and hedgehogs, oh my, rang through Ben's head. "And who takes care of the animals during that time?" He was really hoping she wouldn't say him. He wasn't any good with other living beings; just ask Jeannie, she'd be happy to elaborate on all his faults.

"Well, I guess you do. Sometimes I would help Bunion with them. But it's not often we get any," she added quickly, seeing the frown on Ben's face. "And Jordy can typically pick them up same day they come in."

Ben rubbed his hands across his face, trying to clear enough cobwebs from his mind to keep up with the jumps in Sylvia's thought process. "Jordy is Animal Control," he clarified.

"Yup. And when he comes, he picks up whatever pet stuff is due for release. It's the arrangement we have with them. We get pet bedding, leashes, food, chew toys. After its time is up, he takes it. Whenever there is an animal to retrieve, that is."

Ben held up a hand. "Got it, thanks." The information that Sylvia was providing wasn't going to stick unless he made some notes in the manual at the appropriate places, so he turned back to the office and sat down once more with Bunion.

For the most part, the manual consisted of straightforward advice about how to organize his day and month to make the best use of his time. Spend a little time each day prepping for and transferring old items to the auction area for the monthly auction. Make sure to enter each item that appears into the spreadsheet on a daily basis so you know what to retrieve for each auction. Stock up on Band-Aids for paper cuts until you form calluses. Throw out any perishables in the packages and do not allow them to find their way to the lunchroom, as there was once an incident with a poisoned—well, laced with laxative—coffee cake. Ben made it through half of the manual before realizing that it was past four, and he hadn't seen Sylvia in over an hour. He picked up his tablet and worked his way out to the bullpen to inquire after his wayward assistant.

The readers ignored him so he approached one on the end. "Hey, sorry to interrupt, but do you know where Sylvia is this time of day?"

The man finished scanning the letter in his hands before looking up. "Typically shredding. She shreds at nine and four." He put down the letter and picked up its envelope, looking at an address that was short a line. Google Maps was up on his screen, and he started slowly scrolling through listings for Bourbon Street.

"Thanks."

When Ben found his way back to the shredder, it was humming softly, but not active. The behemoth took up an entire corner of the sorting garage, and was perched on scaffolding that allowed rolling carts to be filled with the shredded correspondence. Sylvia was sitting on the top stair, a half-full bin sitting beside her. There was a piece of stationery in one hand, her chin propped in the other and a small smile on her lips. When she saw Ben standing at the foot of the stairs, she stuffed the letter she was reading in a back pocket of her jeans and stood up, tossing the contents of the bin into the shredder. The shearing sound filled the air for a minute as the machine chewed its way through the paper and then muted to dull humming again.

"Done with the manual already? You read faster than I thought." She wouldn't quite meet his eye as she spoke, one hand checking to make sure there wasn't any paper sticking out of her pocket. Ben decided it would be better to pretend not to have noticed, rather than call her on one of Bunion's cardinal rules, listed on page five: *"NO READING ALLOWED."*

"Not quite, just about done with half and the day's almost over, so I thought I'd track you down and wrap up for the day."

"Sure, sure, have a seat while I finish this up." Sylvia, all smiles again, picked up another box of letters and used it to gesture to the steps. Ben made his way up to the top and sat leaning against the railing. It was impossible to hear over the shearing, crunching sound of the paper, so Ben waited until the last bin of letters fluttered into the machine and Sylvia hit the kill switch, leaving the room silent.

She flopped down onto the stairs beside him, a little too close for comfort. "So, how's Bunion treating you?"

She smelled of vanilla and warm paper, with just a hint of paint thinner. He wondered where that last scent came from, and then realized it would be impolite to lean forward for a better whiff like he wanted to, and shifted as far into the rail as he could. "There's certainly a lot to remember. But there was one thing; she mentioned Hail Mary's before an auction? I was wondering what sort of things we might be able to use to find an owner that the readers missed."

"Well, if something seems particularly obvious, like the reader overlooked the address written on the tongue of a boot, then you get to double-check their research. Otherwise nothing, really, you just store and sell 'em. It's super rare to find something; they hardly ever miss anything." The last comment had been a bit rueful, and Ben wondered what a reader found Sylvia doing to make her sound so bitter about their observational skills, but decided this wasn't the time to ask.

"Have you ever heard of them selling something that someone tried to claim later?"

"Ha. No. After a year or so, no one is looking for anything. It just sits there. The only reason we hold onto journals is 'cause we hope whatever titillating bits are in them are long out of date, and we hold onto expensive jewelry in case someone tries to file an insurance claim. That's it."

They sat in silence a moment, Ben acutely aware that their knees were touching. He hooked an arm around the railing above him and hauled his gangly form erect, not quite avoiding jostling Sylvia. "Well, thanks. That answers my most pressing question." He peered into the hole leading to the shredder. "What were you shredding today, anyway?"

"Letters. Undeliverable and unreturnable; the ones without anything else in them, like photos. Just…letters that never make it anywhere." She shivered, then pulled on his arm, hauling him away from the opening. "Leave 'em be. You'll go mad if you think about them too much."

You'll rarely need to engage in this task. It's really not your area of responsibility, but every once in a while, those idiots seem to get overwhelmed and need a hand. So here are the basic rules of sorting lost mail, should you ever need them.

~ *Gertrude Biun,* Property Office Manual

As Ben drove home, he noticed that the liquor store was still open. After a quick mental calculation involving his new paycheck and how much he needed to be setting aside for his search, he swerved into the parking lot. At the coolers, his first inclination was to reach for the cheap 6-pack of Budweiser, but his eye was drawn to the sale signs below the Peachtree Pale Ale. It had been his favorite beer since he left college. He normally felt guilty spending the money on a microbrew now, but with the sale price, he could allow himself to splurge on it.

When he got home, he stashed five of the beers in the fridge and took the sixth into the living room. The room was nearly empty except for a battered desk in the middle of the floor. The desk faced the one uninterrupted wall. On the left was a map of Georgia, a close-up of Savannah in one corner. The map was riddled with pushpins and these were wrapped in yarn and twine, connecting an aura of papers to the map. There were printouts and news articles, sticky notes and photographs. The map was ragged as though someone had torn it repeatedly from the wall and the perforations created by the constellation of pushpins gave it the look of old lace.

On the right-hand side of the wall was an enlarged map of Atlanta. A handful of pins had begun their march across the surface roads and a few of them were connected by strings. Centered above the two maps was a black and white photocopy of a poster. There were only two lines of text; the top line read *Missing*, and the bottom: *Have you seen this boy?* They framed a photograph of his son, taken from the same photo that Ben had put in his desk drawer at work.

This is where he knew his time was supposed to be spent, at this web of interconnecting data. The job at the warehouse was only a means to the end, a way to earn enough money to have someplace to put up these maps and spend every moment he could sifting through the mountains of data that the police ignored. Those men relied only on their computers to sift through all the tips that came in to tell them if something was related to a cold case. Ben hated that phrase—cold case. It made everything impersonal, like they couldn't even be bothered to care about it anymore.

Ben popped open the beer on the corner of his desk and took a long pull while studying the maps. He was looking for holes and clusters. Tracing from one pushpin to the next, his fingers danced across the strands of the map, and he felt at peace, for a moment, seeing how much he'd accomplished already. After a few minutes, though, he started to feel restless again, so he put the beer down and picked up a large wooden box from his desk. The box had seen better days; it was cracked and there were slivers of wood missing, which made the intricate parquet of the lid uneven.

There was a small stutter in his heartbeat every time he picked up the box, an echo of guilt that he pushed down, hard; a constant reminder. Ben strode to the wall and opened the box, revealing more pushpins. He sorted through them until he found a clear one and placed it on the map where his new apartment was. A second clear pushpin went in for the location of the warehouse.

He turned back to his desk and set the box down, aligning it with the corner of the desk with a special reverence. He opened a thick file that sat in the middle of his desk. There were several strata of papers, each distinctly older than the next. Some were crumpled and stained, the ones on top newly printed. He emptied his beer and returned to the kitchen for another one before starting to go through the pile, his movements practiced and measured. This was his meditation and his prayer. The key was to let his mind drift, to not so much focus on the words as to let his subconscious take them in and start to make connections. He idly twirled a pen in his fingers as he studied the pages, occasionally making a note.

It was in these pages that he knew he would find the key to his loss, find the way to bring his son back to him. Every evening, weekend, holiday, "sick" day, he sat this way and had for almost a year, skimming through the pages of tips and police reports. And as soon as he figured out how to use all the new search programs at work, he would add even more pages to the pile: people who had moved directly after Benny's disappearance, John and Jane Does who might have lived in that area. Any new scrap of data that he could add to the pile of information in front of him that would finally make everything clear.

He sat this way for a while, skimming through the printouts, until he tried to take a drink of his second beer and found it empty. He returned to the kitchen for another and found leftover Chinese when he opened the refrigerator door. He brought the cold lo mein and a third beer back to his desk.

The takeout box was empty when he let out a small exclamation and pulled one of the newer printouts out of the stack. There had been a report of a woman who had forced a blonde little boy who was just his son's age into her car all while the boy screamed about wanting to go home. That could be his son, crying for him. He ripped off a portion of the page with the information and fumbled with the box to pull out two red push pins. At the map of Atlanta, he stuck a push pin into the zoo and pinned the printout to the wall nearby. On his way back to his desk to grab a length of string, he brushed the poster of his son, the caress gentle.

"I'll find you, just wait. I promise."

There is a certain Zen to properly cataloging items. A pattern, a patter, almost mesmerizing. It's soothing, this repetition, but it can also lull you into a false sense of security. And that's the way you misplace things.

~ *Gertrude Biun,* Property Office Manual

Ben arrived at the Center the next morning, bleary-eyed but on time, and made his way to his office, intent on figuring out the cataloging system for the property room. The section of the manual dealing with the computer and physical filing system appeared to take up a large portion of the pages and he had skipped it yesterday. But he'd do anything for a distraction today to take his mind off the dismal failure the rest of his night had been. After he'd found that one promising item, there hadn't been a single other tip, or even anything to correlate with that report of the boy at the zoo.

He unlocked the door to the warehouse and sank into the chair in his cubicle, rubbed his face briskly, and then pulled the manual down from the shelf behind his desk. Opening it to the beginning of the *Cataloging* section on page 19, he waded into the dense handwriting.

It is important to be entirely accurate in the labeling and cataloging of all pieces that enter your domain. There should always be tags in the middle drawer, and if you run out, ask for more from those ninnies at the front desk; they know where the supply closet is. Heaven forbid you forget to order more when the closet gets low. Those women at the front desk think they run this place. It's only because all communication with the high muckety-mucks goes through their fat fingers, but don't you pay their grandstanding any attention.

You should never, NEVER allow your work to back up.

As for the cataloging process itself, each item is labeled with a unique identifying number. It is four two-digit numbers and is structured as follows: Year-Month-Day-Item Number on that day. Or YY-MM-DD-IN. Rarely will you get more than one hundred items a day, and if you do, it is then permissible to allow the Item Number to exceed two numbers.

Ben followed that well enough, but he wondered what would happen when the dual digit year numbers caught up with themselves century-wise in the long-term storage bay. He was sure that things must be sold off long before the century mark, regardless of what they were, but then he remembered Uncle Shem. Something like that couldn't be sold. Not just for the fact that it was human remains, which he was pretty sure was illegal, but regardless of whether his family wanted him back, the people here seemed to be rather attached to him now. It is a welcoming final resting place, though it might do the old man a service to put him someplace people stopped nattering at him.

After a half hour of reading and note taking, Ben stood and stretched his neck, picking up the pad of paper he had attempted to take notes on, with a myriad of crossings out, cross-hatchings, and diagrams. He thought he had the organization of the shelves down, but he was not at all sure about the computer system. Bunion's instructions had been equal parts curse and divination, including such treasures as: *When the entry disappears, it has become part of the microchip mass, and to access it again, it is sometimes needful to restart the machine.* He wondered just how old the woman had been and what state the system was actually in. If it was in as bad a shape as Bunion suggested, then it would be of little use for his personal project.

He went out onto the main floor of the warehouse and over to the 2006 shelves to make sure he had the organizational scheme down. The three towering shelf walls that formed the bay were starting to look sparse as there had already been seven auctions that year. Starting at his right and going around the bay, the shelves contained books, figurines, toys, cloth items, various implements from the garden, kitchen, and household, contraband, artwork, and finally, on his left, the "other" category. In the center of the bay stood a large wooden jewelry case and a file cabinet that contained the photographs and smaller art and prints lost to their recipients.

Each section of the bay was further segregated by month with each month's gleanings carefully separated to help with the search when preparing for the auctions. Ben was grateful for this as he did not want to waste time by diving through the piles of detritus to find the one toy, or fork, or whatever that had gone missing over the interim time.

The clatter of a cart announced Sylvia's presence, and she drifted into sight on her way to the current bay. Her hair was still in the spunky pigtails, but she had a different vest hanging open over a low-cut cotton tee. "Morning, Ben!" she called cheerfully and sailed out of sight on the back of the cart. Ben put down the wooden flute that had been lost en route from Argentina and followed her down the concrete to find her shelving a boxed set of Shakespeare.

"Morning, Sylvia. I have some more questions for you. Mrs. Biun wasn't always the clearest in the manual." More like she was cranky, way behind the times, and a bit batty, but Ben tried to be charitable in his attitudes toward the elderly.

"I'd bet every Cabbage Patch doll in here that you're confused about the computer stuff, right?" She laughed and gave up trying to find a spot for the Shakespeare books on the literature shelf and dropped them in the Rubbish instead. "That's what they used to think of him anyways," she muttered half to herself.

He let out a rueful laugh. "Well yes, she seemed to think the computer was a device designed by the devil to test her very soul." He traced the embossing on the Shakespeare box, flicking off a lingering bit of packing peanut.

"It's not. She got some viruses at some point and she wouldn't let me take care of them, but I wiped the computer before you got here, a fresh start. The database system is super easy, very self-explanatory. Just stay out of the porn and it should work fine."

Ben colored and steadfastly ignored her comment by opening the collection to a colored print in *A Midsummer's Night's Dream*. "I have to ask though—since when was Shakespeare rubbish? All my teachers seemed to idolize him. I certainly think he's a damn fine playwright." A rather well-endowed Pan was entertaining naked fairies, and Ben flipped back to the front in disbelief, wondering what edition this was.

Sylvia pulled the book from his hands and turned back to

the plate. "Not since he died. He was a writer for the masses—strictly low-brow. I didn't have much else to do after...for much of my kiddie years. I read a lot." She turned the cart around and leaped on the back headed toward the bullpen.

Ben stepped out of her way, just managing to avoid the wheels of the cart. "Got it. Watch your speed there, tiger." Her slip had him wondering what it was that had laid her up as a child long enough for her to reach for histories about Shakespeare. She seemed more the type for swashbuckling romances than dusty non-fiction, but then what did he know about what women actually liked reading.

"Watch yourself. If I get all of this shelved I can stop early for lunch. I didn't have time for breakfast this morning. I could eat a cow. A whole one, tail and all." Her stomach echoed her opinions and Ben couldn't help but crack a smile.

"Well, before you hurt yourself, stop by my desk on the way out. The bottom drawer is full of snacks. I can't stand an empty stomach, so help yourself." He turned and started toward long-term storage to try to open the safe for the first time.

"Thanks. You're a lifesaver." She rattled away and Ben heard the bottom drawer open as he knelt in front of the enormous cast-iron safe that looked like it might be as old as the post service itself. He spun the ancient dial around, treating it just like his old locker, and on the second try he got it unlocked.

But before he could open it, he heard Sylvia walk back up behind him. "Ben, who are these people? Is this your wife and kid?"

He cursed himself for forgetting that the photo was in the bottom drawer and paused a moment to arrange his face into as neutral an expression as he could manage before turning to his nosy assistant. He was tired of pity, he was tired of nosy, and he was tired of the constant checking in on how he was or whether he'd made any progress. The hope that he might be able to keep his trouble from his coworkers was fading fast, but he was still going to do all he could to keep them from butting in.

"Yes. We're separated, though, right now." He held his hand out for the frame she was studying closely, twisting it this way and that.

"She's pretty, in a freckly-girl-next-door sort of way. The boy lucked out though; he's got your bone structure. He's going to grow up to be as big as you, I'd guess." She finally looked up from the picture to see Ben's hands clenched around the handle of the safe, his face pale and contorted. He was trying hard not to snatch the picture from her hands and hurl it away from them. He hadn't realized how much it would hurt to hear someone talk about him like he wasn't gone. Just for a moment he had let himself believe her vision of the present, with a growing young boy once more eating him out of house and home, but he couldn't keep reality back for more than a second before the fear that he would never see whether his son would out-grow him crashed back in.

"Ben, I'm sorry, I…" She tried to hand the picture back to him, but he shook his head, not trusting his hands to stop shaking enough to not drop the picture.

"Don't. Just keep out of it, okay?" He turned back to the safe and waited until he heard her walk away before he spun the dial to clear the combination.

His hands shook, and he rubbed them on his knees before standing and leaving the warehouse. He made his way out the front door, waving a negligent hand to the receptionist Judy's greeting and continued around the side of the building until he reached the back of the facility. He wished momentarily that he'd brought his flask with him, regardless of how it would seem on his first week on the job. Alcohol helped him stop shaking, kept him a little bit more numb to the things he couldn't think about. For now, a brief walk would have to do.

A dual set of defunct railway tracks stretched between the rows of warehouses, snaking their way through the industrial complex until they disappeared in the heat haze. The shimmer was worse than normal today, the air quality index screeching off the end of the scale, and Ben coughed at the emissions and soot that immediately invaded his lungs. There had been humidity in Savannah, but not this all-devouring smut that filled the air here. He felt that he'd never get used to its heaviness. A pile of railroad ties was partially obscured by the choking kudzu vines to one side of the tracks and he sat, idly picking at the splinters that threatened his pants leg.

He was remembering the day that Benny was born. Jeannie had been too exhausted to stay awake, her strawberry hair limp on her hospital greens, emitting the soft half snores that had made him fall in love with her. He had held his hour-old son so he could see out the window.

"See, Benjamin, Benny, my boy. That world is a great adventure. One quest after another. It'll challenge you, but don't worry, I'm right here. Always will be…"

Ben started out of his daydream as a man in overalls slammed open the door of the building across from him, lighting a cigarette as he crossed the threshold. The man took a long drag before waving across the tracks to Ben, holding up his pack in offering.

Wrinkling his nose, Ben shook his head and tapped his watch before hauling himself off the pile of ties and turning back toward his office. He took a couple more deep breaths of the Georgia fug before heading inside, somewhat calmer and determined to apologize to Sylvia. It wasn't her fault she had found the picture and chosen to comment. He just wished he had managed to have kept it hidden. He'd forgotten it was in that box at all, to be honest, and he should have taken it home when he found it.

She wasn't in the warehouse or the sorting room, so he poked his head into the readers' pen, gazing about at the moderate chaos of the room before ducking back out unnoticed. He finally found his way to the break room, a large conference-type room that doubled as the auction room.

Sylvia sat on the raised platform that held the auctioneer's podium, poking at a container of yogurt with a spoon. She frowned, scooped out a dollop of the thick, pink substance, and then flung it back into the container.

"Be sure you don't miss, doing that. I'd hate to have to be the one to clean yogurt out of the carpet." She jumped and made as if stand, but Ben put a hand on her shoulder and sat down beside her.

"Ben, I'm really, really sorry. I didn't mean to go poking around like that, but the picture was right there, and I'm always too curious…"

Ben held up a hand to stem the furious tide of apologies and rubbed his hands over his face. "Just, leave it alone, alright? I don't want to talk about it."

"Then I'll leave it alone." Sylvia nodded shortly and picked up her uneaten yogurt. Jumping up, she hesitated before holding her hand down to him, "Do you want to go back to work now?" She didn't seem nearly as miserable as when he'd first walked into the room, and he wondered if these mercurial changes in mood were standard, or if she had been truly that upset at causing him distress.

She stood and dumped her yogurt into a bin, and then

turned to him with a hand extended. Ben decided that the best way to keep her from getting nosy again would be to give her something else to think about for a while, so he grasped her hand and pulled himself upright. His mouth twisted into an involuntary smile as he nearly pulled her slight frame down on top of him, but they both ended up standing. "Back to work, yes. I was going to look in that safe, wasn't I?"

"Yes, I think you were. Care to go see?"

"Lead on." He gave an abbreviated bow towards the door and followed Sylvia back to the warehouse. Treasure was a suitable distraction; girls liked shiny things, and they especially loved showing off shiny things. They stood in front of the safe for a moment before he leaned down toward her and whispered, "Fantastic jewels? Gold? Stocks and bonds? Do you know what the old lady kept in here?"

"Yes." Her eyes sparkled as she tried to suppress a grin and she looked up at him, meeting his eyes squarely. He noticed that they were an unusually clear green. "But I'm not telling. That would ruin the surprise."

Ben rolled his eyes and knelt once more before the old cast-iron safe and pulled it open. He peered in, his face blank, and he paused before he reached in and pulled something out, cradling it in his hand. "Huh."

"Oh, come on, you're no fun! What kind of reaction is that, 'huh'?" She pulled the door out of his grasp and let it swing fully open, and she bent over to look in and then down at his hand. "Huh."

Ben felt his stomach sink to the floor and hoped this was a hazing initiation for the new property clerk. He had enough problems; he didn't want to complicate things at work, too. "Is the safe supposed to be almost empty?"

"Um, no. I don't think so. She used to keep all sorts of

things in here." She nodded at the rag doll in his hand. "She was terrified of that thing. It's a voodoo doll, you know. Was mailed from New Orleans a few years back. Bunion thought it would do someone damage if it was messed with, so she kept it locked up in here. But there was also jewelry, a few valuable books, things like that." She reached over Ben's shoulder and patted down the shelves of the safe. "Nope, not here. Wonder if she put it all back on the shelves?" She bounded up and headed over to the next bay to start rummaging through the jewelry box.

Ben gingerly placed the doll back in the empty safe and closed it, spinning the dial to clear the combination. Kind of like locking the barn door after the horses are gone, he reflected, but it was probably good to keep the voodoo doll in there. "Who should we report this to?" he called over to Sylvia.

"Report this? I don't know." She looked up as Ben walked around the shelves. "Nothing's ever gone missing before that I know of. I swear it was all here last week. I put an engagement ring in there with the rest of them."

"I haven't finished the manual yet; do we have a 'lost property' file? It seems like the same woman who'd label books 'rubbish' might have an 'incompetence' file at the very least." He ran a hand through his hair and shifted his weight back and forth, debating whether he should ask her if she took anything. He was thinking of the letter she had stuffed in her pocket the day before.

Almost as if she had read his mind, she hunkered down and peered around the edges of the safe. "Well, I didn't take it, you just learned about it, and the only other one who had the combo was Bunion. I guess we should figure out who we report this to."

"All I saw in the manual was long and detailed instructions about how to handle what is here, not what to do if something isn't." He frowned, then continued, "I'd have thought it'd be awfully hard to lose something here as this is where all the lost things come. Thought it might have a magnetic pull for the lost or something."

"No," Sylvia ran a hand thoughtfully along a shelf. "No socks here, or hardly ever I should say, and, when we do, we almost always get matched pairs, so not everything lost ends up here."

"Just a little whimsy, I guess." Ben went back to his cubicle and dragged the manual off his shelf, flipping it open to the contents page, trying to figure out which section might have the information they needed. "There's just nothing here. I'm going to find someone who might know what to do. Can you keep looking through the bays, see if you recognize anything that's supposed to be in the safe? I mean, since you probably handled some of it in the past."

She saluted, then spun on her heel and skipped back into the warehouse as Ben made his way to the reception desk.

Judy sat at her desk, the phone clenched between her ear and shoulder as she typed away, searching through the lost mail index. "Five carats, you say? And he says he mailed it to you two weeks ago? No...no, I'm not seeing anything of that weight that's come through here, ever. He didn't insure it? Are you sure he sent it? No, no, there's no reason to use that language, ma'am; I'm just checking. Of course I think he loves you; perhaps it will come in the next day or so, and, just in case it shows up here, we'll put your information into the system. All right now, you have a better day then." Judy dropped the phone into the cradle and rubbed her ear before turning to Ben. "Well now, I hope your boyfriend hasn't sent you fictitious jewelry as well; I'm all out of platitudes."

"Does a safe-full of missing jewelry count?" He linked his

hands behind his back, rocking onto his heels. "'Cause that's what I seem to have."

"I haven't time for silly jokes, Ben, so what's up?"

"The safe in long-term storage—it's empty. Well, empty except for a voodoo doll. Sylvia says it was full. I now have two questions. Can you show me on that little software program of yours how I can look up where things are supposed to be stored, and who in the hell do I report it to if all that stuff is truly missing?"

"You'll have to ask Sylvia about that. Mrs. Biun had a unique way of...organizing that data. And I'd fill out an incident report form, if I were you. No one really to talk to directly about that sort of thing. Maybe the people who come from headquarters to run the auction? I'd bring it up with them next time they come."

"So you're telling me I don't know what's missing in that warehouse, and I don't have anyone to pass the buck to." Ben grimaced, threw his hands in the air, and started back to the warehouse. "I won't stand for it. Lost things don't stay lost. They get found."

Judy's laugh followed him back to the warehouse.

*An exciting aspect to be sure. We have almost
unlimited resources when it comes to tracking down
the proper owners. Of course, when I started here,
I actually had to call offices all over the country to
try and get the information I needed. That's still the
only way to do some things sometimes; technology
simply cannot replace good solid legwork.*

~ *Gertrude Biun,* Property Office Manual

B en found a copy of the incident report form in the back
of his manual, filled it out, and gave it to the receptionist
before spending the rest of the day shelving items and learning
the computer system that tracked every piece of lost mail. This
included not only the items at the Atlanta facility, but the Saint
Paul, Minnesota, facility as well. Each item that came through
his office had to have a description entered and as much of the
addressee and return address as could be deciphered. It wasn't
as easy as it came across, however, for after the basic info was
entered, there was an intricate protocol for handling the search
for the item's owners.

At five o'clock, Ben shut down the computer and stretched, data spreads of cities dancing before his eyes. For once, he had actually managed to lose track of time, and he brushed off the vague guilt he felt at not having thought of his search for the last few hours. Learning his job was integral to continuing said search, he rationalized. Besides, he was just about to get back to it. He called a good evening to Sylvia as she had insisted on shelving the last set of items that night herself.

She waved merrily, brandishing a partially melted spatula. "Have a good weekend! If you need anything, I don't live too far from here. I'd be happy to show you around or something."

Ben smiled, imagining the scenario in which Sylvia had melted the spatula herself. It involved her trying to deep fry ice cream and not having a metal slotted spoon. "Thanks, but I think I'll just spend this weekend settling in."

The short drive from the industrial park that housed the Mail Recovery Center to his apartment was delayed by an accident along the highway, and he was growling to himself in irritation by the time he reached his mail box. He grabbed the few envelopes waiting for him and continued up to his apartment, throwing the mail on the counter as he grabbed a beer from the fridge before sitting down at his desk. He flipped through the maps that he had marked up the night before and pulled out a legal pad to begin marking out his strategy for the weekend. There seemed to be a large number of tips called in around Grant Park and the zoo so he decided to focus his flyers around there. He kicked the lid off the paper box next to the desk and ran his hand across the stacks of flyers, his son's face staring up from the cropped and enlarged beach photo.

Ten years ago, when Ben had just graduated from high school and was trying to decide whether he could survive a school in the south long enough to get his library science degree, all he thought his future held was a long life in the stacks of a library somewhere. Maybe doing some restoration work, but mainly helping young readers find books to fire their imaginations. But then he had met Jeannie and they had a child together, and the librarian job he'd once envisioned began to seem like a very lonely kind of life to lead.

When Jeannie's father decided to retire and asked if they wanted to take over his antique shop, it had seemed like an idyllic life working every day beside the woman he loved in a shop filled with old junk and books. Constant antiquing trips, auctions, and conversations with older antiquarians and young couples looking to furnish their own first apartments.

The phone rang and startled him into spilling his beer over the copies. "Damn!" He grabbed the top few sheets and waved them over the carpet to shake off as much beer as he could. Walking over to the kitchen counter, he dropped the flyers and picked up the receiver.

"What? Who's this?" He put down the beer and grabbed a paper towel, dabbing at the flyers and then the splash of beer on his pants.

"It's Sylvia, Ben. I just wanted to see if you needed any help getting settled in or anything. I hate moving. Figured a cheerful helper might be just what you need."

He took a moment to count to ten so he wouldn't snap at her. He hated interruptions when he was settling in to work, it broke his concentration and he worried he might miss something. "Thanks, Sylvia." He threw the balled up paper towels into the sink. "But I prefer to do this on my own. Plus, I'm kind of busy this weekend."

"I got it. That's cool. Hey, at least you didn't say you'd had enough of the cheerful helper already this week." He made a face but didn't comment. That would be one of the other reasons he'd prefer she not come over. Oh, and the wall full of the search for his son. He didn't really want to explain that all to her. "Anyway, if you need anything, my number should be in the manual; there's a company directory at the back of that. You know, all twenty-five of us or so."

"Got it. I will let you know if I need any help. Don't you have plans of your own? A date or something?" He kicked himself for asking that last and then wondered at the fact that he actually wanted to know whether she was seeing someone.

"Pssh. As if there are boys in this town worth the effort. Nah, I'll just end up working in Gram's yard again. It's the great Garden-Patch War and apparently all hands are needed. You wouldn't believe the amount of work that has to be put into that thing."

He looked over at his desk and the piles of paper, maps, and folders. "You'd be surprised. Anyway, thanks, Sylvia. You go find some fun this weekend, hear?"

"Got it, boss. You too."

The next morning, Ben packed a satchel full of flyers along with duct tape and a staple gun with plenty of extra staples. He threw in a couple bottles of water and protein bars as well, having learned his lesson after one particularly unpleasant day in July when he ended up in the hospital after a day of canvassing the streets of Savannah. After three bags of fluid had been pumped into him, he lied about having someone to take care of him and was discharged to go back to his dank motel room. He grabbed his maps and keys and drove east into the city. Even at eight o'clock, the air was fouled with dust and smog, the temperature creeping past eighty. Ben knew he could cover one city block in about a half hour, and he was planning to be in the city until dark.

He left his car in a rundown parking structure that promised all-day parking for ten dollars and set off in the direction of the park. His goal was to completely cover the park and the surrounding block of streets. Every telephone pole he passed, every boarded window or door, every blank wall received a poster. And it had to be every possible surface; every few feet he would stop and look back, making sure he had achieved maximum poster visibility. His heart leapt every time he noticed a space he had missed, and he would hurry back to fill it in, give it the face of his son.

There was a sort of mantra or meditation to the work, step step staple, step step staple. The repetition and the fact that he was doing something active, something that could bring in a hint of his son, helped him to relax more than anything else he did on his search. He worked steadily as the sun rose, stopping passersby to make sure they saw the picture. "Have you seen this boy? He's five; my son."

He had stopped noticing what the people actually looked like. They were a blur of red and blue ties, dark suits, high heels, styled hair. Occasionally a detail would pop out in particular—a purple mohawk, a brightly patterned umbrella used as a walking stick, a violet muu-muu.

"If you could for a moment, ma'am. Just a quick look; have you seen this boy?"

They all passed by, most of them just shaking their head and not engaging. Some would just snatch the paper as they went by to glance at before tossing it in the trash or gutter within the next block. If it was salvageable, Ben would retrieve the poster, flatten it carefully, and post it farther down the block.

"Have you seen my son? Benny?"

Sometimes he wished that even one would stop for just a few seconds to take an honest look at the flyers he held and actually think about whether or not they had seen his son.

"Maybe you've seen this boy around the park?"

Mothers steered their flocks of children around him. Those were always the most painful. Fingers in their mouths, hands clasped to their mother's pants leg, sitting in their strollers. Every one of them reminded him of something about Benny. He had the same dinosaur toys as the young African-American boy or he always insisted on mismatching shoes as a toddler, like the little girl in the stroller wearing one mini Sketcher and one mini sandal.

"No? Thank you anyways. Have a good day."

He always made sure he was unfailingly polite, regardless of how negative a reaction he received. He didn't want anyone to think he had lost his grip, and it was sometimes hard to keep from shouting at the people who just brushed past him. He wanted people to actually think, to look at the posters. He knew he would be dismissed even faster if he turned into one of those bullhorn men shouting damnation from the street corner.

Around noon he took a small break, walking toward the zoo and getting a hot dog from a vendor at the entrance. He sat on a bench, stretching his legs to try and ease the tension in them while he ate his lunch. Just enough to keep going and then up and at it again.

He and Jeannie had taken their son to this zoo last year. Benny had wanted to see a real, live monkey. Ben could remember it so clearly, just a flash of the three of them standing in front of the gorilla enclosure.

"See, Benny, see how that gorilla moves? It's just like a human really. They're incredibly intelligent. They learn sign language and can communicate with humans just as easily as I talk with you."

"But, Daddy, they're so hairy!" Benny had his nose pressed to the glass, the air so humid and hot that his breath didn't even fog it.

"So is your Uncle George, but he's definitely human, I think." Ben had grinned as his wife slapped his shoulder for maligning her brother, but she let it stand.

Ben finished his hot dog and tossed the wrapper into the trash beside him before heading back to the sidewalks and his flyers. He passed a bag lady pushing a cart full of cans and automatically held out a flyer. "Have you seen this boy?"

She stopped and looked sideways at the poster, eyes scanning back and forth, before settling back on her cart. "'S one of them missing boys, ain't it? Them truck boys."

Excitement coursed through him, an electric tingle bringing him fully awake and out of his moving meditation. He had known that if he just kept asking long enough, he'd find someone who saw something. "Yes, yes, he's my son; he went missing a year ago. You've seen him?" Ben scrambled for his notebook, letting the flyer fall.

"Not him. Like him. Them truck boys. Green truck boys. Green truck comes, little boys go." She started off down the street, muttering, "Green truck comes, little boys go."

Ben stared after her for a moment, then shook his head and stuffed the notebook back into his satchel. He should have known better than to try to get sense out of a transient. They couldn't even keep it together enough to have someplace to live, let alone have a firm grasp on their memory. But that wasn't fair to the homeless population, and he instantly chastised himself, blaming his attitude on the disappointment he felt that she hadn't seen anything after all. He bent to retrieve the flyer he'd dropped and was taping it to the back of a mailbox when a thought started to niggle at the back of his mind.

It was the green truck. Even if the lady was a bit off her rocker, it didn't mean that she hadn't seen something. And he was sure he'd heard something else about a green truck recently, but he couldn't quite place where. As he walked the rest of his route, he absently thrust the poster under people's noses and forgot to say thank you, all the while racking his brain for the reference he was missing. He walked until dusk started to fall and then he made his way back to his apartment. Once inside, he dumped his satchel among the empty beer bottles on his counter, cracked open a fresh one, and sat at his desk.

A green truck. He rifled idly through the tip-line transcripts, taking slow swigs from the bottle until it struck him. The tips from Atlanta. He sat up straight and started flipping pages faster, scanning each page until he found it. A green truck. A man just outside of Atlanta had reported a young boy on a sidewalk picked up by a green truck, though the boy didn't seem to know the driver. Excited again, he started from the beginning of the transcripts and gripped a highlighter in his teeth as he went page by page, trying to see if there was anything else about a green truck.

After two hours, he had no other occurrences, his back was sore, and he realized he was hungry for the first time since he had started his new job. He called the local pizza place, the only number on speed dial, and ordered a medium sausage and black olive. He got up to stretch, walking around his kitchen sipping his beer while he waited for the pizza. As soon as it arrived, he sat back down at his desk to wade through more of the tips. There were over four hundred pages of transcripts, mostly garbage, people looking for attention. He hardly noticed as he dripped pizza sauce on page 270, the smear of tomato and grease blending nicely into a brown soy sauce stain.

He read until he could hardly see the page, and it wasn't

until he sat back when he reached the end of the transcript that dawn was actually breaking. He had found three specific instances of people talking about a green truck with a young boy, though they were in different areas—the one outside of Atlanta, one by the zoo, and the last about halfway between Atlanta and Savannah. None of the boys' descriptions sounded like Benny, but eyewitnesses were unreliable, everyone knew that. Especially if you watched enough crime drama, like Ben had before his son disappeared. Afterwards, he just didn't have the stomach. But here was a lead, a solid lead, and he smiled.

Since it was so early, Ben decided to catch a few hours sleep before calling Detective O'Connor, the man in charge of his son's case, and letting him know what he had found.

"Detective, please, I know you—"

"Ben. Stop. We've been through this more times than is healthy. You really need to stop; leave the investigation to us. We're the ones trained in it. Though, admittedly, it's been a couple weeks since your last proposed lead." The detective sounded tired, strained. He sighed, then asked, "But, whatever. This is a great way to start my Sunday. What color truck did you say?"

"Green. Three times." Ben waited, hoping that this time—this time—his information might actually convince the detective to do something. He had lost track of the number of times he had called the man, insistent that he had found something new in the morass of paper on his wall.

A sigh came down the line. "Did you count how many times other vehicles appeared in the slush?"

"No, but there was someone in Atlanta, a woman, she said—"

The detective didn't wait to hear anymore. "According to the analysis sitting in front of me, there were three green truck tips, four white sedan tips, and ten all popular panel van tips. We've checked this out."

Ben thought he remembered those tips. But this one had seemed real. He'd spoken to someone who had actually seen the truck. "Really? You've tracked down these people and asked them what they saw?"

"We can't track down every anonymous tip, Ben, you know this. We've been over it."

Ben's hand clenched convulsively around the phone, but he tried to keep his voice level. He was not going to be dismissed again. "You should try. How many hours are you putting into this, anyway? One, two a month now? I'm still putting in forty-five or more each week. How can you justify telling me you can't track this stuff down when you're not spending the time to even keep up with the tip line?" Despite his best efforts, Ben was breathing heavily, the anger showing through in his voice. There was a moment of silence on the line.

"I'm going to forgive you that one, Mr. Grant. I have forty cases on my desk right now. Your son's included. But we've hit a dead end. There is no new information coming in to attend to. I go over it as often as I can find the time, to try and find a new thread, but there is nothing there."

"Don't *say* that! There has to be something there, you can't just give up—" Ben's voice broke and he struggled not to let his exhaustion and fresh despair overwhelm him.

Silence again.

"Look, there's someone I think can help you. If you've got a pen, I'll give you her number."

"Is she a private eye? A missing person's consultant? I'm not sure I can afford that right now, maybe if I saved a bit." Ben shuffled papers on his desk to unearth his legal pad and pulled a pen out of the "#1 Dad" mug on the corner of his desk.

"She's...not. Ben, she's a counselor, and I think with the amount of time you spend obsessing over this—"

Ben slammed down the phone. He lowered his head onto his crossed arms and stayed there, taking deep breaths to calm the tide of anger that flooded him. He wasn't like his wife, the suicidal mess. He didn't need some shrink telling him he couldn't look for his son, or worse yet, telling him time after time that what he did made no difference. After a few moments, he hauled himself out of the chair and fell into bed, only to rise four hours later and start over on the tip line transcripts, this time listing on a legal pad all the references to specific vehicles or objects and where they were located.

The next morning, Ben mumbled a greeting to Judy and made his way back to the warehouse. He dropped into his seat, threw his sunglasses onto the desk, and briskly rubbed his face, trying to force himself awake. He had fallen asleep at his desk late last night and had slept poorly for it. A mug of coffee appeared on the desk in front of him, held by a slim hand with something green under the fingernails.

"Judy said you looked like you could use some. Careful though, Byron brews it like his very life depends on the amount of caffeine he can squeeze out of the beans." Sylvia perched on the end of his desk, gesturing with the cup. "Come on, it'll do you good."

"I don't know. Should I accept something from someone with green gunk under their fingernails?" Ben was striving for a light-hearted tone as he reached out and cupped the lukewarm mug in his hands. But judging by the look on her face, he didn't quite succeed.

Frowning at her nails, she started picking at them. "It's paint. It's hard as hell sometimes to get oil paints out from under your nails without dipping your hands in turpentine. Then they smell." She made a face and gave up on the stains. "So, looks like you had quite the weekend. Care to spill the juicy gossip?"

Ben took a cautious sip of the coffee, swallowing a couple times to try and rid himself of the acrid aftertaste and set it gently on the desk. And then ignored her question. "You were right. Coffee of doom they should call that stuff."

She dropped her head to the side, waiting.

Ben tried again to distract her. "Painting, was it? A fence in the garden?"

"No, portraits, of a sort. It's hard to describe. So, who was it kept you out to all hours?"

Since she wouldn't take subtle hints to drop it, he attempted the more direct approach. "I don't want to talk about it. Alright?" Ben pointedly turned to the stack of new entry forms already on his desk.

"Fine. Whatever. I don't need to know her name I guess." She flounced over to her cart and proceeded down the bays. "But next time I advise you to drink some V8 Splash with whatever it was you drank last night. Lots of vitamins and minerals, keeps you from getting a hangover the next day."

"You know this from experience?" he called after her.

"Ah, no, but I've heard people say. They swear by it!"

He lowered his head to the desk and stayed there for a second to let his fatigue settle more fully into his bones before getting up and following her, still clutching the acrid coffee.

"So how much shelving do we have today?"

"Not all that much actually. We might be able to start pulling the next auction materials today. Sound good?"

"Ah, sure. I think I remember that part of the manual."

"It's easy. Here. You finish shelving these, and I'll go get your computer set up."

Ben took his time shelving the books at the bottom of the cart to give the coffee time to enter his bloodstream before trundling the cart back to his desk. "So, how does this work?"

Sylvia already had a few items sitting on his desk. "These all came in during August 2006. They're ready for auction. First things first: determine whether something needs to go into long-term storage." She waved her hands like a magician over the pile. "Does anything look like it might be valuable or volatile?"

He shifted the top of the pile to the side and then squinted at it. "Isn't that a journal there?"

"Yes, sir, you have won the prize! Ding, ding, ding!" She grabbed the journal and tossed it at him. "Fifty years in long-term storage! First, mark in the database that it is going into storage. Second, shelve it. The journals are shelved chronologically as to when they came in. So put it to the far right of the shelf."

"Got it. Where do I put it into the database?"

"Already done, and I'll shelve it when we're done here. Now, the fun part. Go through this database." She called up a program. "And make sure that none of the things match any pending claims in the logs. And take another look and see if there was anything obvious the readers missed, like a license plate or something."

"How does that help?"

"We can access the DMV records and see who owned such and such a car in such and such a state with such and such a plate." She swiveled in the chair to face him. "Pretty neat, huh?"

"Yes." Ben handed her the journal. "Why don't you go shelve this while I get started, then you can double check my work?"

"Right'o boss man. Have fun!" She took the journal and headed down the warehouse. "And put some music on. It's like a graveyard in here!"

He turned to his computer and called up the local oldies station on the internet, starting the live stream.

"Gah! Not this crap!" She came back down the aisle. "Go to 89.1! Lord. Some people's taste."

Ben rolled his eyes and paged over to the Brenau University jazz station. "I thought everyone loved the oldies."

"I do, but just the deep tracks. Much more interesting and musically mature." She came back around the corner into his office.

"Really, now. So you know your music."

"Absolutely. Grandma has an extensive vinyl collection. B-side and deep tracks all the way for me."

"That's the way I've always felt too, but I sometimes enjoy a good A track. Even if they are overplayed. Now. Can you show me what we're actually doing with this stuff?"

Sylvia fished a bagged and tagged framed photograph from the pile. "Okay, we'll start with this. Open the file." Ben typed 06-07-23-11 into the prompt box and waited while the program retrieved the pertinent file. "Okay, first double-check item against description. One framed photo of a couple in front of a house. Check. Next you check the research log. Hmm, looks like the reader tried to search for the address using the house number and the town it mailed from. Hah! But they didn't try searching the town it was mailed to! See, it says in the partial delivery address box that the town was clear, it was everything else that got messed up on the package. So, here's where the fun starts. See the icon of the map? Pull it up. Google helped us put together our own tool for this. Type in what we know—house number and town. Search."

They waited while the list of possibilities started and then continued to grow. When it stopped, there were forty-five.

"Damn. Knew it wouldn't be that easy. Okay. Any other clues we can draw from?"

Ben started to get the same sort of feeling that he had while digging through the lists of tips and names, an excitement he wasn't sure was entirely due to searching for his son, but was also connected to the thrill of the hunt. He scanned the digital ticket for any clues they might had yet missed. "It says there was a G in the street part of the address."

"Okay, that narrows it down. Only street names with a G in them." They applied the restriction and watched the list narrow to fifteen.

"Better, but still not great. What else, what else?"

They racked their brains for a moment, trying to figure out if there was any other way to narrow the parameters. "Is there a program that allows you to search by the kind of house or construction?"

"No. But there is Google Maps Street View! Genius."

Together they put the fifteen addresses into the computer one at a time and pulled up the street view. Fourteen houses had it, but none looked the same as the one in the picture.

"Man, I thought this one had a chance." Sylvia started to dismantle the frame, to file the picture in long term and to put the frame into the auction.

"Hold on, can't we access the white pages for this last one?"

"You just don't give up, do you? Yeah, I think we get unrestricted access or some such to phone numbers. Not sure as I wasn't ever given access to those programs." She pointed to a Yellow Book logo on his desktop and he logged in.

"Okay, time to make some calls." Sylvia picked up his phone and handed it to him.

He grimaced, but knew he'd probably have to get used to it someday. So he picked up the phone and listened to the dial tone for a second before dialing the number. He held his breath.

"Hello."

"Hi, this is Ben Grant calling from the—"

"Psych!"

Ben growled under his breath. He hated this kind of voicemail message. It always struck him as immature and pointless dicking around.

"This is the answering machine for the Geralds. Leave a message and maybe we'll get back to you."

"Hi, this is Ben Grant calling from the Mail Recovery Center of the United States Postal Service. We have here an item, a framed photograph of a couple, that may have been meant for you about four years ago. If you could give me a call back at," Sylvia held up a notepad with a scribbled number on it, "1-800-ASK-USPS, that would be great. Once again, that number is 1-800-275-8777." He hung up the phone and turned to Sylvia. "I hate those kinds of voicemails."

"Really? I always think they're kinda funny."

"To each their own." He hefted the frame. "What do you do with this in the meantime?"

She took it from him and tossed it onto one of his bookshelves. "Pretend they're your cousins or some such until they return that call. Or you call them back, or you give up and put it into the sale."

"I can just give up? Won't I get in trouble for that? What if they call back two months later?"

"Meh, their loss. Obviously they haven't been looking for it all that hard."

"I guess." Ben picked up the squat Santa figurine that was next in the pile. "Well, I'm going to start on this. You go do some shelving or shredding or something and then come back to double-check me?"

"Thought that's what I was already doing." She slipped off the edge of his desk and headed out to the bullpen. "Holler if you need me!"

Ben worked his way through the pile meticulously, double- and triple-checking before he entered it into the sale spreadsheet along with his appraisal of its value. He pulled up a couple sites dedicated to collectables once or twice, but there wasn't anything really exciting. An hour later, he flagged down Sylvia as she trundled another cart into the warehouse.

"Okay, I think I'm pretty well set with these. Tell me if I missed something."

Sylvia shooed him out of his seat and settled in with the trackball mouse, swiftly alternating between screens. Ben grabbed the cart and wheeled it down to the appropriate bay and started shelving. In the second tray, a green Hess truck leered up at him. He picked it up, and carried it back to his office.

"Hey, Sylvia."

"Go away, Ben, I'm not done yet. Do some shelving, or something." She grinned at him.

"Sure. But afterwards, do you think you could show me how that DMV database works?"

This takes a keen eye and a sharp mind. After years and years of practice, I can immediately tell what something is worth. And if it will sell. All those pricing catalogs are useless; the only surefire way to price things appropriately is by personal experience.
~ *Gertrude Biun*, Property Office Manual

That evening, as Sylvia hollered, "Goodbye, don't stay long," from the door of the warehouse, Ben pulled up the DMV database to put what she had taught him into action. He started poking around in the database settings, getting familiar with the search restrictions for car registration by color, partial license plate, make, model, state, and even county and city.

He narrowed his search to the state of Georgia: green pickup trucks, and hit the search button. There were 2,763. In the state of Georgia. It was an impossibly high number, and there was no way he could check out everyone who owned the elusive vehicle. He stared at the screen trying to decide what to do next and then narrowed it down to just the counties surrounding Savannah. There were still 1,579. Better, but still too many to try and track down just on his own. He'd have to get more specific in his search by going back and seeing if there were any other details that the eyewitnesses reported. The printer took a long time to spit out the list of fifteen hundred trucks, but he was determined to bring it home with him to see if anything aligned with the tips waiting at home.

He was just about to log off of his computer when his inbox chimed. He opened the message titled, "Your Report."

Thank you for reporting this problem in the United States Postal Service. Employees like you help us to continually improve the working conditions and service of the USPS. A case log has been opened and you will be contacted within 4-6 weeks to resolve this matter if we find it requires our attention. ~Senior Management.

"Well, someone thinks their time is valuable," Ben muttered to himself as he grabbed his briefcase. Bureaucracy at its finest, but if they didn't think a safe full of missing goods was important, he wasn't going to waste his time on it either. He shut down his computer and shoved the leftover half of a sandwich from lunch into his briefcase, crumpling a few of the Missing flyers. He pulled them out and tried to smooth them. He'd gone through quite a lot of flyers that weekend, a couple hundred at least, and he was angry for ruining even a few. His working theory was that you never knew which flyer was going to be the one to bring his boy home. Plus, all the copying was starting to get pricey.

Tossing the ruined flyers into the recycling bin under his desk, he headed out toward the front door. He passed the industrial photocopier in the hall and he paused. There were still a few good copies in his bag; what would it hurt to run a few off in the office? It would only be a few, not too many, and he doubted anyone would even notice. He made twenty-five copies and thrust them into his bag before hurrying out into the evening.

Ben arrived the next morning with a list of details about the green truck that he had pulled from the tips and planned on diving back into the search engine since the list he had printed had just been too long to wade through in an evening. But as soon as he entered the warehouse, he was derailed from his planned research by Sylvia, who bounded out of his office chair when he walked in.

"Ben! We have a *claim*!" She grabbed him by the arm and towed him over to his computer. "Log in! Geoffrey said he sent the form to you this morning. God, I love these days." Her excitement was a bit over the top for his hangover to handle, and Ben wished she had just taken care of this herself before he'd gotten there so he could just dive back into the database.

Sylvia circled his chair like a caged animal while he logged in and booted up his email. The first email did indeed read, "Claim." He opened it, found the retrieval tag, and headed back into the warehouse to find it. "So I take it we don't get many of these." He told himself he didn't really care, but Sylvia's enthusiasm was infectious. She was literally skipping down the aisle ahead of him.

"Maybe two or three a week. We manage to just return a lot of the mail. Most of this stuff, though, people don't care about. So I really like these days."

It turned out that the object in question was a taxidermied armadillo from 2008, frozen in a state of half-curled agitation. It sat on its back and rocked gently when nudged. Sylvia set it in motion and laughed. "This thing is kinda cute, isn't it?"

Ben grimaced. He didn't think taxidermy should ever be practiced as it always just looked creepy to him. "I don't know.

It's trapped in an eternity of exposed fear. Not sure 'cute' is the right word." He scooped it off the shelf and was surprised by the heft it had. "One armadillo, returned to its rightful hunter."

He returned to his desk with the creature in question and turned to the filing cabinet. "Any other forms I have to fill out for this poor sod?"

"Nope, just the communal log, and then that log over there where you sign it, and then take a photograph of it and upload it to the database, and then I'll go pack it up for you."

A sigh escaped him. It was a ridiculous amount of paperwork just to return something to its rightful place. "Well that's not much at all, now is it?"

"Compared to how these systems used to run, it's hardly anything at all." She reached into the recycling bin to find a piece of paper to write down the claim's address. "In the 1890s, it was all paper forms, and no one knew how to find them again once they'd been filed. This is much better." She flipped over the paper to see what she was writing on and Benny's face stared back at her.

Ben looked over to see what had silenced her and felt the heat rising in his face. He didn't want to share this with her. Not now. But he had been stupid enough to leave those here, so he tried to cover his pain and embarrassment with nonchalance. "Sorry, they were in my briefcase and got messed up when I was on my way out yesterday." He tried to snatch the flyer from her, but she moved the paper out of his reach.

She examined him just as closely as she had been examining the paper. "Don't want to talk about it, huh? Fine. But I'll figure it out, you know." She turned it back over and smoothed it out, grabbing a pen and jotting down the address of the armadillo's owner. "I'll just go get this part started."

Ben stared after her as she left the room and then realized his hands were gripping his chair tight enough to cause his fingers to tingle. She hadn't asked, hadn't pried, like everyone else did. She didn't start offering false sympathy. He told himself that was a good thing, and he didn't want to explain it to anyone, let alone her. But she had hardly even said anything about it. He wasn't sure which was worse. He was so used to people just diving into the burden of his life without asking, but when she saw it, she said nothing, and it had hurt.

Shaking out his hands, he rolled his shoulders to try and release the tension caught there, then turned to the forms on his screen. He dutifully entered the information it requested and then printed out the hard copies that got sent to the filing center of the USPS in Omaha, Nebraska. When Sylvia came back, she took the armadillo from his desk and settled it carefully into the paper nest she had created in the center of the box.

"There. He should be comfy on the ride now, don't you think? Were there any notes or anything accompanying this that need to be retrieved from the files?"

Ben glanced back at the claim log and shook his head. "Just the 'dillo." In an effort to distract himself more than anything, he added, "I really want to know the joke behind this thing."

"I just keep imagining some farmer being pestered by this thing rattling past outside his window all night and running out in his birthday suit, waving his gun around until he finally caught it, and then had it taxidermied in its final retreat as a trophy."

"Ha. So why was it lost in the mail for so long, then?"

"Dunno. Maybe he was sending it to an old war buddy to prove there was actually something under his window all this time."

The laugh that erupted out of Ben was genuine, much to his own surprise. "You think up the craziest things, you know that?"

Her shoulders hunched and she at scuffed the floor with her toe. "It's not crazy."

Ben grinned and leaned back in his chair. "Come on, they're a little crazy, I mean, I'd never be able to think up a story like that."

"You know what's crazy? Let me tell you. Abandoned children, genocide, starving families, drug abuse, and broken homes. That's crazy. And if I make up a few stories here and there to break the tension of the really crazy shit that's out there, how is that crazy? What the hell gives you the right to call how I think crazy?" Her voice had increased in speed, but not volume, leaving her panting at the end of her tirade.

Ben raised his hands in surrender. He had no idea what landmine he had just stepped on, but it appeared to be a doozy. "I didn't mean crazy per se, more unique? I think they're fun. I meant crazy in the unique and fun way."

Sylvia turned and stalked out of the warehouse, the boxed armadillo under her arm. Ben let out his breath in one long sigh and ruffled his fingers through his hair. He couldn't fathom how what he said could have set her off like that, but he'd had the same problem with his wife from time to time, accidentally trodding all over her buttons. In an effort to see if he couldn't find out what button it was he'd hit, he made his way across the way to the bullpen and wandered up to the reader, Mina, who was taking a break and stretching out her back.

"Hey, Mina, quick question for you?"

She bent over into a quick downward-facing-dog position and looked up at him. "Where's your little sidekick to answer for you?"

"Um, that's part of the question. I kind of made a comment about how a story she made up was crazy, in a good way, but she kind of—"

"Blew up?" Mina popped back up and clapped him on the shoulder. "She's from a rather long line of crazies. All worked at one branch of the post office or another, I heard. She even claims to be related to the blind reader herself." Here Mina gestured to the austere portrait of Patti Lyle Collins, which observed all the proceedings in the mail room with a critical eye. "Her grandmother had a stroke last year. Used to work the front desk at a branch, quickest sorter I ever saw, but man could she tell a whopper. Never knew what was truth and lie with her. Well, back to work for me. You, too. And best to lay off the word 'crazy' 'round the little minx."

"Thanks for the advice, Mina." *If a bit late*, he thought. Back in the hall, he heard the distinctive sound of shredding coming from the sorting room and went to apologize to Sylvia, even though he felt her reaction was a bit over-the-top. He had learned a long time ago to just apologize first to a woman; things settled down a lot faster that way, even if he didn't really understand what he had done wrong.

She was perched on the rail of the steps pitching letters in twos and threes so they sailed through the air like Frisbees before being munched by the machine. "Sylvia?" he called up. When she didn't respond he raised his voice a little. "Sylvia!" She slipped off the rail, the box of shredding on her lap tumbling across the platform.

"Jesus! What?" She bent down and began scooping the letters back into the mail crate.

"I just wanted to apologize for earlier. I didn't realize my words were, well, offensive to you. Peace?"

She squinted down at him for a moment, arms akimbo. "Ok, who said what?"

"Well, Mina in the bullpen said—"

"Bet she left out the part where my family had me committed." She dumped what was left in her basket into the shredder and then shut it down.

The situation was making Ben more and more uncomfortable. He was completely unprepared to get drawn into anyone else's emotional mires. There was more than enough for him to be worried about as it was without adding Sylvia's drama to it too. "Frankly, I don't see how that's any of her business anyway. Everyone needs a break now and then."

Sylvia snorted and crossed her arms, leaning back against the shredder. "A break. I had a break alright. I was fourteen and when I came back to school, when the kids found out where I'd been for two weeks, well...suffice it to say, I don't like being called crazy."

"Point taken. Apology extended most sincerely." He didn't want to get involved, but couldn't help wondering what had happened at fourteen that caused her to spend two full weeks in a mental hospital.

Sylvia leapt off the stairs and stuck the landing right in front of him. "Well, now that my deepest, darkest secrets are out of the closet, may we continue with our jobs?"

"Of course. Were there any other claims that came in?"

Sylvia walked past him, barely brushing his shoulder as she went. "No. By the time the readers give up on them and pass them to us, it's unlikely that anyone is actually looking for the stuff. Instead, I got a lot of shelving to do today. How about I bring you a cart and you do the entry, and when you're done I'll bring you another cart and then shelve the one you entered?"

"Sounds like a plan that has me chained to the desk all day and likely to give me a headache." Ben followed her down the hallway to the warehouse.

"Exactly. Once your punishment is done, I'll forgive you the crack about me being crazy." Her shoulders were still stiff with ire, and she didn't look back as she talked to him.

"That doesn't exactly seem fair. I didn't even know it was a sensitive subject!" He stopped rebelliously in front of his desk.

"I didn't say what they said wasn't true, just that I don't like hearing it." She finally flashed him a smile and went scampering across to the bullpen for his first load of the day.

Ben was forcibly reminded of a quote from an old Melville novella he read in his intro level English class. It was about the insanity-inducing burden of working with the lost letters, something about those who died unhoping. He had thought at the time that it was just more old-fashioned melodrama, but after being here for a few days, he could almost see the truth in the passage.

They managed to get through the backlog of carts fairly quickly, which left their afternoon free to catalog items for the auction once more. Focusing on books, they managed to prep sixty items for the next sale.

"I just still can't believe the magnitude of stuff that gets lost." Ben tossed the dual-language copy of Chekov into the box labeled "Lot 34 – Fiction" before logging out of the shared auction document.

"It just seems like a lot because you have to move it not once, but something like four or five times around the warehouse. It's really not all that much. I mean, how many books are in that lot?"

"So far? Twenty. And I've only scanned about half the shelf looking for the appropriate items."

"I think the estimate last year of books mailed through the postal service was in the neighborhood of twenty million. So your twenty? Nothing."

"I guess if you look at it that way." Ben stood to stretch and then picked up the box to take it to the auction preparation section.

"Grains of sand on a beach, that's all this is." Sylvia picked up the armload of stuffed animals that they had also entered. A teddy bear with a worn nose and a missing eye escaped her grasp and fell to the floor with a muffled clatter.

"Did you hear that?" She dumped her armload into Ben's arms and stooped to pick up the ragged bear.

He struggled to maintain a grip on the box that was now piled high with fake fur. "Heard you drop something. What was I supposed to hear?"

"It didn't sound like a stuffed animal. There's something in here." Sylvia shook the bear, but nothing rattled, and it didn't look like there was anything inside but stuffing. She poked its body and arms, trying to determine what it was.

Ben stifled the urge to mutter a curse and started to make his way back to the auction bay, struggling to see over the pile of stuffed animals. "It probably just fell on its eye or something."

"I swear there was something else in here. Ah ha!" She had the bear by the nose and was squeezing. "Something in here all right." She gave it a tweak and nearly dropped it again when an artificial voice box coughed into action.

"I love youuuuu…" It trailed off into silence with a gargled moan.

Sylvia handed the bear to Ben as though it were a child, turned, and walked out of the warehouse. Ben juggled to keep the bear aloft along with the other eight animals in his arms as he turned to take them to their new shelf. He knew how she felt; the decaying recording had sounded so melancholy and despairing, an unrequited love lost in the mail center. As he put them down, he adjusted them carefully so that they were sitting upright and facing each other in a circle. He straightened the bear's head and ran a hand over its ears before heading back to his desk. He cleared his throat a couple of times before continuing the paperwork.

The rest of the week passed in a similar fashion. It seemed the bear incident had cut through the last of Sylvia's ire and she was interacting normally with him again. Or, at least, normal for her. They dropped easily into a habit of cataloging and organizing the incoming objects and then spending their extra time prepping items for the auction. They had one more claim during the week, a painting that appeared to be done by a fourth or fifth grader. It had apparently been addressed by the child as well because the address had been entirely illegible. It was forwarded on to the appropriate grandparent. Sylvia also kept up with her shredding, and those few times she was out of the warehouse, Ben turned on a radio to help cut the silence. As soon as the clock struck five, or sooner if he could manage it, he was out of the office and away home, carefully constructing the new web of data surrounding the map of Atlanta.

On Friday Ben decided to stay after work and explore the resources that were inherent to his job. Not only did they have the DMV database, which was proving a bit too massive to be of help at the moment, but they also had all sorts of other databases at their fingertips. There was photo recognition software, data-mining software, and subscriptions to all the major online databases for news and scholarly pursuits. On a whim, Ben brought up one of the news databases and entered his son's name.

Your search for "Benjamin +Grant" has returned 400+ entries. Display All. Refine Search.

Ben stared at the screen. More than four hundred entries? That didn't seem possible. The Georgian papers hadn't even run maybe twenty articles. He selected *Display All* and started scrolling through the results. The first ten or so were about his son's disappearance, but after that, the relevance seemed to start trailing off. Apparently there was a little known writer/singer/songwriter from Australia whose name was Benjamin Grant Mitchell. Ben returned to his original search screen and selected *Refine Search*. He entered *Missing* into the search terms and hit the search button.

Your search for "Benjamin +Grant +Missing" has returned 47 entries.

Well, he'd been surprised at the four hundred search results, but forty-seven was equally unsettling. So few articles about the time in his life where everything fell apart. It seemed obscene that so few newspapers could have cared enough to run any articles at all. Besides, it wasn't like he expected to find anything new, but he didn't know if some little known, possibly connected news article might spur a new connection in the facts on his wall. But with only 47 articles ever written about the disappearance, it didn't seem likely.

He started scrolling down the page, scanning the titles of the articles.

5 Year Old Missing in Savannah

. . .

Benny Grant Goes Missing, No Suspects

. . .

Nationwide Hunt for 5 Year Old

. . .

Boy Missing, Father Prime Suspect

. . .

No New Leads in Case of Missing Boy

. . .

Stats: Missing Children in 2009

Ben quickly exited the search engine, fighting to breath normally. A statistic. After one year Benny was reduced to a statistical summary. Doing the search had been a mistake; it always was, looking at the media response. All they cared about were ratings. They would pretend they wanted to help find your child, but then they would lose interest, just like everyone else. If he had his way, he'd start his own organization where all they did was help with the search for missing people —especially children.

He rubbed his hands roughly over his face and leaned back in his chair until his breathing moderated, then shut down his computer and left. He needed to get more flyers out, get more data points. That was the only way he was going to help his son, not by brooding over journalistic sensationalism. As he drove home, he started to plot his papering route for the next day.

Ben planned to spend Saturday afternoon handing out flyers in front of the Six Flags park, which wasn't more than ten minutes from his office, a whole twenty from his apartment on Cascade Road. Wanting to be polite, Ben first spoke with the manager of the park, asking for permission to talk with the day's guests.

The manager stopped scribbling on his clipboard and stared at Ben. "You want to do what?"

Ben had lost count of the number of times he had explained himself; managers, police, and belligerent citizens all demanded he explain himself multiple times before they would decide he wasn't some scam artist. "Hand out flyers about my son. He went missing last year."

"Here, show me one." The manager dropped his clipboard and held out a hand.

Ben gave over one of the flyers from his bag and waited, shifting his weight in the small plastic chair. The manager took entirely too long to study the simple image and three lines of text.

"You want to hand this out to our patrons?"

He wouldn't have asked, three times, if he didn't want to. "Yes, please."

"As they come into the park? Forget it. Maybe as they exit. Maybe." The manager flipped the paper back to Ben and he had to stretch to reach it before it hit the floor.

He was irritated by the way the man was treating him, but he still thought this was a good venue. "I will take what I can."

The manager nodded, pleased, and picked up his clipboard again. "Alright, you can stand by the exit. No hassling people as they come into the park, and if they ignore you, you ignore them, got it?"

"Sure thing, thanks. If I may, though, why only as they exit the park?"

"Stuff like this makes people sad. Sad people don't spend money. Wait until they're tired and irritable and their wallets are already empty." It seemed like the man was reading off of a script in his head, already starting to ignore Ben.

"That's…industrious of you."

"Thanks. That's why I run this place and you don't. Now get going. I have a ride with a retainer stuck in the tracks to take care of before the crowd kills us all."

For six hours, Ben manned the exit turnstiles, handing out the flyer to any of the worn and tired families that would take it. As the day wore on, clouds started gathering. At first he was grateful for the shade, but it started raining about five o'clock. Not a nice refreshing rain, but the kind of sticky misting rain that just increases the humidity level and leaves everyone miserable. The families started pouring out of the park, unwilling to deal with the weather on top of each other.

Few people would stop to take the flyer. No one had anything to add to his search. As he was getting ready to leave, Ben asked one of the anonymous-looking ticket clerks if he could speak with the manager again.

"If I can find him." He started muttering into the walkie-talkie in his booth, listening absently to the reply.

"The man says he's busy. Can't see you again."

"I just wanted to thank him, ask if I could leave some flyers at the ticket booths."

The young man muttered again into the talkie.

"The man says you're welcome, but you can't leave those flyers at the kiosk. They make people sad."

"Yeah, yeah, they make people sad. That's the fucking point, to get people thinking." Ben started sneezing, then muttered, "Thanks anyway." He turned and strode to his car, digging through his bag for his keys. He fumbled them and slammed his hands against his car in frustration. A whole day lost to idiot managers who had no humanity and families who couldn't feel empathy for a fellow father in pain. You can bet that if they lost one of their squalling spoiled brats they'd be the first to demand that people pay attention. But they couldn't spare one iota of attention for his pain.

Once in the car, he noticed that he was down to just ten flyers in his bag and he knew he had less than fifty left at his apartment. He wondered when he was going to have time, or money, to make more copies.

Ben spent the rest of the night shifting through his copies of the tip line, the police reports, and interviews and started compiling a list of things he might be able to double-check in his new databases at work. He had lists of vehicles, addresses, names, blurry photos, and multiple suggested timelines. He wasn't sure what he was going to do with all of it, but the whiskey had suggested that the more lists he put together, the better his chances were of finding something significant.

He fell asleep at his desk, head thrown over the back of his chair and an empty whiskey glass tipped over in front of him, along with a mostly empty bottle. When he woke, he frowned, thinking the bottle had been almost full yesterday, then carried it and the glass into the kitchen. His head felt fuzzy and thick, his sinuses ached, and he wondered if he hadn't had just a little too much to drink.

It quickly became apparent that this was not a simple hangover. In fact, he had come down with a nasty cold, and he did not have anything at all that would make him feel better. Even the orange juice container was empty, yet still in the fridge.

Sighing, he drank several glasses of water and munched on toast spread with peanut butter while trying to gear himself up to go to the store. He finally managed a shower and a change of clothes and stumbled out to his car, determined to make it to the Publix nearby before going back to bed. He pulled into the parking lot without incident and stood outside his car for a moment as his equilibrium stabilized.

"Ben?"

His name pulled his attention to the neighboring row of cars and a short pixie-cut lady. Sylvia. That was the name.

"Boy, you don't look so hot." She put her laden canvas shopping bag into her backseat, locked her car, and came over to him.

His smile even felt sloppy to him and it took an effort to stand up straight in front of her. "Actually, I feel quite warm, thank you. I think it may be the fever."

"Hm, might possibly. Do you need some help getting stuff? Carry anything for you?"

"No, no, I'm fine, absolutely." A thought came swimming

up from beneath the fog in his brain. "Wait, why are you here? You live nearby?"

"Yes, yes I do." Sylvia was fighting hard to keep a smile off her face. "Just down Cascade, at the edge of the historic district."

"I live on Cascade too, just closer to work." As he stood there, his sinuses draining, he couldn't help but think how pretty she looked when she wasn't harassing him with stories or questions. He blamed his slightly lecherous thoughts on the fever, since he couldn't yet blame them on cold medicine. "Isn't the historic district a bit pricey for someone with your job?"

"Gee, how tactful you are today." She took him by the arm and started walking him to the store. "If you must know, I live in my grandmother's house."

Even though he was sick, Ben could tell there was something a little vague about her reply. "You live with your grandmother?"

"No. She's…not living there now, but I live in her house and sort of watch over things and everything."

"That's quite decent of you." He absently patted her hand on his arm, thankful for her support. "You know, I'm not as sick as I may seem. I am perfectly capable of taking care of myself."

"I'll believe that when I see it," she muttered under her breath. "Men can't ever take care of themselves."

He shook off her arm when they reached the doorway and made shooing motions. "Go. Can't have two of us sick at work, so you stay away. I am going to blitz this stupid virus with every possible item in the cold war arsenal. So, shoo." He wavered a bit at the loss of the extra stability she had provided but managed to stay standing.

She backed away with her hands up. "Fine, fine, but call me if you need anything, okay? Or if you need to take Monday off, that's fine. I can cover things."

He considered this a moment, clinging to the handle of a cart. "I would if I had your number, but the only number I know is work."

"Well, that won't reach me at all. Here." She rummaged in the pockets of her pants and vest until she came up with a receipt and a pen. "This is my cell phone. Seriously, if you need anything. Chicken soup, a movie, ginger ale, please don't hesitate."

Ben took the proffered slip of paper and stuck it in his back pocket next to his wallet. "Thank you. I didn't realize how much I relied on, well," he paused, thinking of Jeannie, "other people when I was sick to have this kind of stuff around."

She smiled and reached up to cup his face in her hand. "You'll get through it." She straightened up and flung one hand imperiously at the automatic doors, causing them to whoosh open. "I now charge you to launch the nukes."

The laugh Ben managed to dredge up was halfhearted, but Sylvia bowed and waited for him to get into the store before returning to her car.

The checkout clerk just snorted knowingly when Ben unloaded his basket onto the checkout counter. Three kinds of cold medicine, a large container of orange juice, six cans of chicken soup, and a small can of Vick's Vapo Rub. His mother had used it on him when he was a child, but Jeannie had banned it from the house, claiming the scent of it burned her nose.

He dragged himself home and sank onto his bed with a pile of notes and his laptop computer. He opened one of the packets of pills, took the recommended dosage, and then tried to start organizing the lists he had made yesterday and identify which facts fit which program. It wasn't more than five minutes before he was out cold, the laptop sliding from his lap to the coverlet, the notes spilling onto the floor. He woke again around four, microwaved an instant serving of Campbell's chicken noodle soup, sipped at it while he tidied the papers on the floor, then returned to bed with another dose of meds.

The next time he woke was as his alarm went off for work. He felt remarkably better, though he still had a very stuffy nose and a sore throat. He took some decongestant and managed to get to work without incident, walking into his office in time to meet Sylvia bringing in the first cart of the day.

"Well someone is looking much better today. The drugs worked?"

Ben had to clear his throat twice before answering. "Frankly, I think it was more the sleep. I don't think I was awake more than four hours total yesterday."

"That sounds lovely. I love days in bed like that; they do wonders for you." She rattled into the warehouse. "Unfortunately I don't get much of that. I spend so much time here that the weekends are the only time I can do all my errands, visit my grandmother, stuff like that."

"You know, that's so wonderful of you. Too few people visit their incarcerated loved ones." Ben slumped in his chair while he waited for his computer to boot up.

Sylvia paused before replying much more cautiously than usual. "She is not incarcerated. She asked to be moved to the nursing home after the hip replacement didn't really work out. She felt she was going to be too much of a burden."

"Sweet of her. The both of you, too sweet for words." Ben dodged the stuffed piglet that came sailing through the air at him. "What?" He leaned over to retrieve it from the floor and sent it back to her.

"You're just in an impossible mood this morning, aren't you?" Sylvia had to leap to catch the pig on its return flight.

"Just sick. I have often been told I'm quite the ass when I'm sick. Is it true?" He did his best to give her puppy eyes, not hard since they were watery from all the sneezing.

"Humph. We'll have to see. I haven't decided yet." Sylvia dropped the forms from the new items on his desk and wheeled the cart back out of the warehouse as Ben started entering all their information.

He felt progressively better throughout the day and at lunch he stopped at the copy machine to print off another fifty copies of the missing flyer. He felt a faint twinge of guilt when he pressed the Start key, but the heft of the flyers soon calmed him down.

At about four o'clock, Sylvia came skipping back into the room, brandishing a claims form. "We've got a live one!"

Ben stood from his desk. "What is it this time?"

"Looks like it's a photograph. Oh cool! It's from long-term storage, too!" She ran down the hall and skidded to a stop in front of the filing cabinet for older photographs.

"Okay, let's see. It arrived in 2002 and apparently it's a set of wedding photos." Ben came over to help her look for the correct ID tag in the file of photos from 2002.

"Wedding photos? And it took them eight years to realize they were missing?"

Sylvia shrugged. "Any number of reasons, probably. Could you print off the claim form?"

"Sure thing." Ben slipped back behind his desk and hit print while Sylvia hovered over the printer.

"Whoops, out of paper."

Ben continued to enter the claim information into the appropriate logs. "Should be more sitting beside the printer."

Sylvia put paper into the printer from the stack on the left and the printer started to spit out the forms. "Oops. Ben, I think I grabbed from the wrong pile."

He turned around and saw that the forms she was brandishing all had his son's missing flyer on the back. He sat there blinking for a couple moments, then held out his hand for Sylvia to pass him the flyers.

"Maybe not." He flipped the papers over and back, and he started to smile. "This could work." He handed the forms back to Sylvia and started drumming his fingers on the desk. "We could print the flyer on the back of each form we send out, see if we can't get the readers in on it, put it on all of the mail they return, on the damaged mail forms, everything. How many forms do you think we send out in a day?"

"I don't know, maybe two or three hundred?"

"That's two or three hundred people who would then know about Benny." He slapped his palms down on the desktop. "This could really work. What do you think?"

"I think you're the one that's crazy. And I know crazy. You know you still haven't even told me what this is all about." Sylvia snatched the forms back from him. "Besides, we'd totally get in trouble."

"Says who? We're the only ones who see those forms. Get one or two select readers in on it; who's to say it would cause any sort of problem?"

"Fine, we can try and see if they'll go for it, but only, *only*, if you'll tell me what is actually going on with you." She picked up the forms and carried them off.

That evening as Ben was getting ready to go, he stopped by the copier to make up for the flyers that Sylvia had printed on. He paused as he heard someone walking down the hallway. Celine, a reader, came into view and started to brush past him. Instead she paused and backed up.

"Illicit copying, eh?" She grinned, arms crossed belligerently in front of her.

He could feel the heat rising in his face as he struggled to lie. He had always been an awful liar. "I, uh, no. Of course not, just some claims forms from today."

"Mmhm. Sure. At 5:15. No one else is still here; I'm only here because I forgot my lunch box. And you look guilty as hell. What, don't have a poker face?"

Ben stared down at his shoes, hoping against hope that she wasn't going to get him in trouble. "I—"

"You shouldn't use your copy code for that; they'll see that you're copying too much. Here, use this one." She tapped 7845 into the machine and stepped back.

Confused, Ben finally looked up at her. "What's that one?"

"That's the administrative code. No one looks twice at the amount of paperwork those bimbos have to copy every day.

"I, thanks. I guess. Everyone does this?"

"Mmhm. Copy my taxes every year on that thing and an occasional school project for my daughter. It's just easier than going out to find copiers. Matthew copies his manuscripts, Bethany her headshot portfolio for the local theaters, pretty sure everyone's copied at least one thing on here before, if not more." Celine leaned on one end of the copier, arms crossed. "So, what are you copying?"

"I think I'd rather not say."

"Oh please. If it's your ass, I'd love to see it." She snatched the flyer from the top feeder of the copier before Ben could stop her. The grin on her face quickly faded to a frown and she looked up at him. "Ben, is this…?"

And here was yet another person he really didn't want to know. He sighed and held out his hand for the flyer. "My son."

"Oh god. I'm—shit—I'm sorry. Here." She smoothed out

the small wrinkles her grab had caused and gently passed the paper back to him. "Teaches me to put my nose in where it's not welcome."

"No, it's fine. Any other trick to the copy settings?" He typed in the new code and set the copier to thirty copies. He was feeling more comfortable with the whole illicit copying thing, considering they couldn't be bothered to keep watch over their own budget. And if everyone used it, who was he to look the gift horse in the mouth? Now he just wished Celine would drop it and leave him be.

"Nope, that's it. Sorry again." Celine was leaning against the wall now, hugging herself, the frivolity gone.

He felt a sudden urge to explain himself to this woman, a reader he'd never even had a conversation with before today, but there was nothing else to do while the copies ran and she showed no signs of leaving, and he felt he needed to justify himself as she watched his copies spool out. "I left Savannah because that's all people saw me as, the dad with the missing kid. Some even thought—" He shook his head, once more hearing the angry accusations, and then continued. "It was nice for a few days, being up here where no one really knew who I was. Maybe some remembered the news footage from last year. Most don't."

"Not exactly something I'd want to be spreading around if I didn't have to."

He sighed and leaned against the copier. "No, that's not quite it, not entirely. I was just tired of the pity. God, you don't want to hear all this." The copier spat out the last sheet and Ben picked them up, straightening them carefully.

"No, it's okay, really. It's interesting, at least. Wait, that's the wrong word, makes me sound creepy." She waved her hand dismissively through the air at her own gaffe and then straightened up from her slouch against the wall. "What I mean is, I don't mind listening if you need to talk."

"No, I'm done. I really don't like burdening people with this. But thanks. And thanks for the code."

"Sure thing, Ben." She turned and started to head for the front door. "Oh, and Ben? I hope you find him."

A wry smile tilted one corner of his mouth up. "Thanks. So do I."

As he walked back to his desk to grab his satchel, he pondered the fact that telling Celine what was going on had actually felt good. He didn't know if it was the telling, the relief of not trying to keep it from her, or the fact that she took it so well. As he stopped in his cubicle, he heard a whispering from farther in the warehouse. He stepped quietly to the edge of the bays and made his way down toward the sound.

"They just don't get it, you know? It's hard, it's really hard sometimes, to figure out what's real and what's not. I'm not the only one. I read the letters. I know we're not supposed to, but do they really expect us to scan them without actually reading what's there? I mean, come on. We all just pretend that we don't understand what's in the letters, that we're just looking for clues to the owners. But it's all in there. People who don't know their lovers are dead, people who don't want to know. Kids who think Santa is real, kids who think he's fake but are writing because their moms don't think they've grown up. So what if I don't always 'grasp reality,'" Ben could almost feel the air quotes the speaker put up. He peeked around the corner to the long-term storage bay and saw the reader Jillian leaning against the shelves, talking to the urn of Uncle Shem's ashes.

"Seriously though, you think my family would be a little more understanding, a little less judgmental. So what if they don't believe what I believe? They don't have to call me a conspiracy nut-job. Sometimes I just wish I was alone. No, you know I don't mean that. At least I have you to talk to, that helps. Anyway, I should probably be getting home now, the llamas need feeding."

Ben scurried back to his desk as noiselessly as he could and started tidying the papers on it. Jillian came into the pool of light cast by his desk lamp, clutching her purse to her chest. She froze when she saw Ben standing there.

"Oh! Jillian, right? Sorry, didn't know anyone was still in here. Find what you were looking for?" He smiled gently, picking up his bag and slinging it over his shoulder. He knew she would be mortified if she knew he'd been listening.

"I—yes and no. Silly claim from earlier. Was sure there was nothing, and I was right." She took two steps towards the door. "I'll see you tomorrow."

Ben shook his head as she bolted, leaving the warehouse door open. She was an odd duck, but no more so than anyone else he'd met here already, or himself, for that matter. He finished shutting off the lights and headed toward the front door. As he stepped out of the warehouse, he almost ran into Sylvia.

"Oh, for God's sake." He steadied her with his free hand. "Doesn't anyone ever leave this place?"

"I might say the same to you. Making more copies were you?"

"Yes, but if I'm here this late doing illicit copying, and Jillian's here to talk to Uncle Shem over in the corner about her conspiracy theories, what in the world are you doing here?"

"Talking to old ashes, huh? Well, she's always enjoyed their chats."

He hitched his bag farther up his shoulder and planted himself in her way. "I'm waiting."

She pouted. "You are no fun. I want to know what's going on." She leaned forward and poked him in the chest, hard. "For real this time. Enough pussy-footing around."

Ben sighed and rubbed a hand over his face. He still felt like he shouldn't be sharing his story around at work where he had to see the pity in people's eyes everyday, but talking that little bit with Celine hadn't been as off putting as he thought it would have been. "Fine. But not here, can we go someplace else?"

"Sure. There's a great bar just down the road."

"Perfect. I could really use a drink right about now."

They were ensconced at a back table at JR's Lounge shortly thereafter, Ben with a Peachtree and Sylvia with a Guinness.

"Interesting place." Ben was trying to look around without being obvious. And stall. He didn't know how to start since most people he talked to about this already mostly knew what was going on. "You wouldn't even know this place was back here if you didn't know about it."

"That's the best part; the party boys don't know about it. You can come drink here without anyone bothering you. Now. So far I know that your boy is missing and that you and your wife have split. Not surprising really. A lot of marriages have trouble after their children have died. Not that he's dead," she hastened to add. "Missing. There isn't any reason to think he's dead, is there?"

"No, no, but let me tell this at my own pace. I haven't had to…most people in Savannah just knew. Now I have to explain it all again. And, unlike most people, you aren't content with 'My son's missing, what else can I say?'"

"No, no I'm not. Besides, I know it helps take the sting out of things to get them into the open air, no matter how much it hurts to do it."

He wasn't sure about that bit of colloquial wisdom, but he had decided to tell her and he would follow through on that. It was also a sure bet she wouldn't let him leave without a fuss if he didn't tell her. Ben drained half of his beer before he figured out where to start. "I guess I should start at the beginning. Well, when he disappeared at any rate." Ben flagged the bartender and gestured for another beer before draining the rest of the bottle.

You don't see many of these now, but they used to be fairly common. Lazy office clerks don't notice that an envelope hasn't got anything on it and just chuck it into the mail. There is no way for them to be sent to the right person or even returned to the sender. Sometimes they're damned important, too.

~ *Gertrude Biun,* Property Office Manual

On That Day, as he had come to think of it, the wooden box in Ben's hands was smooth, the inlays dating it to at least the 1800s, but someone had replaced the hinges recently and poorly. He probed at the loose nails, deciding he would need to pry out the hinges completely, use filler, and then attach something more period appropriate than stainless steel craft hinges. He hated when people couldn't be bothered to take the time to do something right.

"Da-ad. Can I see the box? Can I?" Benny knelt on the stool behind the counter of his parents' antique shop. More properly, his mother's shop, but Ben was the one who did most of the buying and selling as well as all of the repair work. The five year old teetered as he made a grab for the box in his father's hand, steadying himself against the counter.

Ben lifted the box out of his son's reach, still focused on the repair job at hand. "It's a box. There are plenty of others in the store to go look at. I need to fix this one."

"But I've seen all the other boxes. They're boring. That one has cool patterns on it. Kinda like the Republic symbol from *Star Wars*." He made lightsaber noises as he caused the stool to sway onto only two legs before it resettled with a thunk.

His son's words didn't quite make it through to his attention and Ben asked, "The what?" He pulled pliers from his back pocket and started to gently work the nails loose from their seating.

"You know, the circle with the thingy in the middle that the Republic has on all their uniforms and ships and everything." His fidgeting started to tip the stool to the side again, and Ben placed one large hand on top of his son's head to steady him. He was amazed that his son had only had two trips to the emergency room for stitches by this age, considering how often Ben had to catch him from falling while he was doing something stupid like rocking the stool off its feet. It wasn't like Benny got that reckless behavior from either of his parents, but the boy just didn't care about pain or danger.

"Enough. Sit down properly. Come on, feet out from under you."

Benny sighed, squirming until his feet drummed on the legs of the stool and his butt was firmly placed on the seat. "Now can I see it?"

"When it's fixed. Can you watch the counter? I need to go in the back and get started on this. It's almost closing time; there shouldn't be anyone coming in. But if they do—"

"I *know*. Call for you as soon as they come in." Benny

crossed his arms and kicked harder at the stool as Ben went into the back workroom.

He was careful to avoid nicking the beautiful wood of the box as he pried out the bad hinges. The wood filler was out on his workbench from a project the day before, and he took his time filling the holes, ensuring that every last air pocket was accounted for before using a soft cloth to wipe up the excess and then place the two halves of the box on his drying rack. This was the kind of work that he loved doing, setting everything to rights, bringing out the beauty in an old craftsman's work. It was a kind of meditation to him, finding all the cracks and filling them, refinishing wood so the stains wouldn't show, making each piece beautiful and tidy.

Since his son had not called out to him, Ben went to his odds-and-ends shelf and started poking around for a set of hinges that would work with the mahogany and pine tones of the box. It took him another five minutes to find the ones he wanted, a set of brass hinges that had been too small on the tea caddy they had originally closed. Tossing them on his desk to attach to the box in the morning when the filler had dried, Ben returned to the front of the store.

His son was not sitting on the stool behind the counter. This in itself was not unusual; Benny was like any five year old and had a hard time staying in one spot for long.

"Benny, where'd you go, champ?" There was no answer. Worrisome, but not more so than usual.

"Benjamin Grant, you come out here right now. No games. It's time for me to start locking up. Do you want to lock the front door?" Still no answer. Benny loved being allowed to lock the front door.

At this point, Ben started searching around the store in earnest, opening chests and wardrobes, a soft fear catching in his chest and making his breath a little shorter and sharper. "This isn't funny, young man. Stop hiding. Where are you? Don't force me to call your mother." When this threat failed to get the usual panicked response, Ben really started to worry. He went to the front door, but there wasn't any sign of a boy, just a few shopkeepers on his small side street starting their own closing routines.

"Bernard! Did Benny come out here?"

The grocer across the way shrugged and shook his head. "Haven't seen the little terror. Lose him?"

"He's probably hiding someplace in here I just haven't found yet, thanks." There was no reason to panic anyone else yet, in fact there was probably no reason for him to panic. He was sure Benny must have just wandered upstairs or something. Please let it be something. Ben retreated into the store and went straight to the phone. He dialed the extension that rang the apartment upstairs while he continued to walk around looking in and behind things.

"What's up?" Ben could hear the TV on in the background blasting one of her fitness workout tapes.

"Jeannie, did Benny come upstairs?" Jeannie either paused or muted the tape as the sound stopped abruptly.

She paused and Ben could almost see her scanning the apartment above. He prayed she would tell him yes, Benny was up there making fun of her again while she worked out. "No, I don't think so. He wanted to help you close up tonight."

Ben hesitated before admitting, "I can't find him."

"I'm sure he's just hiding in the furniture again. Remember when he fell asleep in that wardrobe?" Of course he remembered. Benny had been three and Jeannie had panicked. They were about to call the police when Ben had opened the 1894 teak wardrobe and found his son curled up on a fur coat he had pulled off of a hanger.

"I've looked in everything. He's not here."

Jeannie hung up without answering and in a moment he could hear her clattering down the back stairs. She came out of the workroom and briskly started the same search, flipping open lids and doors around the perimeter of the store. Ben headed into the center of the storefront to see if Ben was just hiding under the desks and tables grouped there.

"Weren't you watching him?" And there it was. He had wondered how long it would take her to come around to accusations. Less than a minute, record time.

Biting his lip to prevent a harsh comment, he responded, "I stepped in the back to repair that jewelry box—you know, those hinges? The one you asked me to fix because no one would buy it like it was."

Jeannie turned from the tin sea trunk she was peering into. "You shouldn't leave him out here by himself; you know how he gets into trouble." She let the lid slam down and continued on to the 1920s pine dresser.

"It was just for a moment. I wanted to get the wood filler on it before we closed up for the night and there was no one here. Benny always listens to me when I tell him to stay put."

Jeannie snorted but didn't pursue the matter. "Did he go outside?"

"Bernard didn't see him." Ben slid the heavy oak chair back into the leg well of the desk he had been checking.

"That man is blind to anything beyond his awnings, you know that." She opened and slammed every drawer in the dresser, even though they were entirely too small to fit a five year old boy.

Losing patience with her sniping, Ben slammed the next chair under its desk. "I didn't see him out there. I'll take a walk down to the park, just to be sure. I think you should call the police." By now they were opening the same pieces of furniture for the third time, just in case. The store was not that big and there were not that many pieces of furniture for a young boy to hide behind. And he needed to get away from the anger radiating from his wife. She was acting like he wasn't worried at all, like he didn't care that his son was missing.

Jeannie closed the brass-bound hope chest she had been looking in and held her hand out for the cordless phone still in Ben's hand. "Go."

Ben jogged out the door and turned to the little park at the end of the street. Benny liked to come and terrorize the squirrels and pigeons that occupied the unkempt green space, though he had always been told to never leave the store by himself. The park was empty except for a pair of teenagers necking on a bench. When he asked them if they'd seen his son, they only looked annoyed at being interrupted but promised to keep an eye out for him. But as soon as he turned away, they went right on back to swooning at each other.

His wife was still on the phone with the operator. "Yes, yes, we've looked everywhere." She covered the phone with her hand, mouthing, *They've sent someone out. Anything?* Ben shook his head. "My husband just came back in. He says Benny's not at the park or on the street."

A patrol car pulled up in front of their store and two officers climbed out. They conferred for a moment and then came into the store.

Jeannie disconnected the phone with a "Thanks, they're here," but clung to it instead of putting it back on its charger.

The shorter of the two officers addressed Jeannie. "I understand your son is missing?"

"Yes, thank you for coming. We can't find him anywhere." She turned to Ben and slipped under his arm. At least her anger seemed spent for now, taken over almost entirely by her worry. He pulled her close, taking as much comfort from the contact as she did.

The officers asked all the questions he was used to hearing from the cop dramas on TV—did they have a recent photo, how long had he been gone—and Ben answered them woodenly as Jeannie ran for a picture. It didn't seem real that those TV cops had stepped into his world now, that the questions actually were meant for him.

Jeannie came clattering back down the stairs, a wooden picture frame in her hands. She was struggling to get the back off the frame as she came down and nearly missed the last step, stumbling into the shop. "Here, this was from soccer this spring. He's grown a half inch since then."

The shorter officer passed the photo to the taller one. "That's fine. Does he have any unique identifiers right now? Cuts, scrapes? Missing teeth?"

"No, no, he got a cast taken off a month ago now. He'd broken his arm on the jungle gym at school." Jeannie moved back to lean against her husband.

Ben's mind was only half there, the other half was a mess of questions, like, had he seen anyone on the sidewalk before going back to work on the box, had he heard the front bell chime? He just couldn't remember, and the harder he pushed at the recent memories, the more indistinct they seemed to become.

"The right or left arm, ma'am?"

"Right."

"Thank you." The taller officer had moved off to speak into his radio while the shorter one continued to talk with them. "We're going to call in a few more officers to help us look around the neighborhood while my partner and I start looking around here and your apartment; is that alright?"

Of course it was okay, why wouldn't it be okay? If the officers found him sleeping under his bed or hiding in the pantry, Ben would be ecstatic. The men wasted more time asking questions about security cameras (there were none) and giving Ben and Jeannie instructions about calling their friends before starting their search. The taller one started in the store while the shorter one headed up to the apartment.

Jeannie turned and buried her head in Ben's shoulder, shaking more than ever. "Ben, where do you think he is?"

"I don't know, but we'll find him. I promise." Ben steered her to the stool behind the counter and sat her down, handing her the phone. "Start calling our friends like the officers asked."

She clutched at his arm as he moved away. "What are you going to do?"

"I'm going to go see if there is anything else I can do to help. I have to do something. I feel like I'm going to explode if I just sit here." When she didn't let go, he added, "I'll be right back. Call." He gently removed her hand and headed over to talk with the tall officer. "Officer, are you sure there isn't anything I can do? Go check other places or something?"

The taller man simply looked at him for a moment, and Ben felt as though all his faults were laid bare in that moment, the officer passing judgment on him as a man and a father and finding him wanting. "No. You need to stay here, just in case. I'll let you know if there is anything else you can do. For now, go help your wife call your son's friends."

Ben seethed at the officer's dismissal as he turned away and resumed his search. Jeannie's phone was the one with all of Benny's friends' numbers programmed into it, so it was no use trying to help Jeannie call around. Instead, he paced around the shop, straightening the antiques, brushing dust off of desktops and shelves. It was not what he wanted to be doing, but at least it kept him moving. As the search team started to arrive, Ben moved to the back workshop to get out of the way since they made it clear he wasn't going to be allowed to join them. His wife was still on the phone with one of her church friends it sounded like.

Their friends started arriving ten minutes later and were quickly absorbed into the search force. Everyone was given a copy of Benny's photo, which an officer had taken to the copy center down the street earlier. They dispersed to their respective search quadrants, milling in and out all evening and well into the night.

Every time the door opened, Ben's head shot up and he started to head over. When he realized it was just another searcher coming in for a break or new assignment, he settled back in behind the counter, his mind running over and over the five minutes before Benny had vanished, trying to tell if there was anything at all that might help the search effort.

All night, instead of being allowed to go out with the search teams as he wanted, Ben kept himself busy, making coffee, tea, and putting out snacks to keep everyone fortified. Bernard brought some party platters over from the grocery that had been meant for a customer the next day. When asked, he shrugged and simply said he'd make others. At its peak, the search force numbered fifty officers and volunteers combing the Savannah streets around the store, but they found nothing. Five separate officers searched the apartment and store and declared definitively that the boy was not hiding there. Around two in the morning, the police officers called the volunteers in and told them to go home and rest. Some of them had been on their feet for nearly seven hours. Through all of it, Ben hovered at the side of the men with the walkie talkies, straining to overhear the crackling conversations, his heart leaping at each possible suggestion of a sighting. He forced coffee and finger sandwiches into the hands of people he swore he knew but couldn't recognize through the pity on their faces.

Jeannie thanked them as they left and then sat in a chair by the door, staring out into the dark streets. Ben approached the two officers who had led things all night. "What do we do now?"

"We've put in a call to a detective, he should be here soon, and they're going to release an Amber Alert on the morning news."

"Isn't there something more we can do now? Someone else we can call?"

"If we had caught a single whiff of your son, maybe, but we haven't found anything. Nobody saw anything. There are no cameras on this street that can see your store. We need to stop and regroup. Detective O'Connor is a good man; he's found a lot of missing people. Just hold tight a little longer."

Ben ferried empty platters and cups and mugs back up to their apartment, ignoring Jeannie's silent stare every time he came back down the stairs. The vacancy of it was what frightened him; he knew how to handle her when she was screaming mad and when she became neurotic, but he had no idea how to approach this silent incarnation of his wife.

The detective, when he finally arrived, was a brisk man and going grey, but his eyes were alert and focused despite the late hour. "I know you've gone through this more times than you've cared to today, but please, one more time, what happened this afternoon?"

Ben shifted impatiently and Jeannie rubbed her hands over her face; they were desperately tired, but Ben knew that neither of them were going to be able to sleep anytime soon. So Ben retold the beginning of the story while Jeannie summarized the evening's search efforts.

She finished and briskly wiped a tear off her cheek. Not the first that evening. "He's only five, Detective. Where could he be?"

"I don't know, but it's my job to find out. Now, I want the two of you to go to bed tonight. Try and get some sleep. I know it sounds hard, but you're probably so exhausted at this point that you'll fall asleep as soon as you hit the bed. We'll start fresh in the morning. Give me a call when you think you'll be up to answering some questions."

Ben stood and offered his hand. "Thanks, Detective. Will do."

The detective left and Ben and Jeannie headed toward bed. They lay there silently, barely touching. The detective's prediction held true and Ben fell asleep quickly, though he kept waking up all night convinced Benny was calling from his room for a glass of water or to go to the bathroom. His boy was terrified of getting out of his bed at night. There were monsters underneath that would grab his ankles and haul him away.

At seven, Ben sat up, at first unable to figure out what was wrong, what was missing. Jeannie wasn't beside him, and he padded down the hall to find her curled up, still fast asleep, in Benny's too-short bed. His chest felt tight, and he had a moment of irrational jealousy for his son's bed, the fact that it could offer his wife some sort of comfort while he could not.

He closed the door, careful not to wake her, and made himself some coffee and toast and called the detective. A recording picked up and Ben left a message, simply saying that he was up and ready to get to work whenever the detective was.

Jeannie came out to the kitchen a half hour later, giving Ben a tight smile, but not saying much. She pulled out the SpongeBob SquarePants bowl and filled it with Benny's favorite cereal, without milk, and sat down at the table, poking at it with a spoon and only occasionally taking a bite.

Detective O'Connor rang their bell at nine sharp and Ben hurried down to let him in. Jeannie placed three mugs, creamer, and sugar on the table, still without saying anything. The detective thanked her.

Ben watched his wife putter, wishing she'd say something, anything really, even if it was more recriminations aimed at him. He finally turned to the detective. "Anything?"

"Not yet. It's only a matter of time. I have uniforms out canvassing a four-block radius. Someone had to have seen something, so we're checking everything. Cameras on ATMs, store cameras, every last thing we can think of. We have pictures circulating on the news every fifteen minutes, and the tip lines have been open since late last night. We're moving as fast as we can, but we don't really have much to go on." The second pot of coffee finished brewing and Jeannie filled the mugs. "I was hoping we could start today with a more comprehensive history of you and your family."

"Absolutely. Honey, come sit down, please." She shook her head and kept washing the dishes from all of the volunteers the night before.

Ben watched the detective watch Jeannie. "It's alright. I understand the urge to keep doing normal things. All I ask is if you think of something while I'm asking the questions that you speak up." He got a shrug in return. "We already have all of the basics of what happened. Let's go over his favorite places to go, in case we forgot any yesterday."

Ben waited for his wife to speak, but when she didn't, he responded, "He loves the zoo and that corner park. He always wants to go to McDonald's, you know the one with the great big play area on Montgomery?" The detective nodded and made a brief note in his ragged notepad. Ben noticed that most of the book was already full. How many of those notes were about children? How many were still missing? "We did his last birthday there."

"Anywhere else in particular?"

Again, Ben waited to see if Jeannie would say anything before answering. "Not really, he likes being in the store and at school, I guess."

Another small notation in the account ledger of the missing. "Did he ever have any conflicts with the kids at school?"

Ben couldn't remember, but he thought he would know if anyone had been picking on his son. He was as transparent as a window when something was bothering him. "No, he's a great kid, got along with just about everybody."

Detective O'Connor didn't write anything down about school. "Just about?"

"All kids get into scrapes on the playground, tussles over balls or the like. Nothing major though, no problem cases." Ben vividly remembered convincing Benny to sit still while he applied hydrogen peroxide to his elbow from a particularly rough spill. Ben had to tell him that even stormtroopers in *Star Wars* were man enough to endure the sting of the foaming liquid. After that he had behaved: stormtroopers were the pinnacle of manliness that month.

"Alright. Anybody ever show an undue interest in your son?"

Ben wrenched his mind back to the conversation. "Undue interest?"

The detective gestured vaguely with one hand. "Men in the park coming up repeatedly, customers who paid too much attention to the boy."

Ben tried to think back. All he could remember was a faceless mass and the occasional encounter with a friend. "I never saw anything. Honey? Did you?"

Again, all the men got was a head shake. Ben opened his mouth to say something about her taking an active interest in the conversation but thought better of it. On any other day that would have brought her full attention to bear, mainly on berating him, but he wasn't sure it wouldn't chase her off now.

"Ben, how was your son at home? Any trouble?" The little notebook was nearly full at that point. How many pages did each child get?

"What? No. He is a good kid." Except for his constant pestering for a puppy. When he came back, they would have to remedy that. A small one that wouldn't break things in the store. Or chew on things. He thought he knew where the county shelter was.

"How was discipline in the house? Strict?"

"Well, yes, I guess. He doesn't get away with things if that's what you're asking. He knows the rules." First rule, listen to your parents. Second rule, don't talk to strangers. Had Benny listened to those two?

The detective had filled a page of notes and turned to the back of the sheet. "How did you enforce them?"

Ben shrugged. "Oh, time-outs, no dessert, the like."

"You never hit him?"

A bowl shattered and Jeannie leaned hard against the sink. A cut on her wrist formed a slender line of blood, which began to drip onto the floor, but she didn't raise her voice. "Never." Ben started from his chair and grabbed a towel to press to his wife's wound, though the detective didn't move.

"I have to ask these questions, ma'am. You'd be surprised by the number of young kids that run away from home because they feel they have been treated unfairly." Detective O'Connor didn't meet her gaze, instead he focused on his full coffee cup, which he turned in circles on the table. "Forgive me if what I ask seems harsh. It's necessary."

Jeannie didn't seem to notice Ben's attentions. "This is a good house. We're good people, Detective O'Connor."

"By all accounts, you are. But your husband was the last one to see your son, Mrs. Grant, and we have to rule out all possibilities."

Ben rooted through the junk drawer for the box of Band-Aids and antibacterial ointment while the detective and his wife stared each other down. Finally Jeannie looked down at her arm as Ben adhered the bandage. She ran her fingers over the spot, as if noticing the pain for the first time.

"We're a good family," she whispered. She wandered back toward the bedrooms, and Ben had the unsettling feeling that he would find her curled back up in Benny's bed when he went to look for her later.

"Do you have any more questions, Detective?"

"No, not for now, thank you. You should look after your wife; she's taking this hard."

Ben stared down the hallway. "I've never seen her like this before."

"Difficult times bring out odd faces in everyone, Mr. Grant."

The days after that seemed a blur for Ben. There was a string of no-progress reports from the police, Detective O'Connor always hopeful, but never too much so. Jeannie spent the majority of her time sitting in Benny's room, making and remaking his bed with the Transformers sheets and reading the picture books on his shelves: *Tikki Tikki Tembo; Mike Mulligan and his Steam Shovel; Alexander and the Terrible, Horrible, No Good, Very Bad Day.* After a couple days of sitting around the house and waiting for word, Ben insisted on opening up the shop again. He needed to be doing anything other than waiting.

He straightened up the shop, unlocked the door, and drummed his fingers on the counter. A few customers came in, but it was mainly friends stopping by to ask how they were holding up. He didn't want to turn on the radio because at every news broadcast they were still asking for information on little Benny Grant, now missing three days. If you know anything, anything at all, please call the tip line.

All day, every time the door opened, Ben was sure he saw Benny walk into the shop before he noticed the customer or a friend bringing another casserole. Shop business seemed more brisk than usual, or maybe he was just so used to not doing anything that it just seemed noisier and more crowded than before. It was only after the third person he didn't recognize expressed condolences and pity for his missing son that he realized what was happening. They were gawkers. Vultures. They came because they heard on the news about his store and his son and they had come to feed on his suffering. Ben threw everyone out of the store and locked up early. He decided instead to work on the pieces on the store floor that needed a bit of touching up and brought a banjo to the backroom to clean up. Its metal needed shining and a rust preventative.

He stopped as soon as he realized his workbench was still taken up by the disassembled box and hinges. The design on the cover was slightly raised under his fingertips. Benny was right, it did look a bit like the symbol for the Republic.

Benny was out there somewhere and Ben was in here, unable to do anything but wait. That wasn't in his nature; he wasn't a patient man, content to let others do the work that he, as Benny's father, ought to be doing. He clenched his hand tight around the box and hurled it at the reinforced concrete of the back wall. The delicate inlay fractured on impact.

Ben stalked upstairs and sat down at the computer. Ten minutes later he was printing out a flyer that read, "Have you seen this boy?" above a picture of Benny. The tip line was printed underneath. Jeannie was still in Benny's room and didn't even acknowledge Ben when he informed her he was going out for a while.

He caught the copy center right before it closed its doors, and he made one hundred copies of the flyer. With a roll of duct tape around his wrist, he prowled up and down the streets around his house until he had run out of flyers, posting them at eye height on light poles, postboxes, fences, whatever came to hand. When he was done, he realized he was hungry for the first time since Benny had disappeared.

Back in the apartment, Ben pulled out a frozen dinner and popped it in the microwave. Jeannie drifted out of the back hallway, clutching Benny's charcoal-colored teddy bear as the timer chimed. There were fresh tear tracks on her face and Ben wondered, not for the first time, why she would cry in Benny's room alone, but she refused to cry in front of him.

"Where were you?"

"I was out putting up flyers. I couldn't sit around here and do nothing. I decided I could help this way." He sat down and dug into the steaming meatloaf and mashed potatoes.

"Do you really think it'll help?"

There was a tentative hope in her eyes, a quiet, desperate need for him to promise that everything was going to be all right. This wasn't his wife, the fiery, argumentative woman he'd fallen in love with and continued to argue with for years. This was a woman broken and scared, and he couldn't think of anything to do but try and reassure her. "I'll find our son, I promise. I won't stop until I do."

She attempted a smile but then pulled away and drifted back down the hall to Benny's room. Ben watched her go, frowning. He couldn't remember whether she had eaten that day or not.

There was still no new information. Weeks had gone by and there was never any new information. It was almost as if Benny had disappeared from the face of the earth. The news agencies had lost interest and the search was now a footnote buried in the middle of the broadcast. Then he wasn't mentioned at all.

"Can't you do something? Find a new lead?"

Detective O'Connor sat at the kitchen table, spinning his cup of coffee around and around. "We've tried just about everything at this point. If there was a lead, we would have miles more than we do now, but we don't have anything. We'll just have to wait and see if time turns something up. I know that's hard to hear, but—"

"Hard to hear?" Ben shot a look down the hallway to where his wife was still hiding and struggled to modulate his voice. Any raised voices right now made Jeannie scurry for cover. "It's fucking impossible. A five year old isn't smoke. He can't just disappear. What about the tip line?"

"There's a lot of chatter, but none of it is useful. Dammit, I'm as frustrated as you are right now."

"Could I get a copy of it, maybe try and go over it myself? I know you guys are busy, have other cases…"

The detective was shaking his head. "I'm sorry, Ben, it's against regulations. I can't let you have that record."

"Why? You guys aren't getting anywhere; I should get a crack at it!"

"I'm sorry, no. And, Ben? You two should be settling in for the long haul on this. It's not going to be quick and easy. In fact, the odds now are just not good for you. Do you understand what I'm saying?"

The coffee tasted foul in his mouth and Ben scowled. "You're saying you're giving up hope." It was their job to be looking; they couldn't give up, not on his son.

"No, I'm...trying to be realistic. You should, too." The detective stood. "If anything comes up, I'll let you know."

Ben didn't even show the detective out; he knew the way by now. After rinsing the coffee cups at the sink, Ben grabbed a fresh stack of flyers from the counter and headed out to the streets of Savannah. Each night he roamed farther and farther from home to paper the city with his son's face. It was better than nothing.

He got home a little after midnight and went into Benny's room to try and coax his wife out of it once again. He shook her shoulder and when she didn't respond, he rolled her over onto her back. A pill bottle fell to the floor, empty. It was the tranquilizers the doctor had prescribed for her a couple days after the disappearance.

He didn't remember getting the phone or calling 911. All he remembered was the paramedics coming up the back steps and bundling both of them into the back of a wailing ambulance.

Ben spent the evening pacing in the emergency room. When the doctors came out, they said they had pumped her stomach and given her something to counteract the drugs; she was still unconscious, but they were hopeful. She would need to be watched closely for the next couple weeks and they suggested she stay at the hospital, at least for a few days after she woke up. They told him to go home, to take a shower and get some sleep. Ben nodded, too tired to argue, too tired to even think anymore, and took a cab back to their apartment to curl up alone in bed.

When she was declared to no longer be a threat to herself or others, Ben helped Jeannie back into their apartment, carrying her bags from the clinic.

"It's so good to be home." Her smile seemed real enough, though it trembled with the effort to sustain it for anything more than a brief flash. It was more life than he'd seen in her in weeks, and it made him happy to see it. As happy as he could be, considering.

Ben kissed her on the forehead. "It's good to have you home." He took the duffel bag back to their bedroom and came out to find her flipping through the mound of papers he'd left on the kitchen table.

"What's this, Ben?" She paused to read a passage aloud. "It sounds like bad movie dialogue—I seen him, the other day, at the 7-Eleven on Main Street. Saying he'd been raised by wolves and right sure they wanted him back."

"It's the tip line. I got a copy of it, thought I could help look through it a bit, see if I catch anything the police missed." He started straightening the mess of papers, gently taking the one out of her hand to put it back in its place in the pile. He had developed an order and process while she was still in the hospital and he wanted to make sure the paper was properly sequenced.

"I'm a little hazy about some things on...that day, but don't I remember overhearing that you couldn't have this?"

"Well, that's what Detective O'Connor said, but you remember John, in my fraternity at school? The one who became a district attorney. Well, he was kind enough to get me a copy of the tip-line transcripts. I had to lean a little heavy on the whole brotherhood thing, but he finally caved." Ben moved all of the papers off the table to a single stack on the counter and put his notepad full of notes on top of it. "You wouldn't believe how many people called in."

"Looks like hundreds."

"More like thousands. From all over the state and even around the country. I don't put much stock in those, but there are some interesting patterns in the other stuff. I go out and post flyers every day and spend my time down in the store looking through the tip line. I feel like I'm getting close to something. At least I'm still doing something, unlike the police. They've basically given up at this point."

"But not you."

"No, not me."

Over the next few months, Jeannie saw a therapist three times a week, then twice, and finally down to once a week. She seemed more optimistic, though she still slept in Benny's room every night. She would come home from her sessions talking about carrying on for Benny, making sure he had a life to come back to, making sure she was healthy and whole for him. She was coming back to life a little bit at a time, color returning to her cheeks, and she even laughed at a joke on one of the late night shows.

But she refused to have anything to do with Ben's tip-line project or the papering. She needed to focus, her shrink said, on organizing herself instead. She meditated every morning and wrote letters to Benny that she religiously saved in a shoebox under her nightstand.

Ben wasn't sure how any of that could help. He was certain that finding Benny was the only real way to make things go back to normal so he continued to go and hand out flyers, posting them wherever he could. He scoured the tip line for any reference to their son, begging for more recent transcripts from his friend.

One Saturday afternoon, Jeannie came into the shop while he sat at the counter working on the transcripts and declared she was ready to go back to work.

Ben carefully marked his place before turning to his wife. "Are you sure?" She was still prone to breaking down at every commercial featuring a young blonde boy, and she still wouldn't let him touch her. What if a customer walked into their store with a young boy? How would she react?

She took a ragged breath and nodded. "Absolutely. Doc said it was okay if I wanted to, and I want to do this. It's all part of keeping my life together for Benny. For when he comes home."

Ben considered this a moment more, then decided that if her shrink said it was okay, she could probably handle it. "Alright then. Want the till?"

"Sure." She settled on the stool behind the cash register and ran her fingers over the buttons. "Been a while."

"We've been doing okay." Ben hadn't told her about the constant stream of sightseers, but the the vultures had been careful to buy things as well so they didn't feel guilty for gawking. He wasn't going to complain about the extra money.

"Sure, we always do well enough. Ben, why don't you go take a break, go get a coffee, or just go for a walk, something. I got this." She crossed her arms, hugging her sweater to herself.

"Ok, if you're sure. I'll be right back." Ben started to head to the front door, happy to get a chance to go paper the city in the daylight, but Jeannie called him back.

"Ben, wait, can you take these someplace else first? I can't —it's hard, looking at it. Thinking about it."

"Yeah, of course." He gathered the papers and took them into the backroom. "Better?"

"Thanks."

Eight months had gone by since Benny had vanished. No leads came in, and nothing Ben offered to Detective O'Connor seemed to be of any use. Jeannie was getting calmer, more put-together, insisting that she was focused on making sure the home for Benny to come back to was whole and healthy—always that phrase, whole and healthy. She ran the front of the store while Ben retreated more and more often into the backroom under the pretext of fixing pieces of furniture.

In reality, he spent most of his time at a wall that was usually covered by a rolling cabinet. He had taped up a map of Savannah and had started mapping the tip-line calls and their content. He had gathered newspaper articles, radio transcripts, anything at all that he could find that referenced his son. When Jeannie came back, he was quick to cover everything. He was sure that if she didn't even like looking at the transcript of the tip line, she would really hate what he was doing now. But it was necessary. He was going to find their son; he had promised he would.

Detective O'Connor was due for his monthly no-progress report. He wanted to have something new to show the detective when he came. He thought that one of the tips sounded good; it had come from two blocks away and the caller had actually given her name and contact information.

"Detective O'Connor, hello." His wife's voice echoed from the front of the store.

Ben shifted the cabinet back into place and went out to join them. "Detective."

"Ben. Jeannie. I'm afraid it's the same as every other time. There just isn't anything." The man had his hands clasped behind his back and his feet planted solidly on the floor in front of the counter.

"I understand." Jeannie was staring down at her clasped hands, fighting tears.

Ben swallowed the tightness out of his throat before asking, "What about that molester you guys found last month?"

The detective frowned. "The priest?"

"Yeah, could he have…?"

"No, I really don't think so. Those allegations are incredibly weak and they're coming from one family within the parish who has had an ongoing feud with the man over his sermon material."

"Oh. Well." Everyone was silent a moment.

Jeannie excused herself and went up to the apartment, probably to brew another of her numerous cups of chamomile tea. It was supposed to be calming. All he knew is he had come to hate the smell of chamomile.

Ben took advantage of her absence to broach the subject of a new possibility in the tip line. The two men went back to the workshop and Ben shifted the cabinet out of the way.

"This one, here, from Marjorie Leek. It seems legit. Did you guys check it out? Should I stop by and talk to her?"

The detective sighed and rubbed a hand over his mouth before replying. "Ben, Marjorie has Alzheimer's. She calls any tip line that comes up on her television screen and insists she has seen the person they're looking for. She never has."

"Maybe this time she did," Ben insisted.

The detective sighed. "She's called us over a hundred times."

Ben tried to control his mounting frustration. "But you didn't—"

"Ben, what is this?" Jeannie's voice cut through their argument and Ben winced.

He turned to face his wife, knowing that the wall of information was scattered and disorganized. Not ready for her yet. Once he found something concrete he was going to show her, prove…well, he wasn't sure what he was going to prove, but he knew this wasn't going to sit well with her. "I've been thinking, working with the tips and the information…"

"But, what is all this doing on the wall?"

Ben started over to her. "I needed to organize the information, see it all laid out."

"Get rid of it." Her hands were wrapped hard around the steaming mug and they trembled hard enough to slosh tea over the edge.

She couldn't ask that of him, it would be like him asking her to stop believing Benny was coming back in just a few days. This is how he was going to find their son and she wanted him to just stop? "Jeannie, I'm trying to find our son!" He gestured wildly at the wall, dislodging a pin. Cursing, he stuck it back in its proper place.

"Get rid of it." Her voice cracked. "Right now." She left the workroom and returned to the front portion of the store.

Ben moved to put the cabinet back in place and started to follow his wife.

Detective O'Connor stopped him. "Are you going to do as she says?"

"Why? She'll get over it. I'm doing the best I can to find our son while she sits there and pretends that nothing is wrong." Ben's throat burned again. He cleared it, coughing a few times.

The other man paused before speaking. "I think she's right; this isn't healthy for either of you."

"Not healthy for your job you mean, if I find my son before you, with all your special detective training." Ben regretted it as soon as he said it. But he couldn't take it back, so he instead glared defiantly at the police officer.

The other man was silent a moment, his eyes calm. "You need to take a break from this, Ben. It's wearing you down. Do as your wife says and take that mess down."

"Fine. Later." But he knew he wouldn't. Both of them did and the detective only let out a slip of a sigh before taking his leave.

Ben continued to work on his project mainly at night, after Jeannie had taken her sleeping pill and would be guaranteed not to stumble in and yell at him once again. It had grown to the point that it now hid behind two rolling cabinets in the storeroom and encompassed over two hundred separate pieces of paper with scribbled notes, photographs, and bits of news reports.

His eyes were blurred from fatigue, but he couldn't sleep. Not until he'd spent some time on this spider web of a chart, making whatever connections he could find, organizing and reorganizing the tip line on different hunches to see if a pattern emerged. To give his eyes a break, he picked up the beer bottles that littered his workbench and took them out the back door to the recycling bin. There almost wasn't room in it due to the stack of bottles already there, though he could have sworn that the recycling truck had come by two days ago.

Once back inside, he pulled over a stack of notecards that held the most believable tips and shuffled it. He found this method of randomization often formed interesting patterns that seemed worth pursuing. After five shuffles, he spread the cards out on the table and started moving them around, blindly pushing them back and forth, already knowing most of the content by heart. His eye started twitching and he rested his head on the desk for a moment to wait for the twitch to subside.

"I can't believe you."

Ben's head jerked off the table and he nearly fell off his stool. Light was streaming in the workshop windows and he had an index card adhered to his face with spit. Brushing it off, he turned to confront his wife.

"What?"

"This!" She gestured at the wall covered in paper, the note cards piled on his workbench. "I thought you were going to get rid of it. I thought you were supporting me, us."

Ben scrambled to wake up enough to defend his project, cursing himself for falling asleep at the desk before covering up his work. "I am. This is the only way to find our son. No one else is doing any work. I have to!"

"No, you're obsessing. And I can't be healthy here if you keep this up. The last time I asked if you had thrown this all out, you told me you had, and I believed you. If you're lying to me about this…"

Ben approached her with his arms out. "Jeannie."

"No, Ben." She backed away until she was in the doorway again. "Not—I can't."

"You haven't let me even hold you for months! All you do is sleep in Benny's room, and I can't even put a hand on your shoulder. You call that being healthy?"

"I'm healing, and you're not helping, not with this—this idiocy!"

Neither of them said anything for a moment. Ben's hands clenched and unclenched in frustration. He didn't know how to make his wife see that what he was doing was for them, for their family. How could she not see that? He was so caught up in trying to figure out a way to get her to understand that he missed the next thing she said.

"What?"

Jeannie repeated herself, stronger this time. "I want you to leave."

"But, Jeannie, please." He moved toward her but stopped when she took another step away and shook her head.

"No. This is bad. It's bad for you, and it's bad for me.

Hopefully this will make you see that." She sounded like she was trying to convince herself more than anyone else.

"Where am I supposed to go?" Ben couldn't think, couldn't process this.

"I don't know. But I want you to find someplace else." She paused. "I don't want to see you around the store, either. It'll be too difficult."

He slammed his hand onto the metal desk and she jumped. "Dammit, Jeannie! Not only do I need to find someplace to live, I need to find work, too!"

She flinched but stood firm. "You can have some of our savings to hold you over."

"Fat lot of help that is." All he was trying to do was find their son. She couldn't see that. She didn't understand. She didn't want to understand. He knew it was because she blamed him, even if she wouldn't admit it.

"Ben, I'm sorry, but it's the only way—"

"It's the only way for you to put your head so far in the sand it hits bedrock. I get it. I'll be gone by this afternoon." He turned to his web of information and started carefully dismantling it, making sure each piece of paper and pin was carefully stowed.

Sylvia swirled a shot of bourbon and downed it. She added it to the stack of glasses already on their table. "And then you came to Atlanta."

"Eventually, yes. Took me a month to land here. Staying at crappy subsistence motels, trying to find work while still having time for Benny. And then this job opened up." Ben was feeling a bit worse for wear. It was thirsty work, wrenching your heart out all over again.

"Why did you take it?"

"Hmm?" Ben had been admiring the balanced stack of

glasses they had created. His brain was fuzzy, soft, and it was hard to concentrate on the here and now instead of reliving the arguments over and over again. "Oh. The databases. I wanted access to those databases. Since the police aren't doing shit anymore, and I didn't have any way to look things up before, this seemed perfect. I can finally start doing something with all that information I've been collecting."

"Is it working? Have you found anything?"

Ben shrugged. "I'm not sure yet. I haven't had much time to actually work with the computer much. Spending too much time getting acclimatized to the warehouse. Soon though. I spend most weekends out canvassing still. There's a chance he could have ended up here; there were enough tips from this city at any rate." He lowered his head to the table for a moment in an attempt to keep the world from spinning hard enough to drop him out of his chair. It had been a long time since he'd managed to get quite this drunk and he was surprised at the amount of alcohol it had taken. A lot more than in college, that's for sure.

"Alright you, I think you need to go home." Sylvia gestured to the barkeep to close out their tab, retrieved her credit card, and hauled Ben upright. "I think you need a cab."

"I think you may be right. Just this once. Don't let it go to your head." He weaved to the door, trying not to put too much weight on the small woman beside him. They flagged down a cab and Sylvia poured him into the back seat. "What about you? How are you getting home?"

"I'll get another cab. I live in the opposite direction."

"Oh, right." Ben folded his frame into the cab.

"Before you go though, can I have a stack of those flyers?" She was leaning into the cab, putting his nose even with her breasts, though he was trying not to look.

"Sure, I guess, how many do you want?"

"Oh, I was thinking thirty or forty should do it."

"Are you going to be handing them out? Or what?" He dug through his bag and pulled a handful out. "You can make more copies at work if you need, too."

"More like posting them actually, if you don't mind."

"No, thank you, please. You can have as many flyers as you can stand. Thank you. Really, I mean it. Thank you."

She shrugged, riffling through the flyers Ben handed her. "You know me, I just like to help."

"Actually, you tend to avoid doing work and only do what you feel like." He leaned back into the seat with a sigh, closing his eyes.

"True, but this isn't work. This is finding. And I love finding things." She started to turn away, but Ben leaned forward and stopped her.

"Sylvia? Thanks. This was—thanks."

Sylvia smiled and closed the door to the cab, waving as they drove away.

When Ben rolled over to kill his alarm the next morning, he realized it had been going off for fifteen minutes already. He thought it had only been around eight when he came in last night, but he had tumbled straight into bed. And he slept straight through the night without waking once thinking Benny had just called his name. He lay there for a minute more, trying to decide if that was a good thing or not. He couldn't come to a decision and instead decided he should probably get up and get ready for work.

As he stood, the world very forcibly reminded him how much alcohol it had taken for him to arrive at that dreamless state. After he finished bringing up what little was left in his stomach he felt remarkably better, though definitely not hungry. He dragged himself into the shower and bit by bit prepared himself to face the warehouse and Sylvia.

He couldn't believe how easy it had been to tell her everything. It shouldn't have been that easy, but she had just watched him, actually listened to everything he said. She didn't interrupt with platitudes in order to cut short the pain of the telling. No. She had listened, and he could almost believe she had understood. That was a new one.

When Ben mustered into the warehouse only fifteen minutes late, Sylvia smiled at him cheekily. Even though she had consumed quite a bit herself the night before, she showed no evidence of their debauched evening. As always, she was neatly dressed in tight jeans and another of her omnipresent vests.

"I almost didn't expect to see you here today. You're a mite worse for wear than when I shoveled you into that cab last night." She finished stacking the empty trays in her cart and leaned on it.

Ben slumped into his chair and leaned his head back, eyes closed. "Nothing a morning spent in the bathroom can't fix."

"And water and Advil and dark, right?" She abandoned the cart and came around behind him to massage his temples and head. He sighed. It felt wonderful.

"Actually, I had an idea in the shower this morning that I thought I might run past you." Her fingers paused and when he made a complaining noise, she resumed.

"And what was this watery epiphany?"

"I thought I'd start with Celine when I try and convince the readers to hand out the flyers in the mail. What do you think? Is she a soft touch? Besides, she already knows about Benny."

"Oh." Her voice fell a little and she stopped the massage

altogether and went back around the front of the desk. "Yeah, sure. She's a good one. I think, though, while you try and win our fair reader over, I will go take care of the morning shredding. Let me know how it goes."

"Will do." He watched her leave before getting up carefully and doing a few soft stretches to try and work out some of the kinks. He wondered why Sylvia had been so quick to abandon the warehouse at that moment, but he was soon distracted by the prospect of asking someone for help, something he had not done in a long while.

As he walked into the bullpen, the readers ignored him completely, continuing with their morning routines. Jillian was chugging cup after cup of the acrid coffee; Geoffrey was polishing his glasses to a mirror-bright hue; Celine was busy picking out a donut from the Krispy Kreme box; and Sean seemed to be meditating.

Mustering his courage, he walked up to Celine and offered his advice. "That one has the most icing."

She didn't look up, instead focusing entirely on the box in front of her. "But I don't like icing. I'm trying to find the one with the least."

"Hard to get a Krispy Kreme with no icing, comes pretty standard."

"A girl can dream." She picked up a donut and napkin and proceeded to try and wipe off a lot of the dripping icing, resulting in a rather crumbly donut.

Ben paused before launching into his pitch. "So, I wanted to say thanks for last night."

"Sure thing, every newbie needs to learn sometime. Glad I could help." She started for her desk and Ben trailed after her.

Screwing up his courage, he finally started, "I was wondering, Celine, if maybe—"

"No, I won't go out with you."

Ben stumbled against a desk in surprise. "What? No, that wasn't what I was going to ask."

"Really? That's a damn shame, wasted a preemptive strike for nothing." She settled in behind her desk and leaned back, picking at the donut.

"No, I was just going to ask if you thought it might be possible to, maybe, include my flyers in the return forms, maybe copied onto the back of the informational flyers about why this or that package was opened? Or damaged?"

She set down her donut and faced him, crossing her arms. "Just so we're clear, you're asking me to include an unauthorized communication in official United States Post?"

Ben wondered if he'd crossed a regulatory line but decided he could always play dumb if that turned out to be the case. "Um, yes?"

"Sure. Sounds like a good plan. Reach a lot of people that way." She picked up the donut and took an enormous bite out of it, continuing with her mouth full. "'Course I can't speak for everyone, but I'm in."

He gave an inward sigh of relief. It had been a lot easier than he had expected. "Do you think you might possibly be able to help me convince some of the others as well?"

"What do I look like, your project coordinator? Go ask them your own damn self. I have work to do. And gimme one of those flyers so I can start copying it."

"Yes, of course. And thank you, a lot. I really owe you one for this." Ben fumbled one of the flyers out of his bag and set it in her in-tray.

"Could you not owe me by releasing a certain item to auction for me?"

Ben paused with his hand still on the flyer. "I'm not sure.

I mean, I can look at the piece, definitely. But I thought we couldn't bid on anything."

"Uh-uh. You and Sylvia and the auctioneering crew can't bid on anything. Nobody who has a direct say in determining what goes up for auction can bid. But we lowly readers can. As can our boyfriends. And there is a particular necklace from 1997 that has been sitting back there because it's engraved: *To my love, Celine.* It's time to come to terms that no one is going to be claiming that locket, and my boyfriend should bid on it."

"Hah, right. I'll look for it. Can't make any promises, though." Ben ran his hand through his hair. He was definitely going against the carefully laid out rules in Bunion's book now, but it couldn't hurt anything to at least look at the locket.

Celine shrugged and headed out to the copier with a stack of forms and his flyer. "I know, but it'd be nice. If you get me."

Ben grinned as he watched her begin copying the flyer onto the back of her forms. He had a good feeling about this. "I get you. Thanks, Celine. Sure you won't help me with the other readers?"

"Sure you can't release that necklace?" she retorted over her shoulder as she returned to her desk.

Ben turned to the rest of the bullpen and decided that Jillian was his next recruit. She was just starting to organize the mail in her cart into generic mail and larger envelopes with the few packages sitting on the floor beside her desk.

"Hey, Jillian, can I interrupt you for a minute?" Ben leaned on the edge of the desk. She nodded without looking up at him, continuing to organize her desk. "So, do you—uh—like working here?" He cursed himself for the awkward opening, but Jillian just shrugged, straightening the slumped pile of letters in front of her.

"So I was wondering...that is I just—" and his nerve failed

him. He sat there for a moment trying to figure out how to tell this woman that his son was missing and he wanted her help, but it was much harder than telling a random stranger passing on the street. He didn't have to see their looks of sympathy and pity every day. He passed them a flyer and they were gone. And it wasn't like she'd already found out, as Celine had. It's not like he was having to broach the subject and watch their eyes melt and their eyebrows pinch into that exaggerated look of sadness. A treacherous part of his mind reminded him that Sylvia hadn't reacted that way.

"You know, never mind. I'll catch you later." He turned and started back to his warehouse, shaking his head at his own melodrama.

"Ben, a second?" He turned back but Jillian still didn't make eye contact.

"Sometimes it helps—well—Uncle Shem is a good listener. Try him first."

Ben suppressed the smirk that threatened to cross his face, instead simply saying, "Thanks, I'll think about it." But he highly doubted that talking to a pile of ashes would do him any good. Instead, he made his way back to the warehouse to take care of the data entry for the day.

"Earth to Ben." Sylvia stood in front of him, leaning on her latest empty cart. When he looked up from the entry he was working on, she smiled. "I'm headed down the road to grab a sandwich for lunch. You want anything?"

"Oh? Sure. That'd be great. Could I get a salami on rye?" He reached into his pocket for his wallet, but she waved him off.

"It's on me today. I'm feeling creatively generous. Salami on rye it is."

"Thanks, but here. I know how much I make, and you

probably make less. Take the cash."

She pouted for a moment. "Fine. When you put it that way."

He smiled and waved her out the door. When she was gone, he turned to straightening his desk and saw the pile of flyers sitting there. "Talk to Uncle Shem, eh?" He bit his lip in indecision, then stood abruptly to go stand in the long-term storage bay.

It was silly, talking to an urn. It couldn't possibly do him any good, but both Sylvia and now Jillian had said it was therapeutic. He walked up to the urn, hands thrust into his pockets and shoulders hunched. He stared at it, then opened the lid to peer in at the ashes, replaced the lid, and backed up a step. He paced to the left and right, stopping again in front of Uncle Shem and giving it a hard look.

"Just so we're clear, I don't think this will do anything for me, got it?"

He stared a moment longer, sighed, then stared at the floor. He certainly wouldn't be able to say anything while looking at the urn, it just made him feel childish, like this was all a flight of fancy. He turned his back on Shem and pulled up a Chippendale chair to straddle while he talked.

"It's been nice this last month, no one hovering, no one asking how I'm doing, how it's going, wondering if there's been any word, or leads, or tips. I—I don't know if asking for help will start that up again. I don't want to watch them, the readers and sorters, process the information and make the connections to that haggard man on the TV last year. I want them to help but not feel sorry for me. God, the worst is when they feel sorry. 'I'm so sorry for your loss.'"

"Well, get over it." Ben yelped, whirling to face the bay's opening. Sylvia was peeking around the shelf. "Forgot to ask whether you wanted mustard or not."

A blush of embarrassment rose in his cheeks. "Mustard, definitely. Thanks." He got up, cursing himself soundly that he'd been caught. And that Sylvia had heard his maudlin and self-centered worry.

"And he'd totally tell you to get the hell over it already. Be matter of fact when you ask, look them in the eye, don't get all flustery yourself, and no one will think twice about it."

"Thanks," Ben mumbled. It was sound advice, but it wasn't going to take while she was still standing there with an amused smile on her face. He made shooing motions. "Sandwiches?"

"Leaving now, promise." She grinned and skipped to the warehouse exit. Ben groaned and covered his face with his hands, rubbing briskly. It's not like anyone could say he hadn't tried the whole talking to Uncle Shem thing. It just wasn't for him, that's all. He turned to the jewelry chest and rummaged around until he found the heart pendant that Celine had talked about and took it to his desk to look up its history.

He'd hardly opened the search protocol before his phone rang. He stared at it a moment. It had never rung, not in the two weeks he'd sat there. If anyone needed something, they walked down to the warehouse if for nothing else than to stretch their backs, sore from hunching over indecipherable letters. *How do I answer, how do I answer?*

He grabbed the receiver on its fourth ring. "Mail Recovery Center, Property Department, Ben speaking."

"Heya dude, you the one that left the message on my machine?" The voice on the other end of the line was male and sounded fairly young.

Ben thought quickly, then realized what the man was referring to. "Do you mean the message about the photograph that we found?"

The man slowed down his speech as if he were talking to

someone slow. "Yeah man, that one."

Ben ignored the tone shift. "Yes, that was me. Is it your photograph?"

"Dunno, is it a rakish-looking, black-haired dude and a devil-like skank of a whore?"

Taken aback at the vehemence in the man's epithet, Ben paused. "I—let me check." He turned around to the shelf behind him and grabbed the photo. "It's definitely a dark-haired guy wearing aviators and a tall, thin woman with red hair? Standing in front of a brown two-story house?"

"Yup, that's my photo. Man, how long've you had it?"

"It came in during August four years ago."

"Huh. So Jeff really did send it. Wondered about that."

The man trailed off and Ben set the photo down and grabbed a pad of paper. "Is there an address I can forward this photo along to?"

"What, no! Burn that fucking photo."

Now Ben was truly confused. "I'm sorry? Don't you want it, or the frame, back?"

"Absolutely not. That cunt slept with half my friends, the gardener, *and* my father before I found out. Though I'm pretty sure it was the gigolo her friends hired in Mexico for the bachelorette party who gave me the crabs."

"I—see. So, you don't want the photograph back then?" Ben wondered if all that were true, and, if she had been sleeping with that many people, how he knew who had given her crabs.

"For all I care, you could send it to hell signed, 'Can't wait to see you!'"

Ben sighed. "Well then, thank you very much for your time. Could I get your name please?"

The man sounded less agitated now that he was sure the picture was not coming back to him. "Sure thing. 'S Jerry."

"Last name?"

"Marshall."

"Thanks, Jerry, we'll take care of this for you." Ben tucked the pad of paper under his keyboard.

"Thank you. Burn that fucking thing for me, will you?"

"Absolutely." Ben hung up the phone and stared at the photo in his hands. The couple looked so happy, smiling foolishly at each other, caught by the photographer before they had really posed. The man's eyes were covered, so it was harder to read his expression, but his smile was full, and the woman looked like she didn't have eyes for anyone other than her husband. In fact, she looked a lot like Jeannie did in the picture on the beach. Happy and relaxed. Pictures could be such liars sometimes, he reflected, hiding all the pain and anger and perfectly content to ignore the fact that life was going to get hard the second the camera came down.

Sylvia came back into the room and found him contemplating the picture. She dropped his sandwich on the desk. "Oh hey, did they call back?"

"You could say that."

"So they want it, right? Such a cute picture." The crackle of her sandwich wrapping interrupted her momentarily. "They look so giddy."

"No, no they don't. I believe the phrase he used to describe her was 'devil-like skank of a whore' or something. She slept with everybody on the block and gave him crabs." He heard the sounds of choking and leapt up, dropped the picture frame, and went around his desk to pound heartily on Sylvia's back. She waved him off, swallowed, and dissolved into laughter.

"Crabs. She gave him crabs. Oh, I need to remember that description, too. What was it? Weaselish whore of a slut?"

A reluctant grin started across Ben's face. "Close enough." He carefully worked the picture out of the frame and set it on the edge of the desk to take to the shredder later. The frame he put back on the shelf to enter into the auction logs.

Sylvia took another big bite of her sandwich and spoke around the mouthful. "God, some people. Oh, that is such a great epithet. Think he practiced it often?"

"Only every time he talked about her, I'm sure. Rolled right off his tongue." He was laughing now, along with Sylvia. When viewed more objectively, the man's reaction had been highly humorous, if for nothing else than his choice of language.

"Man." Her laughter slowed and she took a deep breath, wiping a small tear from her cheek. "Oh, I needed that." She perched on the edge of his desk and proceeded to take another monster bite of her turkey club sandwich. She chewed slowly and swallowed before turning back to Ben. "I think you broke a couple ribs with the back slapping there. Hey, if I'd choked right then, would you have given me the kiss of life?"

He started stuttering and turned red, and Sylvia just winked and pranced out of the warehouse, off to bother someone else with her lunchtime. He turned back to his desk to take another look at the photo, but it was gone. The floor was clear, and there was nothing under his desk, so he figured Sylvia must have taken it with her to recycle. The log entry for the locket he'd retrieved was still blinking at him from his computer, so he pulled up his chair and set to studying it.

After five minutes, he was certain no one was going to look for it again, so he dropped it on top of the frame to enter into the auction logs after lunch and took his sandwich down to the break room. When he entered, Sylvia was entertaining a corner of the room, taking bets to see just how much of her sandwich she could fit into her mouth at a time. The breaking point seemed to be four inches of her overloaded hoagie, and the spectators paid up as she chewed.

Ben found his way over to Celine's table and sat down. "So, I found this gorgeous little necklace in long-term storage today that should probably go to auction."

She set aside her Tupperware of bean salad. "I see. And what was special about this necklace?"

The innocent air he adopted as he leaned back in his chair was overly campy. "Nothing much really. It had been put aside because it has an inscription in it, but it's not particularly valuable in its own right, so I put it into the auction."

"Gee, that's great." She picked out a couple of marinated green beans with her fork. "Hope no one comes looking for it later."

"Doubt they will. Nothing traceable at all on the packaging, washed clean by being dropped in a puddle. And it's sat there for so long, it's likely no one will ever want it back."

Celine beamed at him and popped her loaded fork in her mouth. "I have several returns to send out today, a couple damaged packages." She swallowed. "And for some reason, there seems to be extra pages in them. It's weird how that happens. Funny how the universe aligns sometimes, isn't it?" She clapped him on the shoulder as he chowed down on his sandwich.

He finished the bite and hesitated before asking, "Anybody else noticing an abundance of paper in their recovered mail today?"

"It's possible, it's definitely possible. I'll look into it." Celine nudged her open chip bag over towards Ben. He accepted gratefully.

After lunch, Ben returned to his computer to find an email entitled "Your Incident Report."

Once again, thank you for bringing this matter to our attention. We respectfully request that you take an inventory of the area in question and inform us of what is actually missing as soon as possible, preferably before the next auction. Thank you. We will be in touch.

He went to the hallway and called over to the bullpen, "Hey, Sylvia, come take a look at something." Back at his desk, he started counting days until the next auction on the computer's calendar. "Jesus."

Sylvia came around the corner. "What's up, el jeffe?"

Ben leaned back in his seat. "You know how I filed that incident report about the empty safe a week or so back?"

She nodded. "Yeah, what about it?"

"They apparently want us to take an inventory and tell them what's missing."

Sylvia groaned, tugging at her pigtails. "That's going to suck."

"Best part is, we have a 'suggested' deadline." He leaned forward again and rested his chin in his hand, cursing his responsible nature that had made him feel he had to report the missing items.

"I'm not going to like this, am I?" Sylvia propped herself on the desk next to his elbow.

He stared woefully up at her. "Before the next auction."

She leapt up. "But the next auction is in a week!"

"Do we get overtime?" Ben slouched in his chair and contemplated the calendar.

"Only if it's deemed justified, and for some reason, the powers that be never deem it justified." She flopped onto his desk in a mirrored pose then jumped up again and saluted him. "Plan of action, sir!"

He waved his hand in her direction. "Please, I'll take any suggestions."

"Actually, I was hoping you had one." She grinned and relaxed again.

"Ah, well then." He brooded for a moment, hands steepled. How was he going to be able to do the regular responsibilities of his job in conjunction with a massive inventory and still find time for the search? "First things first, grab an extra couple carts. We're going to try and pull everything that's got to go up for this next auction. I'm going to run a report to see what items are supposed to still be in here." Sylvia saluted and started to make her way out of the warehouse. "Ah, Sylvia?"

"Yeah?"

He colored slightly. "How do I run that report?"

She snorted. "How about I do that and you go get the carts?"

Ben wandered into the bullpen and grabbed two carts, pushing one in front of him and dragging the other so that he would fit through the doorway.

"Okay, got two carts. How's the list?" Sylvia sat staring at the printer, which continued to spew out paper. After a minute it stopped. As she riffled through the stack of papers, she mouthed the count aloud.

"Twenty-eight, twenty-nine, thirty, thirty-one. Thirty-one pages."

He pulled the carts up against his desk and leaned on them. "That's not so bad, is it? How many items on each page?"

"One hundred. A page. Organized by date, not type of item, because there was no way to sort for that. So, we have over three thousand items to account for."

Ben stared at her. "There *can't* be that many items in the long-term storage bay! Are you sure you discarded everything that was supposedly already auctioned?"

"Yup." She frowned at the list, leafing through it. "I guess we could cross-check items against the list. I think that'd be the least hassle."

"Absolutely, but it'll take us a month at least to make it through there, let alone get everything else done, like prepare for an auction."

"I don't think it'll be as bad as that; there can't be more than a thousand items in there right now. It shouldn't take all that long to determine that most of this list isn't there." Sylvia started to wander down to the bay.

"Are you sure you got the right list?" He was panicking now. There was not enough time to get the inventory done before the auction, and have the auction ready, too. He needed this job; it was just starting to prove useful in trying to find his son. "Not the list of items already sold at auction?"

"Nope, it's the right one." She popped around the corner holding a journal. "This is entry 487." She came back down the aisle and laid the list down on the table.

"Crap."

"That about sums it up, though I would have used 'shit.' More evocative in this instance."

Ben snorted. "Shit it is then. Let's work on a plan of attack."

"Simple, we'll alternate days, one person entering the new items and prepping for the auction, the other inventorying. We'll mark shelf by shelf. Work for you?"

"Works for me."

"Good, I'm starting in the storage bay; *you* can do the cataloging for today."

"And what about the shredding?"

Sylvia flipped a hand as she walked away. "It can wait. This is more important."

"Well then, let's get started."

They worked amicably for the next few hours, Ben ferrying items from the bullpen to his desk, then to the storage bay, and back again. He made it through five cartloads before he decided to take a break and look for more auctionable items. He poked his head into the long-term bay on his way and caught Sylvia reading a leather-bound journal.

Ben cleared his throat right behind her. "How is that inventory coming along?"

She leapt up from the stool she was sitting on, hiding the journal behind her back. "Great, just great. Made it through," she glanced over at her list on the shelves, "half a shelf?"

"I see. Maybe we should trade now; you go look for some auction stuff to enter."

Blushing, she muttered a reply, threw the journal onto the appropriate shelf, and headed out of the bay. Ben wandered over to the shelf, glancing over his shoulder to ensure that she had truly left, then picked up the journal she had been reading. The front was embossed with flaking gold leaf, reading *Journal*, and it had a matching leather cord that wrapped around it width-wise. He opened it to the first page and found an inscription.

To our darling daughter, with her wild imagination and wonderful tales.

He flipped to the next page and found an immature scrawl, probably a young girl not much out of middle school.

Darling daughter, right. Funny. They just want me to shut up and write in here instead of talking to them. "Here, now you can write it all down," they said. Then they left for the party. A party. Who knows which one...

He skipped to the middle of the journal. The writing had improved somewhat, though the entries seemed to all be about the length of the first one.

Bobby is so cute, I could just eat him up, but Jessica has totally laid dibs on him, though I think he'd much rather be going with me than her fat butt.

Ben snorted, then returned the journal to its appropriate spot in the lineup of journals—chronologically by date received. It had only been there ten years, so it was nowhere near its release date. He picked up the next journal in the line and searched for it on the list. He worked like this for another ten minutes until he heard people start trickling past in the hallway, leaving for the day. He sighed and put the list down to go find Sylvia.

She was at his desk with a pile of auction items, frowning at the computer screen. "Nothing fun in this pile. All totally researched and shelved. No fun at all." She hit the return key and tossed another book into the cart of items to go to the auction storage bay.

"So, it's five o'clock. How late are we staying tonight?" He came around behind her and leaned on the chairback to look over her shoulder at the screen. She typed in the code for the next item, but brought up an error screen. "I think you mistyped that number; I don't think it was the thousandth item cataloged that day, if I'm not mistaken."

"Slip of the keys. I think we should stay as late as we can stand it. Order a pizza or something for dinner." She entered the right numbers and found the hedge clippers she had been trying to look up.

"I was afraid you were going to say that. Alright. Order that pizza and then come help me with this damned list. I think it'll go a lot faster with one of us on the shelf and the other on the list."

"Meat lover's okay with you?"

"Perfect. Girl after my own heart."

"Well, dunno about that. A girl with a healthy appetite maybe."

Ben laughed and headed back into the warehouse with the list as Sylvia picked up the phone to order pizza.

They stayed until around nine that night and returned again at the usual time the next morning. They alternated working on the cataloging, auction preparation, and inventorying together and again spent the evening working, this time with Chinese. And again on Friday, the only change being that this time Sylvia stepped out to get hoagies.

"Lord, do we seriously only have four more work days until the auction?" Sylvia stretched her shoulders by holding onto one of the shelving units behind her and leaning forward.

"I know, only half done with this and about half done with the auction items. I haven't even started to add suggested prices to the auction list." Ben tossed the inventory list on top of the safe and did a few squats.

"Break time, definitely." She dropped to the floor and started doing simple yoga stretches, trying to work the kinks out of her neck from such prolonged hours of abuse. "We're so not going to make it if all we do is work a few nights. I think we'll have to hit it this weekend as well."

"I can't," Ben replied without thinking.

"Why not?" She had her legs spread nearly into a split and was stretching her left arm over top of her head and leaning toward her right foot.

Ben tried not to follow her distracting movement. "I've got things to do this weekend."

"Meaning you're handing out flyers, am I right?"

"Well, yes, and I have a few things to look into that I don't want to delay more than I have to."

"Where were you planning to paper this weekend?" She leaned over to the other side now.

"I was thinking the theater district. Hit the late shows, lots of people at those."

She stood and shook out her limbs, bouncing a bit. "I'll make a deal with you. Saturday, we come here. Nobody's going to want to talk with you during the late shows on Saturday; they're all out to have a good time, and they don't want the downer." Ben started to open his mouth, but she held up her hand. "We'll hit the matinee on Sunday instead—lots of people, lots of families, and they're more likely to stop, because families care more about kids than the trendy hipsters at the late shows."

"But the research I wanted to work on."

"It'll still be there after the auction. Can you really tell me that one week of intense labor is going to make a difference? Be honest."

Her cavalier attitude was starting to make him angry. "You never know what's going to make the difference."

She stood, legs shoulder width apart and hands on her hips, eyebrow quirked. "But you can do without one day of research and come do your friggin' job, mister."

He struggled with himself a moment more before nodding his assent. He couldn't stay mad at someone who looked like Peter Pan lecturing the Lost Boys. All the same, after they called it quits for the night, he headed straight home to his desk covered in papers and the map on the wall. The first thing he did was plan out the area he wanted to cover for the weekend. He was low on flyers, but he could just copy those at the Center the next day. Then he sat at his desk and decided to get up to date on the websites that reported on missing children.

As per usual, he was disappointed in the results. More children listed, but nothing posted about his son and sadly few happy posts. For every twenty or thirty posts about a child missing, there was maybe one response of a child later being found, typically with the estranged parent.

He closed those windows and opened another bookmark. The Take Root website loaded, and he took a moment to examine the illustration of a tree that adorned the home page. It was a site he went to occasionally when he tried to picture what it would be like when Benny came home. It was dedicated to ensuring that children who were returned to their parents were not then forgotten. The found children often needed years of therapy, depending on what the situation was, and Take Root made sure that the parents were aware of this.

Ben liked to visit it and plan the aftercare for his son. He had several different plans, depending on what had happened to Benny. If it was a desperate person who simply wanted a child to love who had taken Benny, the care wouldn't have to be as extensive. A few light counseling sessions maybe; perhaps after a year he might have some readjusting to do, but Ben was sure that his son would fly straight back into his arms.

On the other hand, if some sadistic bastard had taken hold of him, Ben had already researched the best counselors in the area for children's trauma and had even contacted a few of them. They had kindly requested that he wait until his son was returned to him before going ahead with discussions about treatment. They also offered the name of a therapist to help him deal with the separation—that's what they called it— which he roughly declined. He was doing fine on his own.

They had also suggested keeping an eye on the state's clearinghouse for missing children. He hated that word— clearinghouse. It sounded like the children were overstocked commodities or there was a going-out-of-business sale. In fact, this was the nervous center in each state for the information related to missing people. Of course, it would be easier to "keep an eye" out as suggested if Georgia would come out of the stone age and put it online, like Ohio and other states. But no, its clearinghouse was still paper and phones, run through the Georgia Bureau of Investigation. And they had asked him to stop calling. The only thing they kept online that was of any interest was a report of the crime statistics for previous years. And it didn't even include missing persons, so it was obvious to him where their priorities lay. It did, however, include citations written up against runaways.

He logged into his email and saw that he had received another two pages of tip-line transcription from his friend. The first in months. It took a moment to download, but when he opened it, it was just more of the useless and attention-seeking comments that plagued the transcripts he already had.

I don't know about that boy, but when I was at the supermarket, som'un about run me down. Who do I talk to about that?

Of course, he came to me in a dream, wanted me to tell everyone that he's with God now, and you don't need to be looking for him anymore. He's having a grand time hanging out with Elvis.

Benny had always thrown a fit when Ben had played anything by Elvis. He was more of a classic hard rock fan. Or Tchaikovsky. He really loved the cannons in the 1812 Overture and had someday wanted to play them, but he'd never liked Elvis.

He printed out the email anyway and added it to the stack of tips he already had. For the rest of the night, he spent his time refining the list of things he had determined to research on the search engines at work, after the auction prep and inventory were finished.

Time was, these sorts of letters were illegal. They were sent all over the world in an effort to collect as many postal stamps as possible before being returned to their owner; we called them Round the World letters. Now all these kids are sending letters that promise curses and evil will befall you if you don't pass the responsibility along to another person or ten. What kind of children are we raising that think that's okay?
~ *Gertrude Biun,* Property Office Manual

A knock on the door nearly caused Ben to fall out of his desk chair where he had once again fallen asleep. With effort, he managed to not vocalize the line of cusswords streaming through his head, aimed at both himself and whoever had woken him up. He glanced at the time showing on his computer and saw that it was nine o'clock, an hour before he was supposed to meet Sylvia. He stumbled to the door and opened it.

"Thought I'd bring some breakfast, you know, to get us started this morning." The minx herself stood there, holding up a Dunkin' Donuts bag and tray of coffees, and tried to scoot past him into his apartment.

Ben rubbed his hands briskly over his face before standing aside to let her in. "Morning. Wait, how?"

Sylvia arched an eyebrow at him. "My, my, aren't you eloquent this morning. Your address is in the employee database at work. Don't look so surprised to see me." She walked into the kitchen and put the breakfast items down on the counter. "Or is that just a hangover in your pocket?" The empty alcohol bottles on the counter—three beers and an empty whiskey bottle—received momentary consideration before she swept them into the trash.

He frowned, not remembering having drunk that much the night before, but there were the bottles. "You're early." He stumbled back to his desk and started to straighten the papers on it.

"I know." She finally noticed the map and papers on the wall and made her way over to it. "Great interior decorating taste, if I may say so. The black stage effect with the lack of furniture really makes the wall decorations pop." She ignored his glare and continued to study the map, fingering the push-pins. "Tips?"

"Yeah. Hands off, please. It's quite precise." He left the living room and grabbed a coffee out of the tray, hoping she would follow him away from the wall. It was entirely too early, and he was not awake enough to be able to defend against whatever she was going to say about the wall. He wondered, not for the first time, what it would look like to someone who didn't know, who hadn't had someone go missing. When she didn't follow, he returned to the living room, finding her with her nose inches from the wall. "I said, I would appreciate it if you didn't touch that. It's organized in a particular way."

She held her hands submissively in the air and wrinkled her nose. "Oh yeah, I can see that."

"I know what is going on and what it means. So leave it."
He took a sip of the coffee, nearly scalded himself, and swore.
This morning was just getting better and better.

She ignored him and continued examining the map wall.
"What I don't understand is how someone so organized at
work can have something this chaotic at home." She retreated
to his office chair and spun it a couple times. "So, are you ready
to get to work?"

It was an immense relief to have Sylvia step away from
his wall, and Ben could feel his irritation start to fade. She had
delivered coffee, after all. "I have to shower and change first."

She chuckled and spun the chair all the way around. "Yeah,
I noticed those are the same things you were wearing yesterday.
Fall asleep at your desk often?"

"Only when a harpy shanghais my weekend." And with that
he left her laughing in his living room while he went to shower.

The Center was silent as they keyed in, no rustling of mail
or loud Latino radio from the sorting room, no keyboards
or murmured conversation from the bullpen. The first thing
Sylvia did when they got to the warehouse was boot up Ben's
computer and open a radio site on the Internet. The strains of
nineties grunge rock filled the building, and they both relaxed
a little.

"God this place is eerie when it's dead." Ben put down his
coffee cup and picked up the inventory lists.

"Completely. I hate coming in on weekends just for that,
but the music helps. Otherwise it feels almost like you can hear
the stacks of mail whispering." Sylvia shuddered and snatched
the list from his hand and wandered off to the bay. "You're
playing with the shelves today. My throat is still sore from the
dust yesterday."

"Fine with me." Ben completely agreed with her on that particular flight of fancy and followed her to the bay where they had stopped yesterday. "Do we plan on doing anything other than this today?"

"I was thinking of shredding. Haven't done it in a few days ,and it's really piling up."

"Our lunch break then. Oh fun, we're to the stacks of canvases now." When he pulled off the first canvas, a cloud of dust filled the air and he coughed until it dissipated enough for him to read the numbers on the claim tag affixed to the back of the frame. "Okay, 1980, July 16."

"Got it."

"Number thirty-four."

"Check. Next." She drew a line through the item as he lifted off the next canvas.

They worked steadily for three hours, taking the occasional drink and bathroom breaks before Ben called a halt. "I am starving, and I want another hoagie. Why don't you go start doing some shredding while I get sandwiches? I really don't feel like shifting any more paper right now, and I would like to see the sun at some point today." He stretched hard and ended up with another coughing fit from the dust, wondering idly if he shouldn't pick up some masks on the way back to keep from getting miner's lung.

Sylvia perked up at the suggestion of food, slapping the list down on the shelf. "One hero for me!"

Ben grinned. He was astounded at the amount of food she could tuck away, a good trait in a woman in his opinion. "The works, right?"

"They make it any other way?"

Ben dusted off his hands and headed to the door. "Be back in twenty. Think you'll be done shredding by then?"

"Fat chance. Have you seen the bins?" She held her hand above her head. "I think I'll have to grow a few inches just so I won't be buried by the avalanche I'm about to cause. Got a shovel?"

He snorted and headed for the door. "You're on your own."

The line at the deli was longer than normal. The weather was slightly cooler than it had been recently and people were out taking advantage of the pleasant Saturday. He returned after about a half hour and walked into the warehouse with the sandwiches.

"Lunch is served." There was no answer, and the radio station on the computer was waiting to be prompted that someone was still listening.

Ben walked down to the sorting room, thinking that Sylvia must still be shredding. As he opened the door, he could hear that the shredder was humming but not active. He felt his stomach tighten with a small niggling of fear before he came around the side of the device and found Sylvia sitting on the steps. For some reason, the machine instilled an exaggerated fear of someone falling in and getting shredded.

He handed her a sandwich before unwrapping his own. "Sorry I'm late. Finish the shredding?"

"Almost." Sylvia made no move to open her lunch, just sat on the steps staring off into the space between him and the machine. It was unsettling for Ben, and he tried to draw her attention back to the warehouse.

He cast about for a topic that might get her attention and noticed the stack of still-full bins to the right of the shredder. "Interesting definition of almost."

She looked around until she saw the bins still waiting for her. "Huh? Oh, yeah."

"Earth to Sylvia." Ben flopped onto the stair next to her and bumped her with his shoulder. "What's going on with you?"

"It's nothing." She stood and he saw that she was holding a letter written on wide-ruled notebook paper.

Ben held out his hand for the letter. "What have you got there?"

"I said nothing." She went to toss the letter into the shredder and stopped, hand extended, then came down the stairs and handed it to him. She grabbed a box of shredding, climbed the stairs and dropped the contents in.

The letter Ben held had apparently been written by a young girl, with the bubbly and self-conscious writing of someone who wants their writing to be "pretty."

> *Dear Mom,*
>
> *I really miss you. Grammy says you're doing just fine up in Jesus's arms, but I just want to be the one holding you. I'm sorry about the toys everywhere, I will clean them up. If I keep doing everything I'm told, will you come back?*
>
> > *Love,*
> >
> > > *Ruthie*

It was heartbreaking in its simple child's logic. Be good, get what you want. But Ben knew that was not how the world worked from firsthand knowledge. "Sylvia, where did you get this?"

She took an envelope out of her pocket on her return trip and shoved it at him, still not saying anything. It had been addressed:

> *To: Mom*
> *C/o Jesus*
> *Cloud 9, Heaven*

"Man, no kid should have to lose a parent. At least she didn't have to watch her daughter go. There is something distinctly unnatural about a child going before her parents.

It's not right." Ben put the letter on top of the bin that Sylvia was about to carry up the stairs. When she got to the top, she picked up the letter, glanced at it once more, then let it fall with the others into the shredder.

"At least she didn't have to grow up without them. She didn't have to scream in the dark at the monsters and have no one there. She didn't wait and wait for them to come back. She didn't think it was her fault."

Ben opened his mouth and shut it again. He frowned. The girl in the letter had only lost her mother. He wasn't sure now what Sylvia was talking about, but it wasn't that letter. He thought he might be close to finding out what Sylvia was hiding, but he didn't want to scare her off.

"Sylvia, what happened?" He was pretty sure she'd try and run away from talking about this again, so he leaned back against the rails, blocking the way down. She could either talk or jump the last five feet.

"I don't want to talk about it." She slammed the off button on the machine and turned, studying her options for egress.

"Look, you know about my heartache, and they have always said it's good to share. So share."

"I shared damn well enough!" She took the leap to the bottom of the steps, landed awkwardly, and hopped around on one foot, cursing for a couple of seconds before testing her weight. When she found it would hold well enough, she started limping out of the sorting room. She was going to hurt herself more if she kept walking on the ankle, so Ben hurried to block her way.

"If you don't want to talk, fine, but sit down before you hurt yourself any more."

"It's your damn fault, anyway." But she sat down at one of the sorting tables, reaching down to rub the offending extremity.

Ben followed her over and perched on the edge of the table, far enough away that he felt less like he was hulking over her, hoping she would be less likely to try running. "How does it feel?"

"I killed my parents, happy?" she snapped.

He hesitated. "Not exactly what I meant."

"At least, I thought I did." She stopped rubbing but stayed hunched over, not looking at him. "When I was twelve. We were out late, and I wanted to stop at McDonald's and get a happy meal because I really wanted the toy." She snorted. "They were running a My Little Pony promotion, Hot Wheels cars for the boys, of course. But I really wanted that pony."

She paused but Ben said nothing, not wanting to interrupt the flow of words now that they had started.

"I was throwing a fit in the back of the car. Dad was driving, and he turned to say something to me, something about not stopping since it was so late, and a drunk driver swerved over the middle lane. The police said there was nothing he could have done. Even if he'd been looking at the road, nothing he could have done. It was too quick. But I thought it was me. I had caused it." She finally looked up at him. "I went a little crazy. Tried everything I could think of to kill myself because I thought I didn't deserve to live after that. My grandmother didn't know what to do, she was already fairly old by that point. So she gave in to the social worker's suggestion and had me committed. Two weeks of lockdown. And when I got back to school, word got out that I was crazy. Crazy enough I had to be locked up. I hate being called crazy." She ran out of breath. "It feels okay."

"Being called crazy?" He was trying to absorb everything she'd just thrown at him so his brain wasn't quite up to speed.

"No, dumbass, my ankle. It feels okay." She stood

unsteadily and then took two giant steps forward. "Yup, fine."
She started back to the warehouse and Ben scrambled to catch up.

He had known there was something in her past she
wasn't happy about, but this was so far beyond what he had
been expecting. "So you've lived with your grandmother
ever since then?"

"Except for the couple of summers at an internment camp
to keep kids from killing themselves, yeah." She glanced up at
his incredulous face. "Jeez, joke much?"

He threw his hands up in exasperation. "Well, you drop
a bomb like that, it takes a person a moment or two to catch
up. Don't make a joke for the next five minutes or so; I'm
still processing."

"Stop processing, start inventorying while we eat." They
had reached the warehouse and she shoved the list into his
hands. "My turn to climb the shelves in search of buried
treasures."

"But, you're okay now?"

"You mean, am I going to off myself when you turn
around?"

"No, I only meant—"

"It's okay, I know what you meant. But no, no medica-
tion, no suicidal thoughts, the occasionally normal and totally
healthy homicidal thoughts, which my therapist told me were
perfectly natural. Next, 1965, September." She waited for him
to indicate he'd found the relevant page, but when she heard
nothing, she turned to face him again. He was staring at her,
trying to determine whether she was joking again or not.

"Christ, my five minutes not up? No, I'm not homicidal,
no I'm not in therapy, no I don't think I murdered my parents
anymore, and yes, I still carry some scars—small scars—
because of it, but that's it. Stop looking at me."

"Sorry, I just—" He had spent so long wrapped up in his own problems, he'd forgotten the kind of pain other people had to deal with on a daily basis. This forceful reminder was proving quite enlightening.

"And no sorry. None of it's your fault. And 1965, September." She made shooing motions when he still didn't turn the page. "Go!"

"Right, 1965...found it." And that was that, he thought. At least she had finally shared.

They worked until eight that night, stopping for Chinese around five, and made plans to carpool into the "theater district" early the next afternoon. Atlanta didn't have a theater district per se, but a lot of the theaters were around the same neighborhoods. During dinner they figured out where the shows were playing and the approximate end times to better lay out a map of where they wanted to be at what times.

Sylvia printed out another theater's playbill. "Nice, *Wicked* is playing this weekend. Lots of good people there. They like a sob story."

Ben took offense to her implication. "This is not a sob story!"

"Boy goes missing, father keeps hunting after everyone else gives up, but can't find him. Of course it's a sob story. Same as a witch who can't seem to get along with anyone, and is shunned for being better than they are. Good sob stories, all."

"Can you please stop calling it that?"

"Can I call it a heart-wrenching story?"

He thought for a moment before responding. "Yes. That's better at least. Doesn't make it sound like it belongs on the Lifetime channel." Ben took the playbill from her and noted the times on a map of the neighborhood that he had printed from a website. "Is that all of them?"

"Looks like it. The last theater is undergoing renovations, so they're not playing anything."

"Good, looks like the earliest one gets out at two. Shall I pick you up at noon so we can find parking and a good place to stand?"

"Sounds good to me. Now let's get back to those shelves. We're almost there!"

Ben arrived outside of Sylvia's house at ten minutes to noon and stood on her sidewalk a moment to admire the landscaping around the 120-year-old house. It was impeccably painted with neatly weeded and mulched butterfly gardens that surrounded the cozy two-story, plantation-style home. As he went to ring the bell, he noticed a sign declaring the house a historical monument. Made sense for the outside to be so well taken care of, then. They would receive a yearly stipend for keeping it up.

The door flew open and Sylvia stood in the doorway, hair yet uncombed and a smudge of red paint on her cheek.

"Crap, is it noon already?" She glanced at her watch as she rubbed ineffectually at the red stain. "You're early. Serves me right I guess. I'll meet you in the garden out back. There should still be a plate of muffins back there." The door slammed in his face again. Ben's mouth had remained open through the brief tirade and he now closed it, contemplating the lion's head knocker staring at his nose. He shrugged and turned to the back of the house.

Passing through a side gate, Ben entered what he could only describe as a recreation of the Secret Garden. A low stone wall encircled the small backyard, entirely engulfed in ivy, with a tall weeping willow over a small pond and rioting flower beds. The small section of grass that was allowed to remain featured a metal bistro set with a teakettle and a plate of muffins. On one of the chairs was a terrier mix, fast asleep on his back, feet twitching in the air.

As the gate clicked shut behind Ben, the terrier dismounted the chair in one swift roll, coming instantly to attention. It fixated on the strange man in its territory and trotted up to him, tongue lolling, to sit at attention at his feet.

"Well, hello." He squatted down to offer his hand to the mutt, who ignored it and continued to study Ben. The dog stared until Ben became uncomfortable and finally broke eye contact with it. With a single whuff, it sat up on its hind legs and offered Ben its paw. Laughing, he shook it, and the dog trotted to the screen door and let out one sharp bark.

Sylvia's voice echoed from inside the house, "I know, Owney. Entertain him, will you?"

Owney snorted and trotted back to the bistro set, jumped into the chair he had previously vacated, curled up in the sun, and promptly went back to sleep. Ben took the opposite chair and picked up a muffin. He took a bite while studying the dog and was surprised to find the pastry was stuffed with bacon and cheese.

Sylvia came out the back door, wiping the last of the paint off of her hands. "I see you have met my Owney."

Ben nodded, trying to swallow. "I did. Interesting name."

"I've had him since I was thirteen. Right after I got out of the center, Grandma bought me a puppy. I guess she felt I needed company, so we went to the pound and came home with this ruffian." Owney's feet twitched, but he ignored his owner. "His name comes from the mascot of the USPS rail system at the turn of the century—a stray that wandered in off the streets and adopted the whole of the U.S. postal system. Traveled the world. Little terrier mutt like mine." She tickled

Owney's stomach while he dreamed, causing him to twitch off of his chair. The dog shook himself and glared balefully up at his owner until she broke a piece off the muffin Ben was holding and tossed it to him. He wolfed it down and wandered off to inspect the perimeter.

"I couldn't help but notice how stunning the house is. A bit unexpected from a girl who professed her family to be dedicated civil servants forever."

"That's my mom's side. This is my dad's family house. Old Atlanta. We have boxes of photos upstairs that date back to the early days of the city and the building of this house." She slouched into the chair her pup had recently vacated. "I keep the gardens as Grandma liked. Riotously overgrown, but well kept." She leaned over to the nearest bed and ran a hand through the foliage. "It's easier than it looks with this postage-stamp yard. Plus all the hard work to landscape it was done long before my time. Doesn't take much to keep mature plants happy."

"Well, it's lovely." Ben dusted the crumbs off of his hands and stood, both eager to get started, but also somewhat reluctant to leave the beautiful retreat. "Shall we?"

"But of course!" She whistled and Owney trotted to her side. "In you go. I have to lock up. Oh don't look at me like that, I'll be back." She herded the dog inside and locked the back door. "Off we go!"

They circled back to the front of the house and loaded into Ben's car. As she buckled her seatbelt, Sylvia noticed the mounds of flyers on the back seat. "Yeesh, save a tree for oxygen?"

He colored slightly, but defended himself. "I've gone through more than that on some weekends. That'll probably just last us the day since it's so nice out. Lots of people should be walking around."

They chatted amiably about old houses as they worked their way further into the center of the city. It felt odd to be heading out to canvas with another person, but Ben found he rather enjoyed having someone else along, someone whose conversation didn't have to be entirely about what was lost. At least not his loss.

They managed to find a parking garage with a tolerable daily rate close to the theaters and parked. From there, they made their way to the corner that hosted a movie theater and two playhouses, one of which was playing *Wicked*.

"This should do us for a while. We'll move to one of the other corners once the *Wicked* crowd dies down." They split the large stack of flyers into three piles, the largest stack stored next to a lamp post under a loose brick for later.

The first movie emptied out around one o'clock, and they were kept busy until the *Wicked* audience started streaming out of the theater.

"Have you seen this boy?"

"Can you just look at this poster a moment?"

"Do you have a moment of time?"

"Please, have you seen Benny?"

For the most part they were met with polite negatives; about one in ten people actually took a flyer. A few people actually stopped to ask about it: when had it happened, was this your son? Your brother? Then their rhythm was interrupted by a Louisiana drawl:

"Lord, darlin', ain't that just the saddest?"

Ben turned to glance at Sylvia and see who it was that had shown an interest in the flyer. His glance skidded over the man and settled on the redhead at his side. "Jeannie?"

"Jesus. Ben." She quickly released her escort's arm and took a step to the side. "What are you doing here?"

Ben's eyes flicked back and forth between his estranged wife and the man she was with, trying to figure out what their relationship was. Wondering what she was doing in Atlanta when on a Sunday like this the store should be open. There would be lots of tourists on the streets shopping. "Flyering." The man didn't seem like anyone Ben knew, definitely not one of their mutual friends, and she seemed overly friendly with him.

"Yeah, I can see that. Who's she?" Jeannie seemed to fold in on herself, her arms wrapped around each other though the day was warm.

"A coworker. She offered to help." He didn't feel like talking with her. She hadn't wanted any part in this before, so she had no right asking questions now. Especially not with someone who took such pity on them as the Louisiana man had.

"Uh huh." They both paused.

Ben thought he should at least try to be civil for the sake of the third parties in all of this, if for nothing else. Sylvia was starting to look downright antsy. "So, what are you in town for?"

"Oh, I was taking Pierre to see *Wicked*. He'd never seen it before. Uh, right. Pierre, Ben. Ben, Pierre." The lanky man at his estranged wife's side held out a hand and slapped a lopsided grin on his face.

"Heard a lot about you, Ben."

Ben stuck his hands in his pockets. He could already tell there was something about this overly friendly man that he didn't like. "Really? Considering I don't know you and my wife and I have only been apart for a little over a month, that's a lot of talking."

Jeannie took a step to put herself between the two men. "Ben, don't."

Ben was nearly as angry as the night she had thrown him out. He felt it boiling up, and he decided he didn't want to control it this time. He was done being the one who had to watch everything he said and did, not when she made it so clear that even when he did, he wasn't good for her. "What? Don't I have a right to know when my wife's found a new interest?"

Pierre leaned around Jeannie. "Hey, man, we're just friends."

Ben snorted. "Right. Friends. Walking arm-in-arm out of a theater. Gotcha."

"Don't you dare." Jeannie stepped up into Ben's face, tears standing out in her eyes. "It's been seriously lonely since you left. Pierre was friendly when he came into the shop looking for a few pieces for his new house, and we've been spending some time together, that's it."

He couldn't stop himself. "Oh? And whose fault is it that you are lonely? I seem to remember *you* telling *me* to get out."

Ben had expected her to get mad, like she always did, to rise to the occasion and fight, but she just sighed and he could see that there wasn't any anger there, only sadness. "I was lonely even before that. You had completely retreated from me, fallen into your obsession and drinking. God, Ben, you were drinking so much. There wasn't room for me and your wall. Yes, I told you to leave, but that's only because you'd forgotten about me a long while before."

He felt as though his heart was missing beats, and he wanted to scream, shake her, but he had at least a modicum of self-respect left. "You *threw me out*! I was only trying to find our son!"

She was starting to cry now, and Pierre was looking even more uncertain about what he should do. Ben hated that she was crying, and he started to feel his anger ebb. He'd never been able to handle it when a woman cried. That was, until she added, "You weren't doing any good, for anybody. Me, you, or our son. Probably aren't doing any good now either."

Ben's anger resurged, coalescing into a cold hard knot in his chest. He shivered despite the warm day, for the first time actually hating his wife. "At least I love him enough to try."

Jeannie's breath left her in a gasp, and her face was drawn and colorless. "You bastard," she murmured. "At least I know enough to know when I'm beat. And to move on."

Ben didn't care how much he hurt her now; everything was fair game. "Apparently. Into the arms of *Pierre*." He gave the man's name a French accent.

Sylvia tried to work her way between the couple. "Ah, Ben?"

Jeannie grabbed Ben's arm and pulled him away from Sylvia. "You have the gall to insult me when your teenage slut over there has her hands on my son's face?"

"No. You. Didn't." Sylvia grabbed the hand clutching Ben's arm and in one swift twist dislodged it. She shoved the stack of flyers into Jeannie's hand. "I am not a slut. I am not sleeping with your husband—though god knows that if he asked I would probably oblige—but he's too wrapped up in the search for his son to even think twice about any woman. Except you. Still has a picture of you at work. With Benny." She stepped away from the woman and threaded her arm through Ben's. "And I am twenty-four, thank you very much."

Sylvia started to force-march Ben from the corner while Jeannie stood with the stack of flyers in her hand. When they glanced back at the next corner she had dropped them in the middle of the sidewalk and was walking quickly in the other direction, Pierre trying vainly to keep up.

Seeing his son's face start to drift this way and that in the wake of passersby, Ben wrenched free of Sylvia's arm and hurried back to their original corner. He carefully picked up each one, squaring it to the stack, trying to brush off whatever city detritus clung to the pages. His face pointed firmly to the pavement, and he didn't say anything when Sylvia came up behind him and laid a hand on his back. At least he had stopped shaking, even if he did feel like breaking something. She had no right, no right, to be criticizing his efforts to find their son. Not when she had given up so completely. Not when she was doing everything in her power to replace everything in her life that reminded her of the son she had loved and held just a year ago.

Once the pages had been collected and were once more neatly stacked, Ben cleared his throat and stood, staring after his wife. She hadn't looked back. He rubbed his hand over his eyes, dashing away the extra moisture clinging there.

"Ben, hey now." Sylvia turned him until he faced her. "It's okay. I'm sure Pierre is just a phase. A coping mechanism if you will."

"What do I care about Pierre? She hasn't really been my wife for a year now. Sylvia, she was his mother. How can she just…give up? It's not right. Look at her, out gallivanting at a show with a boy toy while her son, our son, he's—" Ben smoothed over the papers again while he waited for his voice to stabilize. "My son."

"Because she is apparently an unfeeling bitch. That's how." Her words didn't hold any venom, though, and he knew they were lies simply presented to make him feel better. "Or maybe it's just the way she copes. She can't deal with the search, the pain, so she pretends it isn't there."

A little bit of the anger still sloshed about inside him. "She has to deal sometime!"

"I agree, but maybe, just maybe, no one can force her there."

"I guess." He looked around him at the crowds passing without even noting their presence. "I think I'd like to go home. This doesn't feel...I just want to go home."

"Good with me, I think I burnt my nose." She stared at it cross-eyed. "Does it look red to you?"

A small smile broke through Ben's misery. He couldn't help but be a bit amused at the image of his pigtailed coworker staring intently at her own nose. "No. I don't think it's sunburned."

"Well that's a relief. I peel like nothing else when I burn. It's embarrassing." She started walking, then stopped. "I don't look like a teenager, do I?"

He shouldn't have gotten as angry as he did with Jeannie, but she had surprised him. It was fading fairly quickly now anyway, with her gone again. "You shouldn't listen to a woman in rage. You should know that."

She stamped her foot at the non-reply. "But do I look like a teenager?"

Ben paused and turned to give her a once over. "No. No, you certainly do not."

She blushed. "Good."

He hesitated before asking her, "Did you mean what you said?"

She linked arms with him again and started walking towards the car. "Dunno what I said. She pissed me off. I stop thinking and just start talking when I'm pissed off."

"Never mind then." If she didn't remember having said she'd happily sleep with him, then he certainly wasn't going to bring it up. Sylvia probably just said it to piss off Jeannie anyway.

The ride home was fairly quiet, Ben brooding over the day's encounter and lost efforts. When they reached Sylvia's house, he walked her up to the door and greeted Owney as the dog came rushing out. He ignored the two humans and headed straight to the herbaceous border of the walkway to relieve himself.

"We weren't gone that long, silly." Sylvia shook her head and turned to Ben. "Well, at least today was educational."

"I'm really sorry about my—about Jeannie. That was uncalled for. And thank you for helping. I think people react better to a young and attractive woman rather than a middle-aged guy looking for a young boy."

"That's not it at all!" Ben raised an eyebrow and she continued. "I don't look like I'm trying to pass a stone when I hand them a flyer. Owney!" The terrier skittered into the house and Sylvia closed the door, laughing.

Ben scowled then muttered, "I do *not* look like that." Muffled snickering answered him and he threw up his hands in surrender and returned to his car. He spent the evening sitting at his desk, staring at the map, telling himself he was picking the location to paper next weekend, but all he accomplished was draining the last of the whiskey bottle at his side. He stumbled into bed, wondering if the next day would bring anything new.

AUCTION PREPARATION

It's important to make sure no one is going to want anything later. Especially journals. The salacious tidbits those things hold could keep the paparazzi busy for decades. Make sure every item is accounted for, and make sure there is absolutely no way to tell who the owner is. Then get rid of it. Something new will replace it in a week.

~ *Gertrude Biun,* Property Office Manual

The center was fairly subdued when he got there, typical for a Monday morning; most of the staff was bleary-eyed and relying solely on the pungent coffee to keep going. As he made his way to the warehouse, Ben noticed the lights were already on and there were voices inside. Voices that he did not recognize. Images of empty safes and stripped shelves danced through his head and he wondered if it was only Mrs. Biun who had stripped them of their valuables, or if there were more thieves among the staff. Well, besides Sylvia, but letters doomed to be shredded hardly counted. He hurried to get inside and confront whoever was in his domain.

There were two people in the bay reserved for prepping auction items. A short, rotund woman was checking things off on a clipboard while an older gentleman was calling out numbers and shelving items.

Ben cleared his throat. "Um, excuse me?"

"Just a tick, dearie, just a tick. Next?" The woman hadn't even looked up and flipped the page on her clipboard.

The old man shelved a Nazi motorcycle helmet. "That would be 06-08-14-72"

"Check."

Ben tried again. "I'm sorry, but I have to interrupt. Who are you and what are you doing in my warehouse?"

The woman rounded on him with a simpering megawatt smile. "Oh, terribly sorry, Tanya's my name. This is Jeffrey. We're from the Minnesota Center. Just brought down the stuff for the auction, didn't you know? And who are you? Where's ol' Pammy?"

"Pammy?" Ben tried to remember if there was anyone in the center by that name, but he drew a blank.

Tanya waved the hand holding her pen. "Shriveled old prune who runs this circus."

"You must mean Mrs. Biun. She retired. I'm her replacement, Ben. Ben Grant." He held out his hand and she grasped it briefly before returning to her clipboard.

"Nice to make your acquaintance, I'm sure. But we have got to finish this up now, boy. Go do what you have to do. We'll talk later." She turned back to Jeffrey, effectively dismissing Ben, and continued her inventory as they unpacked their boxes. Ben shrugged and went to his desk to find Sylvia peeking around the divider.

"Is that little monster here already? She wasn't due until tomorrow."

Ben propped himself up against the wall, interrupting Sylvia's view of the shelves. "It would have been nice if you had told me I was going to have company in my warehouse." Sylvia stuck her tongue out at him and turned to head out to the bullpen for her first cart and Ben followed, unwilling to give up the conversation.

"I was going to tell you today. They must have sped all the way down from Minnesota."

Ben frowned, wondering why there was no mention of them in Mrs. Biun's notebook. More likely he had just missed the reference. "They come every month? With the auction stuff?"

Sylvia snagged their first cart of the day and turned back to the warehouse, only to find her path once more blocked by Ben. She made shooing motions, and he grudgingly stepped aside. He didn't really like surprises, particularly ones where someone was infiltrating what he now thought of as his space. "Only if they're bringing down a particularly large load or something valuable. Jeffrey emailed me last week to let me know they were coming."

"And you didn't tell me then, because…"

She stopped him before they reentered the warehouse. "I don't like her. I was hoping they'd cancel, but they didn't, and I was going to tell you, so don't give me that."

"But why don't you like her? She seemed pleasant enough, if a bit task oriented."

"Watch." Sylvia pushed open the warehouse door and pushed the cart in.

"Hey! Hello, Tanya, Jeffrey. You're here early!" She left the cart at the desk and wandered over to the auction bay.

The man looked up from the vase he was holding. "Next up, 06-08-30-45. Good to see you, Sylvy. Been a couple months."

Tanya ignored them. "Check."

"Yeah, Jeffers, not since you brought down that load of jewelry in May." Sylvia was inching closer to the boxes holding the auction items.

Tanya moved herself so she was between the boxes and Sylvia. "Jeffrey, next item please."

Jeffrey rolled his eyes and pulled the next one out of the box, reading off the label.

Sylvia made another move towards the boxes and around the overweight woman, but she moved again to keep herself between Sylvia and the boxes. "Tanya, darling, what's new with you? What did you bring me this time?"

"Nothing to play with, if that's what you mean. I'll thank you to keep your grubby mitts off the merchandise this month, thank you."

Sylvia gave an abbreviated bow. "As always, Tanya. A pleasure seeing you again."

The older woman rounded on Sylvia and Ben, and she stuck a finger into Ben's face. "You're new here, so I don't expect you to fully understand things. But this child needs to be blessed. She hasn't been to church since her sainted grandmother went to the home, and she simply will not listen to her elders, who know better about these sorts of things. You keep her away from valuables and you keep her away from me; unless of course she decides to become a proper young lady, stop dressing like a girl who can't make up her mind if she's a boy or not, and attend church to figure out where she is in this world." She turned back to Jeffrey. "Next item."

Jeffrey's back was carefully turned to Tanya as he struggled to contain a laugh and the next call number was muffled through his clenched teeth. Sylvia simply bowed again to the woman's back and retreated to Ben's office.

She hoisted herself up to sit on Ben's desk, legs swinging.

"See? And her rants never make sense, either! One day I'm the child of the devil, the next I'm a tramp, and she always thinks I'm going to steal her auction items."

"What happened to make her think that?"

"One auction, a glass unicorn that was up for sale was broken between one day and the next, and I tried to tell her that we get birds in here all the time and sometimes they knock things over, but she wouldn't believe me. And since I was the one to try and explain things, I was the one who got the blame. Personally, I don't think it was birds; I think it was Jillian. She likes unicorns and sometimes comes in to look at the shelves to see if there are any there. But it could have been a bird." She scuffed her shoes on the carpet. "Stupid old cow."

Ben sighed at Sylvia's cross expression, already familiar with how much ill it bode. "How long do I have to put up with this feud?"

"They're only here for a day, usually. They'll unload their stuff and then they leave, so just today. Thank god."

Ben was thinking the exact same thing, though he had to admit, Tanya's wrath was highly amusing, if almost insensible. Sylvia jumped off the desk and stomped out, muttering something about shredding and Tanya's face.

After he had been entering data for about twenty minutes, Tanya and Jeffrey came around the corner and presented themselves at Ben's desk. "All present and accounted for. Everything should already be appearing on the inventory for the auction this month."

Ben carefully minimized the search window he had open to the long list of green trucks. "Thanks. Say, do you guys stick around for the night on these runs or do you head straight back? Quite the long drive." Ben leaned back in his chair, stretching his tall frame as best he could in the cubicle.

Jeffrey opened his mouth to say something, but Tanya overrode him. "Not this time. We've been asked to hang around and help you with the inventory of your warehouse."

Ben's chair straightened with a thump and he frowned. "That whole long-term storage thing? Sylvia and I finished that this weekend; we have a list of everything that appeared to be missing."

Tanya propped her plump arms on her hips and turned to survey the warehouse floor. "That's a good start. Obviously we'll need to double-check your work, make sure you didn't overlook anything while we inventory the entire rest of this rat maze."

Ben was sure he couldn't have heard right. "The whole warehouse? Why? They didn't tell me that the whole thing needed to be inventoried, just the long-term storage."

Tanya shrugged. "Who am I to argue with the anonymous voice in my email? It said to hang around down here until the auction and get the entire warehouse inventoried. That leaves us nearly four full days, maybe even staying through Friday if we don't quite finish up. Apparently there are concerns about some missing items." The way she said this last part made it blindingly clear who she thought the culprit was, and the suspect and her pigtails were currently shredding up a storm in the sorting bay.

Ben rose to the defense of his absent coworker. "There are a couple hundred missing items in the long-term storage bay that I'm sure Mrs. Biun took with her as she left. The rest of the warehouse should be pristine. Or at least everything since I got here. I can't vouch for any work preceding my tenure."

Tanya patted him on the arm. "Hush now, no one's calling you into question. This happens every ten years or so to each warehouse. I'm due in about four years myself, if the pattern holds true. Guess they decided with the changing of the guard here to hurry things up a bit. Don't worry, when my time comes it'll be you who gets to do the violating." She smiled, but it slid off her face too quickly to be sincere and she turned to Jeffrey. "Are you ready to get started? I want to get going on this."

Without waiting for an answer, Tanya turned and strode into the warehouse. Jeffrey looked at Ben and shrugged, conveying an abashed apology for their intrusion, before following his boss to the back bays. At that point, Sylvia brought in a cart for his attention.

"I actually ran out of shredding to do. Could have sworn there would have been more backed up what with our inventorying and all." She noticed the frown on his face and followed his gaze to the back of the warehouse and listened to an echo of the Minnesotan accent. "They still here?"

"Yes. And they're going to be here for a few days, at least." Ben started unloading the cart onto his desk, making a tower out of the trays.

"What? Why?" she hung off of his shoulder. "Can't you make her go away? Please?"

Ben shrugged her off and settled into his chair to start the entries. "You seem to get along with Jeffrey fine. Can't you just ignore her?"

"I can try I guess." She paused and straightened her cap. "So, why are they going to be here longer than their usual drop off?"

"They have apparently been assigned the undesirable task of inventorying the entire warehouse. Top to bottom. Every item."

"Shit." Ben raised an eyebrow at her strong language. "I mean, that has got to suck, royally."

"I figure they'll be in and out before the actual auction hits, and then they'll be gone. It's not like there's going to be anything really missing in here anyway. Except for that stuff that was in the safe that we already reported." Sylvia was now standing at the edge of his office space and staring into the warehouse. He had a sudden flash of concern about what else might be missing in the warehouse. "Right, Sylvia?"

"Hmm? Oh, yeah, right. Is there anything I can do for you that is not in the warehouse?"

Ben struggled not to laugh as she nearly vibrated with discomfort. "Sure, why don't you go see if the sorters could use a hand, or the readers even? You keep saying how much you'd like to eventually be one."

"Thanks." She scurried out, throwing one last glance over her shoulder. Ben could understand her not liking Tanya if all their interactions went the same way, but this excessive dodging of the pair from Minnesota was starting to get, well, entertaining, if he was honest with himself. He turned back to his recording and shelving, having to go and fetch all the carts himself as Sylvia didn't show her face in the warehouse for the rest of the day. There was about an hour left at the end of the day that he spent chasing down more items for auction and doing a little research.

At five, Tanya and Jeffrey showed no signs of slowing down, so he wandered over to them. They had barely taken a lunch break.

"Hey." The steady rhythm of their back and forth paused and Tanya glanced over at him before picking up her patter where she left off. "I was just, uh, checking to see when you guys were going to be headed out tonight."

"Benji, we have a whole warehouse to inventory before the end of the week. We'll be here a while; 07-04-18-76."

He shoved his hands in his pockets, nose wrinkling at the

diminutive. "It's just Ben, thanks. What time did you get here this morning anyway?"

"Around six, why?"

"Just thinking you are gonna wear yourself out if you keep working like this." That, and he didn't particularly want to leave her alone in the warehouse. Despite the fact that if there were items missing it wouldn't be his fault, he sincerely wanted to be here to oversee their work. But at the same time, he was feeling the pull of his wall of information, which felt sadly neglected after his busy weekend.

"Well, *Ben*, if you weren't so used to the southern easy way of life, you'd be used to the kind of hard work we can do if called on. Jeffrey, check?"

Jeffrey waved the sheaf of papers he was holding at her. "Check." He turned to Ben. "And if you saw the rat hole we are staying in down here, you'd want to spend all your time here as well."

"Jeffrey, you hush. We are government servants and must use our expense account wisely." She turned on Ben next. "These shelves are an absolute disaster."

He crossed his arms defensively. He was starting to understand why Sylvia had made it a point to avoid the warehouse today. "Well, it's not like I shelved any of it. I've been here less than a month."

Tanya shook her head sorrowfully. "It's that dratted Sylvia girl, I know it is. No good role models in her youth, bet you ten to one. She's trouble, she is."

Ben stood a little straighter. "Hang on, now, she's been nothing but helpful since I started here. She's the very spirit of helpfulness."

"She's a damned menace is what she is." Tanya slammed down her list to emphasize her point.

Ben was furious now. "Do you have any proof of that?"

The woman stood on tiptoe to get in his face. "Besides her trashing my auction items, you mean?"

"I asked for proof, not conjecture," Ben snapped.

"Not yet, I don't, but don't you be surprised when I come up with more stuff missing than can't be accounted for. She's a sticky-fingered little wretch, and she should be put back in her place. Or fired, better yet. She's utterly incompetent." Jeffrey opened his mouth and then thought better of it and returned to peering through his sheets of paper, ostensibly counting the number of items left unaccounted for.

Ben was furious. Here he was confronted with a woman who obviously had no familiarity with logic, and for some unfathomable reason she had determined to hate Sylvia. "Fine then, I'll keep her out of your way while you're here. But don't expect me to boot her entirely from the warehouse as I need her assistance in finishing the preparations of my own auction items as well as logging the daily intake. Who, by the way, is covering your job back in Minnesota in your rather sizeable absence?" He regretted the crack as soon as he made it, but he hadn't been able to help himself.

Tanya gave him a black look and took a step towards him, raising her hand.

Jeffrey stepped between them finally. "It's a huge job, no question. We have some trainees and interns who are working on things and sending daily reports. Also the readers know to check in on them from time to time."

Ben waved his hand dismissively. "Well, good. Wouldn't want you to get behind while you're trying to prove we're all dishonest crooks down here in the South."

Having calmed a bit, Tanya replied, "No one is implying you are crooks. We are simply looking for inefficiencies, discrepancies, and the occasional incompetence. It has nothing to do with your honor. You'd think it was precious to you southern gentlemen."

Ben threw his hands in the air in frustration and strode back to his desk. It appeared that Tanya was a woman it was very easy to make an enemy of, though he wasn't sure how Jeffrey had survived as long as he had. Some miracle of willpower, Ben assumed, or lack of personality. He wasn't quite sure yet. Regardless, he hurried out of the office, eager to be away from the harridan and back home with the comforting stacks of reports waiting for him on his desk.

The next day Ben didn't see Sylvia at all. The morning passed uneventfully, his meditative data entry and shelving accompanied by the constant patter of the inventory going on down the way. The duo had finished one bay and were well into their second. Ben was flabbergasted at their speed and determination; the hotel they were staying at must have been truly horrible if Jeffrey had acquiesced to Tanya's desire to speed through the process.

Around lunch, he poked his head into the break room, the sorting room, and the bullpen but still couldn't find his wayward partner. Everyone he asked said they remembered her asking if there was anything she could do for them and disappearing again when they said they didn't. One of the readers, Byron, even admitted telling her he wouldn't give her a research project even if he did. She wasn't cleared for it.

Ben hadn't heard this term yet. "Cleared for it?"

Byron looked around conspiratorially and leaned in. "You actually need a security clearance to be a reader. You know, just in case."

Ben was amused at Byron's reaction. "Has that ever mattered?"

"Once, I think. Sometime in the 1940s a letter went astray from one of the scientists on the Manhattan project." The reader smiled dreamily. "Imagine holding a piece of history in your hands like that."

"Fascinating. I wonder, had it been censored yet?"

Byron shrugged, and turned back to his pile of waiting letters.

By the time it came to close up the office for the day, Ben was a little worried; it wasn't like Sylvia to so completely disappear. She seemed to thrive on constant attention and putting herself where she didn't belong. Even deliberately making people uncomfortable. And, oddly, it was this intrusiveness that he missed. He checked on Tanya and Jeffrey one more time, but they just waved him off, Jeffrey with a polite shrug and Tanya with a gruff, "Go on, get home."

So Ben left them to their work and headed back to his apartment. He stopped on the way home to pick up more Peachtree Ale since he had finished his stock the night before, and as soon as he got home, he cracked one open and sat down at his desk. He turned on his radio to the only station he still listened to, 95.5 WSB, news and talk. It wasn't like he even really listened to Sean Hannity and, later, Herman Cain. He just liked having the noise on in the background. In fact, if he ever did truly listen, he'd probably just end up pissed off at something the political commentators said.

He sipped his beer and tried to decide how his evening would be best put to use. He would prefer sitting at work and running through the list of possible searches he had put together from the tip line or making copies, but he didn't particularly want to be doing that with the harpy from Minnesota hanging over his shoulder. With out that option, he was at a loss. He shuffled his papers a few times, logged onto the tip sites and started scanning them, but between his irritation over Tanya and his worry for Sylvia, he was just too distracted.

Food might help his concentration, he decided, but he really wasn't at all hungry despite the fact that he'd eaten lunch early that day as an excuse to try and hunt down Sylvia at work. And then he started wondering about Sylvia again. He didn't have her personal email, so he decided to call her just to make sure everything was okay.

He scrabbled around his desk for the phone number that she had written down the day he was sick and finally found it under a stack of whiskey-stained notes. Sitting down with the phone in one hand and the number in the other, he dialed the first three numbers and then hung up. *Should I call her?* She had obviously been at work as other people had seen her. Ben just had not seen her. Did that warrant a call to her house during the dinner hour?

Maybe she wouldn't be home and he could just leave a message or hang up. But best to call her anyway, in case something was wrong. Most days you couldn't pry her out of the warehouse. So he dialed again and finished his beer as he waited for the dial tone to resolve itself into the simulacrum of a human voice informing him that the number he had just dialed was not answering.

After the third ring, however, there was a click on the other end of the line, a pause, and a cocky, "Sup?"

"Sylvia?"

"Oh, hey, Ben. Something up?"

"Not really, just didn't see you at all today, and since I'm ostensibly your boss, I just thought I'd check in, make sure you were still alive." He got up to go get another beer while flipping through a stack of takeout menus.

"Aw, Ben, that's sweet of you. But I'm fine, just avoiding the plague in the warehouse. I'll come back to you as soon as the harpy and her puppy leave. I love Jeffers, don't get me wrong, but that woman…oh, I could just, just choke a tree!"

"Choke a tree?" He tried to picture the little pixie with the badly dyed ponytails and newsboy cap wrapping her arms around a hundred-year-old oak and trying to choke the life out of it.

"You know what I mean."

"I do. But it's not that bad; they ignore me all day unless I butt in. You could come back to the warehouse tomorrow. Please? There is just too much to do without you."

"So this is all just because you've learned you can't live without me?"

But Ben had stopped listening to her. A news bulletin had broken through the usual inane chatter on the station.

"The police have just arrested a man on the charges of abduction and murder for several counts. Sources are saying he kidnapped and held several young boys. Updates in an hour. But now, back to your host."

"Sylvia, I'll call you back. I have to check on something." Ben hung up without waiting for her answer. He immediately dialed Detective O'Connor's number, still memorized.

"O'Connor."

"It's Ben."

"Jesus, I knew you'd call as soon as you heard a news report." He sighed. "We don't know anything right now. Hold tight."

"Just tell me, is it true that he kidnapped young boys?" Ben clutched the phone, mouthing *please god* over and over while he waited for an answer.

The detective paused a moment and Ben could just imagine the man slouched in his desk chair, hand over his eyes. It was the same posture that had greeted him the last couple times Ben had dropped by the precinct unannounced to check on progress before he moved to Atlanta.

"Can you just leave this alone till we know more?"

Ben seriously considered it before replying, "Could you?"

"I'm not going to tell you everything," the detective warned.

"Just something. Please." Ben tried not to sound like he was begging and failed.

"Fine then. And don't go running off to everyone telling tales. We stopped a guy with a broken taillight, and there was a boy sitting on the bench seat crying. Turns out the boy was snatched. We arrested the guy, but he's retarded. Literally. IQ lower than sixty the shrinks say. We searched his property and have found one other…boy so far."

Ben heard the hesitation and realized what the detective didn't want to say. "Dead."

"Yes." It was delivered crisply, as though in a report to a senior officer. No emotion.

"And?"

"We're going to keep searching. If there's two…"

Ben struggled for breath, glad he was sitting down. After a moment, he straightened a little in his chair. "You said a bench seat; what was he driving?"

Again, the detective hesitated. He was weighing his words carefully tonight. "I'll never hear the end of it if I tell you."

At his words, Ben knew with certainty what it was. "A green truck."

"More rust than green, but yes," the detective admitted. Both men waited for the other to make the next conversational gambit.

"Detective?"

The sigh was audible over the line. "Yeah, Ben?"

"Thanks." At least Detective O'Connor was honest. He never lied to Ben about what had happened before, nor did he try and avoid the truth now.

"If or when we know any more, I'll call you. But don't wait by the phone; it'll be a while."

Ben hung up without saying anything else. The phone rang almost as soon as he'd hung up. He stared at the receiver in his hand for three rings before he hit the talk button.

"Ben? Ben are you there?"

He didn't answer. His mind was still turning over the reality of the green truck and missing boys.

"Ben? Goddamn it. Answer me." Sylvia's voice was tight and worried.

Wrenching his attention to the voice on the line, he answered, "I'm here."

"Shit, I thought you'd had a heart attack. Your voice had gone all funny before you hung up." She sounded relieved now that he was talking. Would she still be relieved when he told her what had happened? Would she understand?

"Close enough."

"What happened?"

"Are you listening to the news?" Still, he wasn't sure he wanted to tell her.

She snorted. "Do I ever?"

"They just arrested a guy for kidnapping young boys. In a green pickup truck. In Atlanta." He wanted to stop thinking. He considered his beer bottle for a moment, then set it down and pulled down a fresh bottle of whiskey. He poured a couple fingers into the only clean water glass.

"Do you think...?" She sounded worried again.

"Yeah, I do." Of course he did. They finally found the green truck, and it leads to a murderer of small boys. Why did it lead to a murderer? Was that better than a molester? Or an insane woman who thought Benny was her son?

There was silence on the line.

"I'm coming over." Sylvia's voice was a little shaky.

"No, Sylvia. It's okay; I'd rather you didn't." That wasn't what he wanted. He wanted to be alone, to think.

"Fuck you, I want a hug." And she hung up.

He dashed another measure into the glass and tossed it back, dinner forgotten. He wished Sylvia wasn't coming over. Then he could get drunk. He didn't want to be drunk in front of her. He poured another shot.

But he still hadn't tasted it by the time his doorbell rang. And though he didn't call out, the door opened to reveal Sylvia carrying two medium Little Caesars pizzas. She walked in without saying anything, dropped the pizzas on the counter, and walked over to where he was still standing in front of the shopping bags from the liquor store. In one glance, she took in the open bottle of whiskey, the glass in his hand, and his stupefied expression.

"That's no way to treat good whiskey." She put the cap back on the bottle before taking the glass out of his hand and putting it on the counter. "No way to treat your liver, either." A slice of pepperoni pizza was put into his hand, and when he didn't take a bite, she proceeded to lift his hand towards his face before he broke away from her.

"It's not good whiskey, it's cheap whiskey." He considered the slice of pizza she had handed him. "Why did you pick up pizza?"

"I was hungry. There's a Caesars on the way, so I got their premade five dollar special."

The scent of fresh, hot grease finally brought him to ground, and he slumped to sit against the floor cabinets and took a bite of the slice she had forced on him. Sylvia grabbed the box and sat beside him and they didn't say anything else until they had each had two pieces.

"My son loved Little Caesars, cheese though, not pepperoni."

"Got one of those, too." She reached up to the counter and pulled the second box down to them and opened it.

They were quiet again while they contemplated the cheese pizza until Sylvia picked up a piece and folded it in half lengthwise. "So, a green truck, huh?"

"Yeah, unbelievable." Ben picked up another slice.

"You mean unintelligible. What the hell does a green truck have to do with anything?" She took an enormous bite of the pizza and stared at him while she chewed.

Ben dragged himself off the floor and to his desk. He had to admit, the pizza was making him feel less fuzzy, and he wiped the grease off on his pants before paging through his notes. "Here. Here and here. Reports of young boys getting into green trucks."

Sylvia took the pages from him with the reports of the truck. "How many pages of this report do you have?"

Ben started digging around on the desk looking for the rest of the transcript to show her. "About two thousand now, and they're tip line transcripts, why?"

"Three references to a green truck out of what could be around ten thousand tips." She threw the pages back on his desk, not caring where they landed.

"And a report I got from a homeless woman while I was papering earlier this month." He carefully placed the pages back into the pile of important papers.

Sylvia crossed her arms and stared him down. "And how many other reports of cars are there?"

"Detective O'Connor asked me the same thing. I don't remember now." Ben didn't like where this line of questioning was going, again, but he waited her out.

She sighed. "Of course there was the stereotypical white panel van, too."

"Yes."

She started pacing in front of his desk now. "So how do you know this is the same green truck? How do you know these reports are not just of fathers picking up their sons in the old family pickup?"

He shrugged, refusing to let her get to him. "I don't; I just feel it."

"You want it." She rounded on him, sticking her finger in his face.

He batted it away. "Of course not, I just think that this is all the same guy, in my gut."

"Well, sometimes that is all investigators have to go on. Maybe yours is more accurate than the layperson's." She wandered over to the kitchen to grab a box of pizza and came back to collapse on the floor beside his desk, failing the presence of any additional chairs. "So tell me, how did they find him?"

"Broken taillight." He thought about the irony of that for a moment and let out a small dry laugh. "Doesn't that seem to be the thing that keeps bringing people in? Small traffic infractions."

"Guess you should be careful driving or you'll wind up accused of mass murder or something, eh?" She nudged his knee with her elbow and winked. Ben only raised his eyebrow. "Right, sorry. Serious mood. Continue. Can I grab one of those beers?"

Gesturing his assent, he continued. "So he had a boy in the truck with him, one he'd grabbed. They found one other body so far."

"So far?" Now it was her turn to look uneasy.

"In cases like this there's frequently more than one." Ben slouched further into his chair, resting his head on the back.

She wrinkled her nose at him. "God, you sound like a textbook."

"Might be because I've read more than one." He gestured to the pile of criminal investigation books and missing persons case studies piled beside his desk. Fat lot of help they had been, with their doomsayers time charts and statistics.

"So, do the detectives think Benny is one of them?"

"Detective O'Connor told me to buzz off for now. He didn't say anything, but—"

"There's always the possibility." She brought back two beers and handed one to Ben. "To the investigation then. May it speed along."

They tapped bottles and each took long pulls.

Ben stared at his bottle and started picking at the label. "It'll be weeks still. With the search, testing...god, testing takes forever in this state. I know from before." He put the bottle down, more to keep himself from shredding the label all over his desk than anything else. It certainly didn't need any more paper added to it.

"So we wait. Do you want to go out again this weekend after the auction and paper some more?"

Ben thought about it while he drank. "I think I'd like to wait and just see what happens first. With..." he gestured vaguely at the pages mentioning the truck, "this."

They ate while listening to the political talk program on the radio. At the hour, the host changed over to yet another political junkie.

Sylvia made a face and went to turn it off. "How can you listen to this stuff?"

"I don't really listen. I just kind of like the noise when I'm here. I'm used to a full house, lots of racket, between a five year old and working with my wife." Ben shrugged. "Then there were all those people around."

They were quiet again, which suited Ben just fine. He

didn't really want to think, talk, or eat; he just wanted to sit for a little while.

Sylvia gave in to her garrulous nature and broke the silence. "Do you mind telling me more about him?"

Ben took another sip of his beer before answering. "You really want to know?"

"Yeah, I do." Sylvia stood and stretched before sitting on his desk, trying to even the height difference between them.

Ben nodded, took another pull on his beer, and then rolled it back and forth between his palms. He didn't look up at her. It would be easier to talk about him if he didn't have to see pity welling up in her eyes.

"My son was born on Saint Patrick's day. We used to joke that no one would realize it was his twenty-first birthday because everyone would be so drunk. I thought he was ugly at first, all wrinkled like an old man, but after a day or so, his skin smoothed out and he was just the sweetest little cherub of a boy. Had the cry of a mule though, kick, too. He grew so fast…"

Sylvia didn't prompt him, rush him, or ask questions. Not like everyone else who had ever asked about his son. She simply waited until Ben finished his beer and set it down.

"He didn't really like sports, but he loved being outdoors or in the workshop at the antique store. Jeannie was terrified that he'd hurt himself while he was in there. I never thought he would. He always listened to me while we were there and knew what he was allowed to touch and not. Heck, his bassinet stayed in there most days while I worked on restoring and pricing items while Jeannie was out front. Kept the customers from getting distracted from the merchandise, she said." He dropped the empty bottle on the table.

"But, he was my little prince. Sure, he was trouble, any healthy boy is, but not too much. Just enough. I remember, this one time, I'd gone out front to help carry a wardrobe out of the store for a customer and that boy thought he'd help out. I had been refinishing a table with a linseed oil coat, and he picked up the brush and proceeded to coat it and the floor liberally with the stain. Got it just everywhere, and it is not easy to clean up. All over him, too. I laughed so hard when I saw it, thanked him for his help, and handed him over to his mother to go wash up, as she was already headed to the apartment to make lunch. This was just before…"

He trailed off, and then stood abruptly, leaving his chair to spin behind him. The whiskey bottle was still sitting on the counter and he picked it up, pouring another measure into his glass.

"Hey now, Ben." Sylvia got up off the floor and joined him in the kitchen. "Is this that friend you keep ignoring me for, then?" He stared at her, not comprehending. "What bottle number is this for you this week?"

Confused, he stared at the bottle. "Two, why?"

"Two full ones?"

He shrugged, not really caring. "Maybe, I don't know."

"Things are a little clearer." She walked over and took the glass out of his hand and downed the shot.

"Hey, I was going to drink that!" Ben tried to take the glass back from her, but she resisted.

"Maybe you were. Now you're not. I think you may want to look at your drinking habits." She wrested the bottle out of his hand and ducked out of range.

He was getting irritated again. He didn't like how comfortable she was getting in criticizing him. She wanted to know about his son, and he was telling her, and she repaid him by taking away the one thing that numbed his pain enough for him to think and sleep. "My drinking habits are fine."

"Really? I walk in here tonight and you're drinking by yourself, standing there with an open bottle. When I came over with breakfast you had spent the night sleeping at your desk. I bet you do that often." Ben started to protest, but she overrode him. "And you look half dead from a hangover when you come into work in the morning. Every morning." She put the glass in the sink, out of his reach, and then recapped the bottle.

"It helps me sleep at night."

"Obviously not well. Ben, I'm only concerned about what's healthy for you. This," she waved the bottle in his face, "this is not healthy."

Even in his distracted state he knew hypocritical reasoning when he heard it. "You were drinking with me tonight. And the other night."

"I don't drink myself to sleep every night." She threw the bottle in the trash under the sink.

"I don't."

"Prove it." She stood there, bracing herself in front of the sink, waiting to see if he'd go for the bottle in the trash or submit to her judgment.

He was silent. He had kept telling himself that the booze was only for the short term, until he found his son, until the pain lessened and he could sleep without it. And then he realized what utter bullshit that was. He heard Jeannie's voice again yelling at him that he was always drunk. He sagged against the counter, wondering just when it was that his drinking had gotten so out of hand. Wondered if it was possible to deal with his pain any other way.

Sylvia saw his face collapse and walked over to give him a fierce hug. "I care about you. You're the first boss I've had I actually *like*. And I've seen this kind of behavior destroy people before." She tilted her head back to look him in the eye. "There are healthier ways to deal with the stress, you know. Much healthier. Exercising, getting a hobby."

Their faces were less than four inches apart, she still held him tightly. His hands tentatively came up to her shoulders so he felt less awkward being held by the diminutive woman. "But I feel like I'm wasting time if I'm not working on finding my son. That's the most important thing. Okay, maybe I can cut back some on the drinking. I think you're right in that regard, but I can't give up what little time I have for the search to do anything else."

"You're not wasting time. You're living. You should live a little. Spend time with friends, make friends, people who care."

Ben considered her words carefully, trying to decide if she was saying what he thought she was trying to say. "Like you?"

She pulled herself closer in to him, turning their standing embrace into something a bit more intimate, her eyes downcast and demure, an odd look for a woman who was normally so direct. "Yes, like me."

Ben bent forward and closed the distance between them, landing a tight-lipped kiss on Sylvia's forehead, testing. Sylvia leaned into him and murmured. "I lied. I knew what you were talking about, and yes."

He sighed, pulling back just enough to make eye contact again. "Now you've lost me."

She refused the eye contact at first. "Last weekend. I meant what I said about you." She finally looked up at him, her eyes curiously bright, eager almost.

"Oh." He hesitated a moment longer, trying to decide whether it was a good idea or not, him being her boss and all, then he bent forward to close the half-foot gap in their heights, and carefully touched his lips to hers. He noticed briefly that they smelled minty and made his mouth tingle before she wrapped her arms tight around his neck and rose on the tips of her toes, nearly suffocating him with the force of her returned kiss.

She pulled back briefly. "You know, this is not what I meant when I suggested you take up other activities. I was thinking along the lines of a gym or continuing education classes." He kissed her again before she could say any more. It had been over a year since Jeannie had allowed him to touch her, a year since he had felt any kind of human contact that wasn't at its heart just an empty consoling gesture. It felt so good to touch and be touched that he prayed she wouldn't stop, wouldn't pull back. He hesitated, and she redoubled her advances, pinning him roughly against the counter.

After that they quickly began shedding clothing, his hands fumbling the buttons of her vest, her's smoothly undoing the row of buttons down his wrinkled dress shirt. They barely made it to his bedroom, where he didn't even have time to think that he hadn't changed the sheets since he'd moved in.

An hour later they lay diagonally across the mattress, Sylvia curled up next to him with her head on his shoulder. She pulled at the sheets until Ben shifted enough for her to cover herself before she started getting chilled in the draft from the air conditioner. They didn't say anything, and Ben absently ran his fingers through her short mop of hair, which had come out of her pigtails.

His brain, for once, was quiet, not screaming with recriminations or demanding he make his way out to the living room to work. "You look older with your hair down."

"If my hair is down, it gets in the way." She brushed it impatiently out of her eyes and curled up tighter to him, throwing one of her legs across his thighs. They didn't say anything else for a while; Ben was content to simply lay beside her, relishing in the feel of her skin on his.

He had almost drifted off to sleep when she stirred. "Ben?"

"Mm?" He struggled to bring himself out of the sex-induced fog.

"Tonight. While we were talking. You never said his name."

He was almost instantly awake, the last bits of endorphins and alcohol speeding from his system. "What?"

"Benny. You never said his name. I just thought it was interesting."

Ben sat up, ignoring her muffled complaints as she flopped over onto the mattress. Swinging his legs over the side of the bed, he sat with his back to her. He hadn't said his name, was that true? He thought back over the entire course of the evening, and she was right. He hadn't. It unsettled him, but he wasn't quite sure why. It's not like he had forgotten his son's name. No, he just hadn't named him once while talking about what their life had been, the happiness of those times. Benny had become the missing poster boy; that's all he was anymore to Ben. It was almost like that cheerful, troublemaking boy was fading, being replaced by the over-photocopied face on the poster.

Sylvia reached out to place a hand on his shoulder, but he shrugged it off. He knew this was a mistake when he had started. Sleeping with his coworker, his younger coworker, but he hadn't expected it to hurt. He had just wanted to forget and feel good, for just a little while. Now that was fading and something worse was taking its place, worse than he had felt than before she had come over.

"You should go home; we have work to do tomorrow." He refused to turn and face her, to watch her face fall as he dismissed her. He couldn't bring himself to watch the pain he was passing to her, and he desperately needed to be alone.

"I thought—" She stopped herself and studied his back for a moment before acquiescing. "Alright, Ben. I'll go. See you in the morning?"

"Yeah. Sure." At that moment he wanted to do nothing so much as rush out into the night, searching and searching, and calling Benny's name to prove he wasn't being forgotten, slowly replaced by an ink and paper version who never lived. The last thing he wanted to think about was having to return to the warehouse in the morning and the loud Minnesotans and piles of unending lost items which never found their proper home.

Sylvia quickly gathered her clothes and made her way to the bedroom door. He waited until he heard it shut behind her before he curled back up in bed, his held-back tears making his face ache.

Now, these are the days to live for. Once a month, every month. The bated breath, the auctioneer's hammer strike, the blessed release as an item is won, frequently after a struggle...nothing is more powerful. And nothing illustrates the greedy weaknesses of the human soul more poignantly.

~ *Gertrude Biun*, Property Office Manual

The next morning Ben seriously considered not going into work. He didn't know what had possessed him the night before, though he felt like blaming the alcohol. That would mean he wasn't responsible for taking advantage of Sylvia, not really. It helped that his entire body was blaming the alcohol, especially the several shots he'd gotten up to get after Sylvia had left. At least she had wanted him; it wasn't like it was a pity fuck, or so he told himself. She'd as much as said she wanted to screw him last weekend. But with his current life situation, how could it not be a pity fuck? He didn't think he could handle it if it was, and he was afraid if he had to face her, that's what she'd tell him. A one-time pity fuck.

He dragged himself out of bed and sat in the shower for a good twenty minutes before he felt together enough to get in the car and stop at a Krispy Kreme for a large coffee and two donuts, his usual breakfast. Back in the car, he took one bite of a donut, chewed slowly, tried to swallow, and threw the rest of the donut out the window for the birds. The coffee went down better, and he actually felt his eyes open.

The office was already in full swing by the time he got there, and Judy tisked his hour-late arrival. "Auction this week, Ben, but you must have things together well enough to afford to be late, I see."

"Actually, yeah. Thanks. Want a donut?" He waved his donut bag in her general direction.

"Ah, hmm, no, thanks. Oh, Krispy Kreme? I guess I can take care of that for you." He handed over the second donut and headed back toward his office. "Oh, and by the way, the auctioneers are here today getting set with the inventory for the month."

He turned to walk backward while still talking to her. "Thanks for the warning. Haven't met them yet. Are they good people?"

"You mean less antagonistic than Tanya? Yeah. Actually a fun pair of boys from just north of Savannah. I think they're, you know," she held her arm in the air and let her hand fall limp. "But they're good boys. Always polite and they're good auctioneers."

Ben decided to ignore the rather poorly mimed slur on the men's sexual orientation. "I see. Thanks, Judy. Enjoy the donut." When he made it to his warehouse, he opened the door just enough to hear what was going on inside, but not wide enough to draw attention to himself.

"I said, next item, Jeffrey."

"Can't a boy finish a conversation, woman?"

Ben had no trouble identifying the first voice as Tanya, but he didn't know who the light tenor was that responded to her in such an amused fashion.

"We're almost done with this. Another hour, and you can chat all you like before we head back north. Jeffrey?" Despite herself, Tanya sounded somewhat tolerant of the interloper. Ben wondered what his trick was.

"Jesus, hun, you have got to relax." That was another new voice, this one more of a bass.

"You watch your mouth, mister. I don't care who you are, you shouldn't be taking the Lord's name in vain. And I can't relax down here in this godforsaken heat. Now enough, go do your work and leave us to ours."

Ben rubbed his temples with his free hand and tried to summon up the patience to deal with the people behind the door. He finally kicked the door all the way open and strode in.

"Morning, Tanya, Jeffrey."

"Hey, Ben," Jeffrey returned. Nothing from Tanya, which Ben was rather grateful for this morning. He wasn't sure his body could handle another irritant on top of the hangover.

The two new men in the warehouse were huddled over the shelves of the auction staging bay but turned at the sound of his voice.

"Ah, you must be Mister Benjamin Grant. So nice to meet you." The smaller of the two men was dressed in a pink short-sleeved dress shirt and tan slacks and hurried up to him to shake his hand. "I'm Larry, and this is Steve." He gestured to the taller and slimmer man behind him.

"Don't we know you? Larry, don't we know him?"

Ben opened his mouth to reply but was cut short.

"He does look familiar now that you mention it."

"But where, that auction in Maryland?"

"No, definitely not Maryland; he's a Georgia boy."

"Yes, yes, I can see that. But not Atlanta, no."

"No, not Atlanta. Savannah?"

"Savannah, yes, but not an auction either."

By this time Ben thought he knew who they were, but he decided to wait out the verbal memory flood. It was much easier to go along for the ride than try to get a word in edgewise.

"No, a storefront. I'm remembering an armoire." He gave the name the French pronunciation.

"No, not an armoire, a chest."

"Chest! Yes, that gorgeous piece we picked up for that dear, Mrs. Peterson, wasn't it?"

"Absolutely, from that little antique shop. You were the oh-so-helpful man behind the counter!"

Ben paused to be sure the two men were done, then nodded his head, which he immediately regretted. "That's me alright. Hard to forget two customers such as yourselves."

"We are that, aren't we, Steve?" The smaller one jabbed his elbow into the side of his companion who laughed.

"Yes we are, Larry."

"So," Ben clapped his hands together and rubbed briskly, trying to force himself more awake and praying that he would have a moment soon to get to the aspirin in his drawer, "you two are my auctioneering team, then?"

Steve draped his arm over Ben's shoulder, his touch feather light. "Have been for ages. We know how this is supposed to go, so don't you fret none. Is all the merchandise accounted for and transferred to the holding area?"

"Yes, I was going to do a double check today, but I think it's all there." Ben wasn't sure he was comfortable standing that close to anyone else, especially not with the man's cologne playing havoc with his headache, but he felt it would be rude to duck out from under the arm.

Larry snagged Steve by his free arm and started towing him toward the auction bay. "Fantastic. We'll just go through and order it for the show then. Put all the big ticket items at the back end, keeps the little fish on the floor longer and the big hitters never bother showing up on time anyway."

Ben shoved his hands in his pockets and rocked back. "Well, I'll leave it in your capable hands. I'm just going to go take an aspirin and catch up on my paperwork for a moment."

"Poor darling. Looks like someone had a rough night, hmm?" Larry winked at him and then turned back to the shelves, waving a negligent hand at Ben. "Go, honey, go. We don't need you. We'll holler if something doesn't line up right. But you go drink some coffee. I find that usually does wonders."

Ben's mouth curled into a half smile. "Thanks for that. Have fun boys." Even through his hangover and guilty feelings from last night, he found the two men amusing. Though he hoped they'd quiet down once they settled into their jobs.

Larry and Steve went back to the shelf full of collectibles they had been discussing when Ben came in, arguing over whether to group all the animal statues in one lot or sell them separately.

No sooner had Ben sat at his desk, with his head in his hands, trying to block out the noise of two separate couples working, then Sylvia banged into the warehouse with a cart full of items.

"Good morning, Ben!"

Ben looked up briefly and then away. "Thanks." It had been years since he'd had to deal with any kind of morning-after conversation, and he just didn't know what to say anymore. Particularly to someone technically his subordinate whom he suspected of sleeping with him out of pity. It was easier to try and ignore that it had ever happened.

"I said, good morning." She crossed her arms and leaned on the cart, frowning. "Though for you it doesn't look so good."

Rubbing his temples, he felt he should apologize for something, though whether it was for giving in to the situation, or drinking more after she left, or just how sorry he was feeling for himself right now, he wasn't sure. "I'm sorry."

"For what? Finishing that bottle after you kicked me out last night? That would make anyone mighty sorry the next morning."

Ben tried to drag his stomach under control and squinted up at her. He decided to test the waters just a bit and see how she felt about the whole thing. "I'm sorry for, well," he lowered his voice so no one else could hear, "taking advantage of the situation last night?"

"Taking advantage, gee, that's funny." She pushed the cart roughly against his desk, turned on her heel, and started to leave, but turned back. "The only mistake you made was kicking me out, idiot. You have no idea what you missed out on." The crash of her cart briefly interrupted his warehouse invaders before they went back to their tasks. Noisy tasks with lots of shouting back and forth. Or at least it felt like shouting to Ben. After he was sure Sylvia had left, he looked at the cart she'd left behind. There was a bag from Dunkin' Donuts in the top rack on top of a copy of Tennessee Williams's plays that had seen much better days. *Hope this helps this morning. I have a feeling you'll need it...* was scrawled across the bag in permanent marker. He peeked inside and found a multigrain bagel, still warm from toasting, and a packet of veggie cream cheese. It left him more confused than ever; a nice gesture balanced against her definitely irritated response to his apology didn't help him figure out what had really gone on the night before besides the obvious.

Ben grimaced and tossed the bag into the bottom drawer of his desk. Maybe at lunchtime he'd feel like eating something, but now was not the time. Instead he turned on his computer and while he waited for it to boot up, he drained the last of his coffee.

After entering all of the items in the cart, he went in to the warehouse to shelve them as he hadn't seen Sylvia again. He went to the bullpen himself to get the next cart, but she wasn't there either. He felt like he needed to apologize again, this time for this morning. And for asking her to leave last night, as she had made abundantly clear.

But by lunchtime, he still hadn't seen her. He had no idea where she was disappearing to this week, but people were sure they had just seen her, and she was apparently getting all her other work done as the shredding pile disappeared at some point. So he sat down to eat the bagel she had left him while trolling through news websites, looking for articles about the new development in his son's disappearance.

It took him a moment to realize that Tanya and Jeffrey were standing over his desk. When he finally did look up, Jeffrey grinned. "Off in some fantasy world?"

"Not exactly." He shut the window he was currently reading from—which had said the exact same thing as every other news service—and stood to stretch. "Are you guys done with the inventory already?"

Tanya cut Jeffrey off. "Of course. This was nothing. You should see the amount of pictures we have piling up on our shelves at home. Talk about an inventorying nightmare."

Ben felt relieved to see these two out of his warehouse. Maybe he'd feel less overwhelmingly irritated once they were on the road home, and Sylvia would come back to help in the warehouse, which would be excellent, what with the auction coming up so shortly. "Well, good job to the both of you then. Hope you didn't find things too out of order."

Tanya shrugged before brushing some non-existent dust off the sleeve of her cardigan. "Mostly what was gone was what you already reported being stolen from the long-term bay; jewelry, etc. But there are a surprising number of photographs missing as well."

"That's...interesting." Ben felt a bit more uneasy about the missing photographs as he suspected he knew where those were going. "So, what's the next step from here? We're all done, right?" He certainly hoped they were, he wasn't sure he could handle many more days where he had to constantly watch his back while using the Center's resources to search for his son. Or thickly accented voices echoing through his warehouse from open till close.

Tanya sniffed, one eyebrow raised as if she found his eagerness to be finished distasteful. "I will turn in my findings to the auditor. He will decide what happens from here."

Ben was sure he hadn't come across a mention of an auditor in Mrs. Biun's manual, but it sounded distinctly ominous. "What's an auditor?"

"*The* auditor, darling. He'll get here the day after the auction. He goes from postal facility to postal facility and audits the branches, making sure they're running on task and efficiently. He'll know what to do about these things going missing. I'm sure he'll fix the little blonde...ahem...the problem." Tanya straightened her sweater set to cover her verbal gaffe and

Jeffrey just rolled his eyes.

Ben was even more worried. If this woman was so out to get Sylvia, regardless of what had just happened between them last night, Ben was determined to figure out whether the woman was going to make things difficult on her. "You're just giving him the list then, right?"

Tanya smiled, sickly sweet and full of poison. "And my perceptions of your facility and competencies, of course."

Ben could feel the bagel solidifying in his stomach. Perhaps he should have waited a little longer to eat anything. Or perhaps he should have found a useful job somewhere that wasn't quite so stressful. "You know I only just got here."

"And so far you are doing just fine." The woman leaned over to pat him reassuringly on the hand. "But I report my observations of all the workers attached to the warehouse. Just a fair warning."

Now he knew she was planning on bad mouthing at least Sylvia, if not himself as well. This was the last thing he needed to add to his guilt trip and hangover. "Thanks, I think. Headed home now?"

"Soon as I walk out that door. I cannot understand how you folks operate in this heat all the time." Tanya fanned herself as she gathered up her purse and started to head to the door.

Ben shrugged. "Some things you can get used to."

"And some things you can't. Come on, Jeffrey."

Jeffrey started to follow Tanya automatically, but caught himself and called after her. "I'll be along in a moment. Go get the air conditioner started; I forgot my pen back in that last bay."

"Sometimes I think you'd leave your head behind." Tanya left the warehouse, letting the door slam behind her.

Ben squinted at the tall man, unsure whether he was absent minded or wanted an excuse to talk. "Your pen is in your shirt pocket."

Jeffrey shrugged and perched on the edge of Ben's desk. "I know. I just wanted to let you know that I'm supposed to turn in a report, too. You don't need to worry about anything. Tanya can be a little overzealous at times, but she's really good at heart. Particularly when she's in cooler weather."

"I'll take your word for it." They shook goodbye and Jeffrey had started to walk out when Ben remembered his manners. "Jeff?" The gangly man paused. "Thanks for that."

"Of course." And they were gone. The noise level subsided considerably with only the two men in the auction bay murmuring to each other. There was the occasional outburst of joy when they found something interesting, but for the most part, they kept it to a minimum volume.

Ben went to check his email for the tenth time that day, and when there was no message from Detective O'Connor, he checked his phone. Still nothing. The worst feeling through this whole ordeal was always the waiting, when something seemed to be panning out but all he could do was wait for someone else to tell him what was going on when he couldn't be out there in the field himself. It drove him up the wall. He was just about to go back to the news sites when he heard his name being called from the back of the warehouse.

"Benjamin, oh Benji!"

"Ben." He got up from his desk and made his way over to Steve and Larry. "Ben is just fine."

Larry was rubbing his hands together briskly and watching Steve carefully load a cart with items from the shelves. "Sure thing. Sorry. It's just we're ready to move the auction items into the break room now and get things set up."

"That's right, my manual said something about the break room doubling as the auction house. Do I need to go do it, or do you guys know how it all gets set up?" Ben hoped they didn't need his help as he would prefer to be doing everything in his power to keep up-to-date with what was going on with the green truck case.

"No, no, like I said, we've been doing this for years; you just unlock this back door that leads to the room and start helping us haul tables and bring stuff in. Trust us, we've got this." Larry picked up a vase full of dried flowers and waited for Ben to open the secondary door to the warehouse. After he had gotten the door propped open, he turned to get an armload of stuffed animals. He tried to console himself with the fact that keeping busy would make the time go faster, but it didn't help much.

The break room was already mostly cleared of the lunch crowd, and Steve and Larry made short work of the last stragglers by suggesting quite loudly that the shift managers were coming right behind them. The tables all needed to be relocated to the back half of the room and set up in tight rows to display most of the goods, while the chairs were brought to the front and set in rows facing the podium and one small table. During the rearranging, the duo somehow produced a locking display cabinet for all the jewelry and valuables.

After the furniture was placed to their exacting specifications, they shooed Ben back to the warehouse with the cart to get more items. It took ten trips to bring out all of the items for the auction, from books to dolls and figurines, hunting knives, and a child's bow and arrow set. Once all of the items were in the room, Steve and Larry started arguing over what order to display them in.

"The vases should go together as a lot."

"Nobody will buy them as a lot."

"They buy books as a lot."

"But people like having lots of books. Vases, not so much."

"There's only three of them."

"Fine, try and sell them in a lot. Just don't forget I told you so later."

They wanted all the big-ticket items placed on the last few tables so people actually had to see all of the smaller stuff before they saw the jewelry and valuable statues or paintings. They had Ben move several of the items multiple times before they were happy with the arrangement.

With the combination of physical activity and caffeine, Ben's hangover was receding, but he was hungry now and wanted to be done with the constant, irrational changes. "Is this it?"

Larry flapped a hand at him in irritation. "Don't be so unhappy with us, Ben. This is an art, not a science. Everything must be arranged in its proper place in order to ensure maximum sales."

Ben rolled his eyes behind the men's backs. "Sure, I get it."

Steve snorted and fussed at the dry flowers in the vase. "I'm not sure you do, but that's okay because we get it and we're the ones getting this thing working. So you can just go home now while we finalize the inventory paperwork and item sheets."

"If you guys think you'll be okay for the rest of it." The offer was made out of habit, but he was happy to get back to his house and keep doing research on the murderer.

Larry came over and clapped a hand on his shoulder. "Of course, we'll be fine. We just wanted to borrow your muscles for this part of it. We really do prefer to be left on our own. It's soothing; the calm before the storm, you might say."

Ben smiled, happy to be on his way, and went to grab his

bag from his desk before heading out. "Okay, then. See you in the morning."

Larry and Steve waved him off and turned to the radio they were inspecting, debating whether it still worked. As Ben reentered the warehouse, he thought he heard voices again, but he tried to convince himself that it was just the echoes of the crowd that had invaded his space earlier. But as he approached the long term storage bay, he recognized the voice as belonging to Sylvia.

"It's just...awkward. That's the only word I can think of. I'm not sure if he regrets it or me or what. But he was a dick this morning, that's all I can say." She paused as if listening to an answer, but when she continued it was without a pause in her train of thought. "Maybe I just came on too strong. I should have been coy. I just don't like waiting, you know? No, you can't know, how could you?"

Ben backed slowly out of the warehouse, so that he felt certain she hadn't heard him, before going down the hall and around the corner through the main entrance, making sure to make a lot of noise. When he had gathered his stuff for the night, he made his way to Uncle Shem's urn, but there was no one standing in front of it any longer.

He pulled out his cell phone and dialed Sylvia's number, more anxious than ever to straighten out what had happened last night, but it went almost straight to voicemail. Two rings, which meant she looked at the caller ID and then rejected it. Calling a hook-up was a lot less angst-inducing when you could just listen to the messages on a machine to determine whether you wanted to talk to anyone instead of shutting them down with the reject call button. Actually knowing someone didn't want to talk to you instead of just letting the call go to the message machine was worse.

Ben headed home, stopping briefly along the way to pick up Boston Market takeout—the turkey dinner. He hoped the tryptophan in the turkey might help tonight because he wasn't quite sure how he was going to sleep; he was pretty wound up between being worried about Sylvia and wondering whether his child's body was just now being excavated from the soil of some pervert's farm. And he was all out of alcohol. Besides, Sylvia's words the night before about drinking too much still stung.

He ate in front of his computer again, checking news site after news site, doing a new search every ten minutes, hoping for a new development. He left the radio on and ended up falling asleep to it, his head thrown back against his desk chair.

He just about slid out of his chair at seven a.m. when there was a station break, and a new talk personality came on. He glanced at his watch, swore, and bolted for the bathroom. It was his first auction day, so he couldn't be late.

After a quick stop at the drive through at Dunkin' Donuts, Ben stumbled into the auction room just before the doors were supposed to open for the preview. The bidding wouldn't start for another hour yet, but the potential buyers had this hour to inspect the merchandise more closely and make notes on what they wanted to bid on.

Ben took up his position next to the valuables case where he could assist anyone who wanted a closer look at any of the particular items. Steve drifted by at around a quarter after eight and tutted at Ben's appearance but didn't say anything. Instead, he made his way through the attendees, occasionally greeting people whom he seemed to know passingly well.

"Excuse me, honey, does that radio work?" A gray-haired lady had laid her hand on Ben's arm and was pointing to an older-style radio next to the valuables cabinet.

Ben frowned, trying to decide if the auctioneers had

established that yesterday. "I think it does."

"I want to be sure before I bid on it. Can you plug it in for me?"

Ben waved Larry over and briefly explained what was needed.

Larry smiled at the older woman and gave her an abbreviated bow. "Sure thing, ma'am. I'll take over your post, Ben. You know where the outlets are better than I do."

"Ha, right, after less than a month. Come on, miss, let's see if we can figure out if this thing still works."

Ben wandered along the edge of the room until he found an outlet and plugged the radio in. It turned on with a pop, blasting static into the room. The volume control seemed to be stuck, so he rapidly spun the tuning dial until the sounds of a news radio program filled the room. "It seems to work alright, though the volume control is shot."

"That's okay; I like it loud. That way I can listen without my hearing aids."

"Well, then, this is just fine for you."

The woman made some reply, but Ben was now ignoring her. His entire attention was focused on the news report currently blasting through the room.

"The police just released his name. Leonard Moscovich is considered a suspect in eleven kidnapping and ten murder cases involving young boys. The police have barricaded his entire farm and are now digging up various areas in an effort to determine whether they have found all of the bodies."

Ben finally looked up at the old lady as she shook him. "I said that's enough, young man. You can turn the damnable thing off now. People are staring."

"I'm sorry." Ben switched off the radio and hurried to place it back by its lot placard. He started back to his post, changed his mind, and left the auction room, going straight to his desk. Eleven boys. Was that even possible? It was a horrifically high number of young lives cut short. But at least he now had a name.

His hands shook a little as he called up the advanced version of the white pages that he had access to, which included all addresses that the post office received for mail forwarding, etc. After searching for Leonard Moscovichs in Georgia, he was left with ten possibilities, only one of which lived near Savannah. In fact, his address was about equidistant between the two cities. Leonard had apparently lived with a Lena Moscovich, now deceased.

Sitting back in his chair, he ran his hands through his hair a few times, and left his hands on top of his head. He stared at the screen wondering what this man, the last face his son had probably seen, looked like. There was no indication in this database so he minimized the window and opened several of the other databases. The Department of Transportation confirmed that this Leonard's mother did indeed own a green truck. A '95 Ford F-150 to be precise. However, none of the other databases yielded any results, so he turned to the ultimate researcher's friend: Google.

Now that the name was public knowledge, news agencies were scurrying to gather material on the man. The only pictures that accompanied the articles, however, were blurry distance photos taken as Moscovich was taken into the police station or excised from his school yearbook. They didn't help Ben; he wanted to see the bastard's face.

He closed the browser window in disgust and sat staring at his cursor. Should he do it or not? Skip out on work to go to the farm crawling with officers, where his son had probably been killed, see what there was to see, maybe talk to the investigators? Or stay here and play auctioneer to little old ladies and used book salesmen.

In the end, he decided he didn't really have a choice. He copied Moscovich's address onto a Post-it and shut down his computer. It didn't matter that his first auction continued on without him. There was nothing for him to do now except to figure out who this guy was. He had to know what kind of a monster could have killed his five-year-old son.

He was halfway down the highway before he realized that he hadn't told anyone he was leaving. It probably wouldn't have made a difference anyway as he really didn't have any idea what happened at these auctions except that Larry and Steve would take care of everything. So what did they need him for?

The driveway to the farm would have been invisible on any regular day; there wasn't even a mailbox on the little two-lane highway. But today it had a police car parked on the highway's shoulder with an officer standing at the end of it. Ben pulled over onto the shoulder and parked. It took a couple minutes before his breathing was under control and he felt his legs would support him when he got out of the car.

The officer's full attention was on him as he walked the ten feet back to the driveway. "Excuse me, sir, this is a restricted area. You'll have to go back to your car and leave."

"This is the Moscovich farm, isn't it?"

"Yes, sir, it is, but I'll have to ask you to leave. This is an active crime scene." The officer's hand was now on his radio.

Ben took a step forward but stopped when the officer held up his hand. "I know, I just have to...is Detective O'Connor here? He knows who I am, please."

"Hold on." He switched his attention to his radio. "Is there a Detective O'Connor on the premises?" He listened to the squawking that resulted from his query. "There's a guy here asking for him."

"Benjamin Grant," Ben supplied before the officer could ask.

"Says his name is Benjamin Grant." The radio squawked again and the officer frowned. "Ten-four." His attention came back to Ben. "He'll be right out."

"Thank you, thank you so much."

Ben waited impatiently, pacing back and forth across the tar-coated gravel at the end of the driveway. Images of possible torture and murder scenes filled his head as he paced, each one more gruesome than the last. The officer alternated between watching him carefully and scanning the surrounding area. After about ten minutes, Detective O'Connor appeared from around the bend.

"O'Connor!" Ben called, waving. The officer glared at him, so he quickly amended himself. "Detective!"

"Ben, what are you doing here? *How* are you here?" The detective patted the officer on his shoulder, and the man walked off a few feet to continue watching the road and the sparse traffic along it.

"I heard it on the radio and…" He made a vague gesture in the air. "Well, I just had to come take a look for myself. I couldn't not."

O'Connor frowned and squinted at Ben. "I thought we were doing a better job keeping this location from the media."

Ben shifted uncomfortably, well aware of the fact that he had probably broken a few laws to get his information. "You know the media; they always show up eventually."

"But they're not here yet. You are." The detective placed himself firmly between Ben and the farm driveway.

"I, uh, whitepaged it." Ben hoped this excuse would satisfy the detective and he would start talking about something important, like if Benny was buried somewhere up that gravel driveway.

"I see." The detective wiped sweat off of his forehead and came off the defensive. "This is an active crime scene, Ben. I can't let you past here."

"You have to! I mean, you at least have to tell me, my Benny—"

"May not be one of the boys here." The detective placed himself more firmly in Ben's path, as if he expected him to make a run for it and start digging for himself.

Ben's frustration was difficult to keep in control. The man simply refused to give him any information, even though it was Ben's tip about the green truck that had led them to Moscovich. Well, maybe not led, but certainly reinforced the discovery. "But the truck fits the description, and they said there were eleven bodies. Eleven!"

"And there are over one hundred missing boys of the age range that we're finding. You have to be patient and let us do our jobs! Go home and do yours. Unless I'm mistaken, this is a work day and last you told me you had a government job." Detective O'Connor turned and started back down the driveway.

"Wait!" Ben reached out and grabbed the detective's shoulder, trying to get him to listen.

The detective rounded on him, knocking Ben's arm aside, finally getting angry. "Look, Ben. I can't tell you *anything*. Do you get that? It's part of my job. Do I wish I could? Sometimes. But I have been looking at little skeletons being unearthed all day, and unless you want me to charge you with obstructing an investigation, tampering with evidence, assaulting a police officer, and whatever else I can come up with to keep you out of here, *go home*."

Ben stood dumbfounded while Detective O'Connor rubbed his face roughly. For the first time, Ben could see just how tired the detective was. There were bags under his eyes and lines that hadn't been there the last time they spoke. "Is it that bad?"

The detective didn't raise his eyes from the gravel when he answered. "Yeah. It's that bad."

It took Ben a moment to get the words out around the sudden constriction of his throat. "I'm sorry. I'll go home. Can you just keep me updated?" All those little skeletons in the ground. Ben thought he could almost see it himself.

"If I ever learn anything." This time when the detective turned around and started walking away, Ben didn't try to stop him. Instead, he went back to his car and baked under his windshield for another ten minutes before he thought to turn on the car so at least he'd have air conditioning. He still wished he could go down that driveway, but he wasn't willing to push his one connection to the case any further than he already had. He was afraid it would break entirely.

That being said, he also didn't think he could go back to work and face the crowd, so instead, he drove back to his apartment. All the way home he couldn't stop thinking about tiny skeletons in shallow graves. They danced in his head, and every one of them had a broken right arm and was just the right height to walk into the kitchen counter corners.

He swerved into the liquor store and bought the cheapest bottle of whiskey they had; there wasn't much left in his debit account. As soon as he was through the door, he opened the bottle and sat at his desk. He automatically reached for his cell phone to put it on its charger and realized that he'd left it at work. Cursing himself because that was the number Detective O'Connor had to get in touch with him, he rummaged under the papers on his desk until he found the landline phone that he hadn't yet bothered to activate and reached for his wallet. He still had the emergency phone card Jeannie had insisted he carry at all times. It was wedged behind all of his other cards, and he'd forgotten about it until now.

After taking five minutes to figure out exactly what order he had to dial the various numbers in, he was ringing through to Sylvia's phone. She picked up on the second ring.

"Hello?"

"Hey, it's Ben."

"Where in the hell are you?"

He cringed at the fury in her tone, but he pushed on. "I had to do something."

"You should be here. We don't have enough people here. We had to pull Byron from the bullpen, and he's pissed."

Ben didn't particularly care about what Byron thought, but he needed his phone for when Detective O'Connor would call. "It was important. Look, I left my cell phone at work. Could you bring it by?"

"Have you started drinking today?"

He glanced at the bottle of amber liquid in front of him. "Not yet."

"Then come get it your own damn self." And she hung up on him.

Ben slammed down the receiver and fumed for a moment before grabbing his keys again and heading out the door.

LIVE ANIMALS AND
OTHER CONTRABAND

*I cannot understand how people think they can send
things through the mail that are blatantly dangerous. Ammunition, poisonous snakes, firecrackers
going off in the back of postal trucks. You name it,
we've had it. They put our lives at risk for a little
fun, and that's not right. More often than not, it just
turns into a damned mess, if you ask me.*

~ *Gertrude Biun,* Property Office Manual

Ben made it back to the Center just as Larry and Steve finished
pushing the last table into place and Sylvia had picked up
a broom to get the worst of the debris off the floor.

"It's over already?"

Sylvia glared over her shoulder before she resumed stabbing
at the floor with the broom. "Yes, it's over. You just took off,
Ben. This is your job. Where the hell did you go?"

"I had to go find out...you know what, never mind." Ben
was still seething from the phone call and didn't much feel like
justifying himself. "I don't have to explain myself to you. I had
a personal emergency."

She stopped sweeping and gave him a level stare. "We all heard the radio broadcast, Ben."

He hunched his shoulders and tried to get around Sylvia and into the warehouse. "So what?"

Sylvia planted herself in front of him, broom propped upright against her shoulder. "You heard a broadcast about a man and a kidnapped boy and you go tearing out of here. I know what you were thinking. At least, I know what I was thinking, and I have less of a response to such stimulating information than you do."

Larry and Steve until this point had been trying to not eavesdrop over by the coffee machine, but Larry could no longer contain himself. "What, what were you thinking? A dick move there, Benjamin, leaving us here." He turned his attention back to the coffee, trying to pretend he hadn't just busted in on the conversation.

Sylvia glared at Larry and turned back to her boss. "Well, Ben, was he there?"

Ben sighed and slumped into a chair still in the middle of the room, burying his face in his hands. "They don't know; there's too many boys, god, there's too many."

Sylvia regarded him for a moment, her anger starting to subside at the sight of his collapsed frame. "How many?"

"More than ten. Including the one they found alive in the guy's truck. But they're still looking. God, so many boys." He was starting to wonder himself why he'd gone out to the farm. It was torture, plain and simple, to make himself confront all those lost boys, but if he hadn't, he'd never have forgiven himself for not trying to get to Benny, wherever he was.

Larry piped up again, "And what is your relationship to the radio broadcast and kidnapped boys?"

Steve finally broke into the conversation. "You really don't know? I keep telling you, you need to read the newspaper we get, but no, all you want are the comics."

"Apparently, yes, you were right. I should read the papers. But what's with him, it looks like someone killed his puppy."

"It's more likely someone killed my son." Ben stood and stormed out of the break room and slammed his way into the warehouse.

At his desk, Ben paced back and forth fuming, wondering how anyone could be so calloused, so self-absorbed, to have missed the radio broadcasts, the television news, and the newspaper articles from the last year, particularly if they lived around Savannah. It was only a year ago, and a man who had interacted with him before, who knew his face, couldn't remember that his son was missing. If not him, who would remember? Who would remember the face on the poster? If they had known about it when it happened, would they have known something, seen something, that would have Benny back home already?

He wrenched open his desk drawer, grabbed the cell phone, and then stopped, staring at his computer, which was patiently waiting for him, the USPS logo twirling back and forth across the screen.

Leonard Moscovich. Ben was here, he might as well take advantage of the reasons he signed up to be there in the first place. He woke up the computer by slamming the space bar. Starting up the most basic of his search programs, he entered the son-of-a-bitch's name. Leonard Moscovich, Lenny, Mosy. What nicknames did your friends have for you?

The search just covered known address, any forwarding requirements, other names at the household, any incidents. The only other name at that address was a Lena Moscovich. Wife? Mother? Daughter?

He pulled up the DMV database, but before he could start snooping, Sylvia slammed a stack of ledgers on the desk. Obviously not all her anger had been dissipated by the news.

"If you're here, you better go take care of the credit slip for Larry and Steve. They need your signature to get paid. And if you're too busy wallowing to do your job, you can at least make sure they get paid for doing theirs." She turned to his computer screen. "Is that work? Or pleasure?"

"Neither." Ben minimized the window before Sylvia could get a good look and crossed his arms, leaning back in his chair. If she was going to continue to be angry, so could he. She had no right to judge him for going after information about his son, regardless of who he discommoded to do so.

"Masochism is a form of pleasure, you know. And that new auditor is going to show up any moment and catch you with your pants down wanking away on this machine."

He was appalled at her use of language, but more so over the image of him taking gratification from the search for his son. This wasn't pleasure, it was torture, and he wished to God he didn't have to keep going, that his son would appear and he could be done. "Sylvia!"

She colored a little but stood her ground. "What? It's not like these activities are getting you anywhere, and sitting in front of that computer too long *will* make you go blind. And it makes you feel better for a very short while. Try and explain to me how this is not masturbatory?"

Ben turned his back on her and idly straightened his shelf, trying to seem busy, trying to get her to leave. He hated that he was arguing with her, but he wasn't going to apologize to her or back down. And she should know that. She was the one who needed to back off the subject and leave him to his search. "It's not...I don't expect you to understand."

"Oh? You think not? How do you think I spent the time after my family died?"

"Medicated." He hated himself as soon as the word came out, but he couldn't take it back.

Sylvia didn't say anything. She simply turned and left him alone at his desk.

"Damn it!" That morning he had been worried about having to apologize to her over sex, but that paled in comparison to the apology he owed her now. He had crossed her one hard and fast line: don't make fun of the crazy. He hadn't meant to, it had just slipped out. But he knew if he went to try and find her now, he wouldn't be able to; she would have slipped into whatever hidey hole she had around here when she was trying to avoid him, and she wouldn't come out until she was good and ready.

He decided instead to go back to his DMV search while he waited for her to calm down enough so that approaching to apologize for his crack wouldn't get him beheaded. Apparently Leonard wasn't supposed to be driving; the state had only issued him an ID card due to restrictions. "Restrictions, like what? Sight, hearing…" Ben scrolled through the screens before coming to a little box at the bottom. It read, *Mental Impairment.*

Ben sat back in his chair, running his hand through his hair. "Mental impairment? What kind of mental impairment has you killing boys?" He emailed the entire file to himself to look over later and had just started scanning the program list for his next source of information when the door to the warehouse opened again to the sounds of bickering.

"He didn't sound at all well. I don't think we should bother him."

"I don't know about you, but I want to get paid, thank you very much."

Larry came around the corner of Ben's cube and slapped a paper down on his desk. "Thanks for your help. Sign here." He stabbed the paper and kept his finger there until Ben had found a pen and signed, but Ben wouldn't let go of the paper until he at least tried to set things right with the two men.

"Look, guys, I'm sorry, but this thing came up, and I just had to...go see."

Larry deflated a bit and turned to Steve, ignoring Ben. "Come on, let's get out of here, leave him to his...thing." The two left without saying goodbye.

Aware of the departing couple and how angry they had seemed, Ben called after them, "Looking forward to next month!"

"We'll be here!" Steve called, then the door closed.

Ben had just decided on searching the criminal database next when Sylvia came back in.

He hurriedly stood, nearly knocking over his chair in the process. "Look, Syl, I'm sorry, okay? It just came out, and I didn't mean it."

"Freud would beg to differ, but stuff it. The auditor just showed up." She added under her breath, "Prick."

Ben's anger flared again at the insult. "Look, I said I'm sorry!"

Sylvia snorted and crossed her arms. "Not you. Him. You're a dick. There's a difference. He had the gall to ask me if it was take your daughter to work day." She scowled and turned her back on Ben. "By the way, I'm officially pissed off at you and will refuse to communicate with you whenever possible. I will do my work, you do yours. Dick. But no one deserves to face this bigot without a warning."

"Grant!" The voice was a full tenor, and it echoed off the walls of the warehouse.

Sylvia ducked around into the long-term storage bay, pretending to rearrange the journals so she could look through the shelves.

Ben righted his chair and sat back down behind his desk. "Over here."

"Ah. Good. This is a nice location. Alright, up you get." The man was a little under five and a half feet and could have passed for a Sean Connery stand-in.

"Excuse me?" Ben exited out of all the search programs before the man could come around the side of the desk. He had a feeling the man wouldn't approve of his use of government property.

The man jerked his thumb over his shoulder. "You. Up. This is my desk for the duration of the audit."

Ben remained where he was, unwilling to cede any territory to this intrusive older man until it was absolutely necessary. "I wasn't informed of this."

The man fussed with his briefcase, setting it down on top of a pile of forms. "You should have been sent an email last week."

"I wasn't."

The auditor propped his hands on his hips for a moment, one eyebrow raised. "No need to be difficult. We'll get you a temporary desk to toss in here someplace."

Ben made one more attempt to hold his position, unwilling to give up all of the search programs installed directly to his machine, unlike the network-based logging system. "I need my computer."

"So do I, boyo. It's what I'm here to do."

Ben finally stood and came around the desk, standing close to the man and forcing him to detour around Ben to actually reach the chair. If this man was determined to make his life difficult over the next few days, Ben would return the favor, and if he was fired, so be it. He had burned enough bridges today that he wasn't sure how he was going to keep working there after this auction.

The man settled in at the desk, changing the height of the chair and logging in to the administrator profile on Ben's machine. "The name's Reg, by the way. Since we'll be sharing air and all in here for the next few days."

It was an awful name, Ben thought, appropriate for a some-what prickish man. Sylvia had been right with that descriptor. The man invaded a room like he had something to compensate for. "Well, Reg, what am I supposed to do while you have my desk, my search programs, and my databases?"

Reg waved a hand dismissively, his attention already on the monitor. "Go organize something. I hear the long-term storage is in disarray; maybe you can do something with that."

The last thing Ben wanted to do was give in to orders from this punctilious man. He was the kind of man that if you gave him an inch, you'd end up getting his coffee for the rest of your time together. "I actually believe my assistant is already working on it."

Reg looked up, exasperated at the fact that Ben wouldn't leave him be. "I don't know what needs doing today; you do. I'll know in two days. Until then, just get out of my hair and let me work."

Ben made his way out of the warehouse and down to Judy at the front desk.

"Judy, there is a...a...well I hesitate to call him a gentleman, in my warehouse, at my desk."

"For the next week or so, yes."

Ben paused, deflated. "No one told me." He had hoped she'd tell him it was a mistake and he could kick the man out of the warehouse.

Judy started shuffling papers on her desk, looking for her message pad. "I could have sworn I sent you a message."

Ben rubbed one hand over his face, trying to let go of some of his foul mood. "I never got it. At least, I don't think I did, but it's been crazy back there the last week, what with all the people in and out."

"It's shit like this that's gotta be fixed!" the auditor boomed from behind Ben.

Ben whipped around and then took a step back to put a more comfortable distance between himself and the auditor. He was thwarted by coming up against Judy's desk, hard. "Jesus Christ! Don't you know you shouldn't sneak up on somebody like that? You'll give them a heart attack."

Reg leaned in to the neutral space Ben had tried to create. "Are you always this jumpy, Benny-boy?"

"Drop the Benny-boy, won't you? It's Ben. And I'm only this jumpy when people are sneaking around behind me."

Reg smiled and wagged a finger in the diminished space between them. "Careful, someone might think you're paranoid."

Ben slid to the side to get the finger out of his face and retorted, "Only because we have someone like you nosing about in our business."

Judy interrupted with a prim, "Ahem." Both men turned to her, Ben seething, Reg bemused.

"Ben, your temporary workstation will get here tomorrow. Reg needs access to our databases, which are only accessible by hardline, for a while. I'm sure he'll be done with that part of his review shortly."

The auditor grinned and slung his arm around Ben's shoulders. "See, my boy, this fine specimen here has things all under control. Bet she has her husband similarly pinned under that pert little thumb of hers, just like us."

Judy lost what little amusement was left in her face. "I wouldn't know, considering I don't have one."

"Well, don't worry, dear, your man catching days aren't entirely gone yet; you're still plenty fetching." Reg turned Ben away from the front desk as Judy, furious, opened her mouth to inform the auditor exactly how she felt about her man-catching days. "Now, Ben, I need you to walk me through your intake process, show me how the things are cataloged, etc. I know you're new here, so I don't really expect you to know everything."

"I've been here a month already." Ben tried to shrug off the older man's arm but couldn't quite manage.

"Yes, but the U.S. Postal Service is a large and complex beast. Someone who hasn't been with us for more than a year can't possibly be expected to understand all the little nuances." Reg continued to tow Ben down the hallway.

"I think that is an unfair assessment of my abilities, thank you very much." He finally succeeded in stripping off the older man's arm and continued down the hallway to the warehouse under his own power.

Reg hurried to catch up to Ben. "Stop your griping. I will only need your space for a few days. Besides, this is all for your own good. How can you know what you're doing wrong if someone doesn't tell you?"

"By making my own damn mistakes and having access to my computer to do so." Ben hated the man's condescending tone. From the sounds of it, the man believed he was the be all and end all authority of the post office, rules and regs memorized and obeyed to the letter.

Sylvia popped out from around one of the shelving units

and turned to the auditor. "You know, he does have a point."

Reg patted her on the head, dislodging her cap. "He'll be able to continue just fine with his work on a secondary computer. And what exactly is it that you do? I don't remember seeing you on the staff list."

"As I told you before, my name is Sylvia, and I should damn well be on that list considering I have been working here for five years." Sylvia turned and stalked deeper into the warehouse to get away from the older gentleman, and Ben didn't blame her retreating for one moment. He wished he had a valid excuse to get away from the man himself, but he had nowhere to go except home. And without a computer, there was no way to get any work done for the Center or his search.

"Wow, you are really good at making new friends, you know that?" Ben went over to his desk to get a few of his things out of Reg's hands, like his snacks and the photo of Jeannie and his son from the bottom drawer. The sounds of a folding table being set up echoed back to them through the warehouse. "In fact, I don't really think you need me at all anymore today, do you?"

"What, nothing to catalog today?" Reg started settling himself in behind Ben's desk.

Ben shook his head as he tried to get all of the papers out from under the auditor's briefcase, juggling everything and mentally cursing the man blithely sitting there with his hands behind his head. "We had the auction this morning, and everyone was pretty well tied up with that."

Reg finally took his case from Ben and set it on the floor beside the desk. "Well, it looks like you were working on something when I came in."

"Nothing much, just some research for a project." Ben knew he wanted to avoid that line of questioning. Besides whatever ramifications it might have for his job, he just didn't want this man knowing anything about Benny. "Nothing that couldn't be put off till later."

"Well if you're sure there isn't anything you could be doing, I guess it would be nice to have the place to myself for a bit." The auditor settled into Ben's chair and put his feet up on Ben's desk.

Ben gritted his teeth at the gall of the man and strode from the warehouse. Sylvia wasn't far behind, but she didn't say anything until they reached the break room. "What are you going to do with your new found freedom? Chase down more improbable leads? Or stand on some street corner getting sick handing out flyers again?" Ben ignored her intentional jabs and started to leave the Center, but she followed close on his heels. "You know, you still haven't apologized for leaving us this morning."

He pushed through the front doors and waited until Sylvia was standing in the muggy heat with him before answering. "What do you want from me? I'm sorry you couldn't handle things by yourself. It's not like I know a damn thing about this place anyway. All I want to do is make just enough money so that I can keep looking for my son and do just enough so I don't get fired so I can keep using the databases."

She studied him a moment before responding. "Well with that attitude, I doubt you'll be keeping it much longer, and for that I'm sorry." Sylvia didn't wait for him to make another comment and returned to the building.

Ben waited until the door had closed before rubbing his hands over his face. She didn't get it at all. No matter how much he had thought she cared, how well she listened to him talking about Benny, it had all been a mask for her just not getting it. And how could she? She wasn't a parent; her own parents had died when she was too young to understand the sacrifices they had made on her behalf. She would never understand the amount of pain he was in and the fact that he would do anything to make that pain go away, even for a little while.

Taking a deep breath, he managed to open the door of his car, but then he didn't know where to go. He wanted to be at his desk with the search engines at his fingertips, learning everything he could about Moscovich, but that was no longer an option. The search engines he had access to on his home computer were childish in comparison to the ones at work, but they were all he had now, so he headed back to his apartment.

When Ben got home, he dumped his bag on the kitchen counter and went straight to his computer. He fidgeted while it was booting up, then jumped up to turn on the radio. He needed noise, some other human voice, just something to break up the silence and the whirring of his computer fan.

Once he was connected to the Internet, he typed in all the identifying information he had found on Leonard Moscovich. There wasn't much from before that day's news; the first two pages of results were simply news articles about the arrest and discovery. Ben started printing out every article and picture. After an hour of reading and printing, he started affixing the new pages on his wall. He even drove an extra-large push-pin into the map at the Moscovich farm.

Then he went back to his computer and started to dig deeper. He backtracked school records, newspaper articles, anything he could think of that was open to the public, which was a surprising amount. He found out that Leonard had been on the football team in high school for a season, though he had not done well enough academically to maintain a spot on the team. There was also an editorial ten years ago citing Leonard

Moscovich as a case study for how the local school system had failed children with learning disabilities.

Everything Ben came across he printed and then stuck to the wall, the papers starting to form clusters: childhood, high school, adult life, news reports. And finally, an update saying that Leonard Moscovich was going to be arraigned the next day at the Atlanta courthouse at noon.

Ben stayed at his computer for most of the night, taking breaks to get another beer and use the restroom, but not sleeping until after dawn had broken. His alarm woke him not an hour later for work, and he briefly contemplated destroying the chirping box, but he knew he would not get back to sleep anyway, and he didn't have the money to afford a replacement.

Luckily, it was a Friday, meaning it was casual dress. Unofficially, of course, but it seemed to be by consensus. He dowsed himself in the shower, struggled into an old pair of jeans, and stopped at the Krispy Kreme to get himself the largest coffee possible and a few donuts. He was planning how to attack the city databases to get more information about Moscovich as he pulled into the parking lot and only remembered that Reg had taken over his systems when he saw the older man firmly planted at his desk.

"Good morning, Ben. Say, when's the last time you gave this old baby a tune-up?"

Ben winced at the overly jovial tone, replying, "Not in the month I've been here," before he wandered down into his warehouse with his coffee and donuts. He found a camping stool that had been lost two years ago, pulled it out, and reclined against the bookshelf of 2008 to try and nurse his hangover, in reality it was more his still-drunkenness, in peace.

He was just finishing the second donut when Sylvia found

him crouched in his hiding space. "Planning on working today?" She had her hands on her hips and glared at him from under her cocked hat.

"You know, I was thinking about it, but there still seems to be a royal ass in my chair." Ben leaned back and closed his eyes.

Sylvia grabbed the coffee cup out of his hand and picked up the empty bag from the donuts and turned to drop them in the trash can.

"What do you think you're doing?" Ben struggled off of the low stool, reaching for his still half-full coffee cup.

"Getting you off your ass." Sylvia let him take the coffee cup back now that he was standing. She balled up the empty bag and tossed it in the bin. "I could really use your help today trying to keep up with the readers. With the auction this week we were going to be behind anyway. And then you disappeared and the auditor took over your seat. You have no idea what this place can get like when we get behind."

"What, you mean there'd be something like work?" Ben drained the last of the coffee in one gulp and tossed out the empty cup.

"No, you never catch up. And you have to stop saying things like that where the auditor can hear you," Sylvia hissed.

"Frankly, at this point I don't really care. The fact that someone can just walk in and take over my office and determine that I can't do my job after being here less than five minutes is ridiculous."

"Yeah, well, we work for the government. They like oversight. This person gets raped by that person and that person gets raped by that person, who in turn gets raped by the president. It's standard American procedure." Sylvia poked and prodded at Ben, trying to get him to leave his place of solitude, but he wouldn't budge. He did not care for a pint-sized woman trying to tell him what he should or should not be doing, regardless of the fact that all her arguments were spot on.

"Maybe I'll get lucky and the auditor will decide they don't need me." Her persistence had him a few feet out of the shelving units.

"Well, they definitely need somebody, even if it's not you. Look, are you going to help me at all today?" She paused in her attempts to get him to cooperate and stood between him and his stool, hands on hips.

"Probably not." Ben made as though to return to his hideaway and Sylvia grabbed his arm.

"Look, I know you're distracted, but this isn't helping anything!" She held tight, trying to make him meet her eyes. "I bet I know what you're doing when you go home now. You're snooping on that Lenny guy. Obsessing over him, aren't you? That's why you took off when you heard. You had to find out everything you could about him. What did you do? Go to your police friend?"

Ben steadfastly avoided her gaze. It was eerie how well she had come to know his habits in such a short span of time. He wondered if he was that obvious, or if she was just that observant. "Kind of."

"Jesus! Look, you're going to lose your job here—which I know you like to take advantage of—which is allowing you to search for your son and keeping you from living in a hovel on the streets of Atlanta. Why can't you just let this go for the few days you're under scrutiny? Seriously." She finally grabbed his chin, forcing his face to look down at hers.

"Because this is it. I mean it could be. And I just have to make sure that everything...happens I guess." Ben finally met her eyes and saw the tears she was holding back. He couldn't tell whether she actually cared about him or if she was just frustrated with him.

Sylvia dashed away the standing water in her eyes. "It's all going to happen anyway."

Ben was silent. He could admit, at the root of everything, that Leonard was going to get his due from the justice system, that the boys would all be identified, and that his ministrations didn't actually make a difference. But he couldn't help the fact that he had this constant compulsion to keep trying, to keep researching, that maybe he would be the deciding point, in some obscure manner, that would bring his son home.

Their staring contest was broken by shouts from the doorway to the warehouse. "Stop it! Don't let it get away!"

"Where'd it go?"

"There!"

Celine and Byron slammed into the warehouse, closely followed by Jillian. Whatever they were chasing skittered across the floor and threw itself under the shelves of the closest bay. Sylvia and Ben hurried over to see what was going on, Ben grateful for the distraction. The three readers had surrounded the shelving unit on its three free sides on their hands and knees to try and figure out where their prey had gone to.

"What is it?" Sylvia crouched down herself, all the reprimand in her voice having been replaced by excitement.

Celine was panting. "Some kind of lizard. I opened the box and it just leapt right out. Who mails a lizard?"

"Idiots. That's who." Byron had gotten all the way down on his stomach trying to see into the gloom.

Sylvia got up and disappeared into the next bay, coming back with a flashlight. "Lizards can go days without food. That's probably what someone was thinking when they stuffed him in there. Why'd we get the package?"

Celine gave up and sat back. "The address was fake, no return."

"Poor guy." Sylvia took Celine's place and laid down on her stomach. "Ben? I think there is a terrarium in 2007, can you go get it?"

He went to retrieve the container, trying to picture what kind of person had so little regard for the animal's life that they sent it through the U.S. post. The glass rectangle didn't have a lid, so he grabbed a roll of mosquito netting from the next bay over and brought it all back. "Here it is." He placed the glass box next to Sylvia and stood back to unroll the sheeting.

Sylvia flicked on her light and spotted the critter backed up against the wall. "Got him." She wiggled forward and stretched out her hand towards it. A muffled hissing reached their ears.

"Careful, it's probably poisonous!" Jillian was still crouched down, trying to see what was going on.

"Hardly. I do believe that we have been graced with a dragon, folks." The scrabbling of claws and more hissing came from under the shelf and Sylvia yelped. "Just a claw, don't worry." After a bit more scrabbling she managed to haul out her prize. She dropped the flashlight and used both hands to pin the critter's front legs to his sides. The brownish spiky lizard had a huge bristling beard that glowed in bright shades of red and orange. "Well, aren't you pretty."

Ben nudged the terrarium forward and Sylvia carefully lowered him into it. Ben spread the fabric over the top and around her arms, which she then removed quickly. "I got it."

"Jillian, could we have some packing tape, please?" Sylvia poked at the scratches on her hand, but none of them looked like they had actually broken the surface.

Byron was studying the lizard. "A bearded dragon, right?"

"I think so. I've always wanted one." Sylvia left off studying her hands and leaned down to the cage. "But they usually have black beards. This one is different."

Ben cleared his throat, almost unwilling to bring her attention back to him, but he felt he would be safe from her recriminations now that she had something small and scared to take care of. "A sunburst beardy."

Sylvia jumped, almost as if she had forgotten he was there. "A what?"

"A sunburst bearded dragon. My college roommate had one. They're rare." Sylvia smiled up at him, and Ben hoped that she might be forgiving him a little bit, but then her face clouded up again. It was apparently going to take more than an assist on a rescue to get back into her good graces and keep her from haranguing him about his search methodologies.

"Look, I'll take care of this little guy. You should go do something useful." She turned back to the terrarium. She sprawled on her stomach, feet in the air, and smiled at the runty lizard. The dragon had let its beard collapse and was now trying to hide in the corner of his tank. "Valiant, that's your name. Proper name for a dragon, don't you think?"

Ben could tell she wasn't speaking to him, but he decided to answer anyway. "Apt, too, what with his dash to freedom."

She glared up at him. "Look, why don't you go make sure all the bays are straightened up after the inventorying from this week so if the auditor decides he needs to make a spot inspection or something it's all right there."

"Fine. I can do that." Ben stormed away from the group surrounding the poor terrified lizard. He went first to long-term storage, reaching up a hand to idly run across the journals. It was almost like he could feel his computer calling him, but a peek around the corner showed Reg still firmly ensconced.

There would be no making progress on his research for now, so he decided to actually take Sylvia's suggestion.

He came around to a chest of drawers and opened the first one. It was where they kept all of the firearms that came through the Center. He vaguely remembered something from the manual about needing to keep all firearms for thirty years in case they ended up being needed for a criminal investigation. There were four in the drawer.

Back at Ben's desk, the auditor turned on the morning radio news report. They were talking once again about the arraignment hearing for Leonard Moscovich. Ben forgot about the the lizard and the auditor as he heard the reporter listing the crimes Moscovich had been arrested for. Twelve counts of kidnapping and eleven counts of murder. All victims under the age of ten, all male. All Ben could see was Benny's face, hear Benny calling him for help in the middle of the night because of monsters under the bed. Those monsters had been more real than Ben had been willing to believe.

Ben realized he was staring at the guns. One was a little pearl-handled revolver, only good for making an elderly woman feel protected on her way home from church; there was also a long-barreled revolver out of a Wild West movie and two black pistols.

The radio continued its inane chatter, the disk jockeys expressing surprise and shock as they rehashed, again, the traffic stop and the terrified young boy found in the truck. They had no idea what the horror was really like, for a parent, a father, living every day hoping for some answer, only to be presented with the worst of their nightmares. And then they cut to an interview with the little boy.

"Can you tell me what happened? With the man in the truck?"

"He said he had baby animals at his farm and that he'd let me feed

*and pet them, so I...I got in his truck. I knew I shouldn't, but I really
like animals. My mommy took me to the zoo last year, and I really
like the baby zebra,s and the man said he had baby horses which were
better than baby zebras and I could pet them..."*

Ben couldn't see the drawer he was clutching as a wave of
black crossed his vision. It could have been Benny talking on
the radio. They had seen the same baby zebras, though Benny
had dragged his family along to look at the monkeys instead.
And this man, this abomination, had tried to take this little boy
from his family, had taken eleven other little boys just like this
one, just like his boy, had probably killed his boy.

The interview had ended and the jockeys came back on.

*"Did you hear that his lawyer has already filed a not guilty by
reason of insanity? He's claiming Moscovich had no idea what he
was doing. Mentally retarded or something like that."*

*"That's what they're saying. Personally, I don't believe it. But
watch, he's going to get sent to some looney bin instead of executed
like he should be."*

Not guilty by reason of insanity. The words rattled around
inside Ben's head. The monster was going to try and get away
with it, after killing all those boys, all those boys who had just
started to grow out of their fear of the monsters under their
beds, whose unsubstantiated fear was replaced all at once with
the monsters in the real world.

He looked around on the shelves to see if there was any
ammunition, finding only one box.

The bullets were obviously too big for the pearl handled
shooter, but he wasn't sure about the other three. He struggled
to get them open, giving up on one of the pistols as he simply
couldn't figure out where the release was. The bullets were
too small for the revolver, but they seemed to fit okay in the
magazine of the last pistol.

He returned the clip to its slot, hoping the sound was masked by the chattering voices resonating through the warehouse from the auditor's general vicinity. Ben slipped the gun into his pocket and headed towards the exit. He had no idea what he was even planning to do with the gun, not really. He knew he wanted to get a better look at Moscovich, and if he was prepared, who would blame him, really? He'd be a hero for taking out such a villainous character. He would be Benny's hero for taking out his killer.

"Where you off to? Not lunch yet, is it?" Reg called out as he passed.

Ben didn't even slow down as he responded. "Nope, just trying to find someplace I'll actually be useful. Later." He banged his way out of the warehouse and exited through the rear door of the Center. He didn't want to have to explain to Judy why he was taking off so soon after getting to work.

Once he was in his car, he took the pistol out of his pocket. Throwing his briefcase into the back seat, he cradled the black metal. It was heavier than he had expected. The weapon was covered in a thin layer of dust, which he cleaned off with his shirttail until it gleamed dully. He could barely make out the etchings on it, but he was pretty sure it read *1911*, though he had no idea what that could mean. He had never wanted anything to do with guns, had made excuses not to spend afternoons after high school plinking with his friends because he had thought it was a waste of time. Now, he wished he had gone at least a couple of times so he wasn't quite as unfamiliar with these tools. Not if he actually got a chance to do what needed to be done.

He put the gun on the passenger seat under a windbreaker that he hadn't needed since March but had never gotten around to taking out of the car. He turned on the radio to the news station, waiting until they started at the top of the hour to recite the current news articles.

...and as we promised you before, we will be coming to you live at noon from the arraignment of Leonard Moscovich, the man accused of kidnapping eleven boys and killing ten, at the Fulton County Superior Courthouse. That's right, we said eleven. What kind of mind could be capable of this, I hear you asking? Let's go to our in-house psychologist. Dr. Borden, what kind of disturbances could this man be suffering from?

Possession might be able to account for the atrocity of it, or maybe complete sociopathy, but whatever it was, Ben was sure it was pure evil, and someone should make sure he couldn't do it again. He pulled out of the parking lot and started to drive toward the middle of the city, vaguely recalling where the courthouse was from his hours of staring at the map on his wall.

Well, Jim, we have to take into consideration the fact that the victims here are all of the same type. Young boys. This would seem to indicate a pattern or fixation on this population. It is entirely possible that he suffered some trauma at that age, and in killing these boys, he is trying to cut that out of his life. Or perhaps he's just a psychopath and this is his way of feeling things.

Ben snorted. As if anyone could "just" be a psychopath. He reached over and turned off the radio, weary of the second-guessing, the second-rate hack job psychology. The man was a sick bastard, that was all. A sick, murdering bastard. Ben glanced over at the passenger seat frequently, checking to make sure that the gun was completely covered. He wasn't sure what the gun laws were in Georgia, but he was pretty sure they weren't lenient.

He had to circle the courthouse a couple times before he found parking, but he finally found a spot and fed the meter.

He had about a half an hour before the arraignment was supposed to take place, so he found a bench that faced the courthouse door and sat, his windbreaker draped over the gun in his lap. He kept going over every detail of the case, of his son's disappearance, of Moscovich's life, and every point at which they might have intersected and brought this monster into their lives. Every cruel thing the man might have done to his son flickered through his mind. He could only think of one thing that would make it all stop.

After a few minutes, he had to remove his hand from the handle of the gun and stretch his fingers and pop his wrist. His palms were sweaty, as was the rest of him. The bench was in the sun, and the temperature was well over ninety. He leaned his head back, then rolled it around, trying to stretch out the muscles, but snapped upright at an increase of sound coming from the courthouse. He nearly let the gun drop out of the windbreaker but caught it at the last second.

However, the noise was just a bunch of news vans pulling up, readying their equipment for their first live shot of Leonard. Ben checked his watch and found it was just now noon, which meant that it would still be a few minutes before the killer was brought out of the courthouse to return to jail. He figured there was no way he could be released on bail. Not with ten dead boys in the ground. He would be cuffed, with an escort, which would make it more difficult to get close to him, but this needed to be done.

Ben wandered back to the steps of the courthouse and started milling between the news crews. There were radio and television, as well as print reporters of all kinds. Boom mics were being lifted and camera batteries checked. He fingered the trigger of the gun wrapped in the windbreaker in his arms, wondering if Leonard would look at all like his pictures online. He had to be sure that he was taking out the right man, the murderous bastard, who must have made his son's last moments on this earth a terrifying agony.

When the noise on the steps escalated again, Ben knew for sure it was because Leonard was coming. The reporters descended on the group leaving the courthouse, shouting.

"Leonard, why did you do it?"

"What was the decision?"

"Mr. Moscovich, is it true you killed your mother, too?"

The man was hunched up with his lawyer's suit coat over his head, the green tweed distinctly clashing with his orange jumpsuit. Ben started to push his way through the throng of people, trying to angle his movement to intersect the besieged party as it hit the street. Abruptly, he was in front of the man and staring into heavily lashed, frightened eyes.

This wasn't the hard, twisted man Ben had expected. He was a nothing, a scared child in a grown-up body. He clearly could not understand what was happening around him, the noise and the people inundating him in stimulus he couldn't comprehend. Ben let the gun fall to his side as their eyes locked, Moscovich's empty of the cold evil that Ben had needed to destroy. Then the crowd swept past him and Leonard was loaded into the waiting police car.

After Leonard had pulled away and the reporters were grumbling about the lack of comments from the publicly condemned, Ben finally tore his eyes away from the direction the car had taken and started to stumble back to his car. He threw the windbreaker and gun onto the back seat, filled with loathing and horror. He peeled out of the parking spot and headed for home instead of work, unable to stomach being around any other people.

His traitorous brain kept going over what had happened, replaying the terrified expression on the round face of the captive, the shouting mob of reporters. He could still feel the steel in his hand, the pressure of his finger against the trigger. And then his mind made the leap, and he started to imagine what would have happened if he had actually been able to fire the pistol. Screaming, running, blood at his feet. He'd never seen anyone shot in real life, but he could imagine it. He might have actually killed him. The blood in his mind was so vivid he could smell it, and his stomach revolted.

He yanked the car to the curb and opened his car door, trying to stop heaving.

He sat with his hazard lights on for another few minutes, head back against the headrest, and tried to breathe normally. When the light-headedness had passed, he pulled back into traffic and changed directions, heading back to work. The desire to be rid of the gun outweighed any desire he had to be alone.

Ben wandered back into the warehouse and went straight to the long-term bay. There was now overbearing opera music rattling through the warehouse, sounding German in origin. He pulled the clip out, trying to empty it with shaking hands.

Reg's voice came from behind him. "Hey there, Ben, going over the long-term stuff?"

"Yup." Ben hastily set down the now empty gun in its drawer and slammed it shut.

"I could have sworn that I didn't see any guns up in the next little while for auction. Just admiring them?" The auditor strode forward and slid open the drawer. He fingered the pistols for a moment while Ben held his breath. He kept reminding himself he had a perfectly legitimate excuse for handling the firearms. He was their keeper, after all. And nothing had happened. Absolutely nothing. His stomach churned over at the thought of what had almost happened. What kind of person was he if he could even think about taking another man's life?

"Just checking to make sure there weren't any signs of rust or anything. You can't sell a gun that doesn't work." Ben's newly empty stomach combined with his revulsion and his head swam. He put a hand out to the shelf to steady himself.

"Oh, well, this won't do. Can't have a man of your stature go down, we won't be able to shift you out of the way! You eaten yet today, boy?"

Ben gritted his teeth at the now overly solicitous man. Why couldn't he just remain uninterested and aloof, particularly at this moment? "I am no boy."

"Well, I guess that crankiness means you could use some lunch. Come on, let's get that darling little assistant of yours to go get us some sandwiches. I need to do your interview." He went to grab Ben's upper arm, but Ben stepped out of his way, giving a mocking bow out of the bay to disguise his shaking.

"She would hate to hear you call her a little darling," Ben informed the man's back as they headed toward the desk.

"It is most ridiculous how women take these endearments as something offensive. Reflects nothing whatsoever on them. Harrumph." Reg stuck his head out of the warehouse. "Sylvia! Sylvia! Oh, there, excellent. Come now, be a good girl and retrieve some sandwiches from the deli. I ordered already. You just need to pick them up."

Sylvia's voice echoed from the hallway, "And you need me to pick them up because?"

"Because I'm about to do Ben's evaluation, and the poor man is falling over from malnutrition!" The auditor shut the door before Sylvia could answer. "Alright now, let's get down to it, shall we?"

"Fine, I guess." Ben dropped himself back into his own office chair, gesturing the auditor towards the folding chair propped against the cubicle wall. He didn't have the patience to pander to the man today, nor the stability to try and balance his large frame on the small chair. How he was going to concentrate on an interview when the image of Moscovich's frightened face kept flashing across his mind, he had no idea.

"Ha, I see how this is going to go then. Don't mind if I do." Reg retrieved the chair and tried to settle into it. "Damn uncomfortable things. And no matter the weather, always cold. Why is that, d'you think?" Reg paused while pulling out a notebook.

"Because they're metal."

"Herm? Oh, quite, yes. Now, let's see. You've been here how long?"

"One month, says so on my paperwork."

"Sure, sure, just easier to ask you. Now. Sylvia is your assistant, correct?"

Ben was unprepared for the question, having been trying vainly to mentally prepare himself for questions about his work, not about Sylvia. "She is more of a Center gopher. She helps me, she helps readers and sorters, she does the shredding. Frankly, I think she secretly runs the place sometimes."

"I see, yes, but she works closely with the objects and the mail?"

Ben crossed his arms, even in his distracted state picking up on the fact that Reg was asking loaded questions. "We all do."

"Mmhm. Well, has anything ever seemed to go missing?"

"You mean besides the whole safe full of valuable objects?"

"Actually, seems to be there wasn't a whole lot that was valuable in there. The last clerk kept an odd assortment of things in there like a voodoo doll, and," he consulted a list at the back of the binder, "a set of false teeth, several ancient 'round the world' letters, and a tiara set with glass stones."

"Really?" This wasn't the first that Ben had heard about the missing items; he had seen the list of items that had wandered off and there was much more on it than that. "Nothing valuable at all?"

Reg waved a dismissive hand. "Oh, of course there was about seven thousand dollars worth of jewelry as well. It was just the other stuff that seemed odd."

Ben shrugged and tried to force himself to relax, knowing that his defensiveness was only going to get himself, if not Sylvia, in trouble. Focusing on how much the little man across the desk irritated him seemed to help him get the image of Moscovich's terrified face out of his head. "Well, if it's gone, it's gone. I haven't particularly noticed anything else."

"Alright. How does Sylvia seem to you? Mentally, I mean."

Ben shifted his weight back and forth on his chair, picturing his assistant's flighty outbursts and dramatic over-reactions to such questions. "I thought this was a review about me."

"Why so agitated?"

"I just...I really don't like talking about people behind their backs; it's dishonest."

Reg nodded sagely and made a note on his pad of paper. "I quite understand, honor and all that, refreshing to find someone around here with your principles. Especially as some might question the relationship between an older man and his young pretty assistant."

For the first time, Ben was thankful that he and Sylvia were unhappy with each other. It made it easier to lie to this man about them having slept together. "Frankly, you've seen how cold she is to me."

"Yes, yes. But one never can tell in situations like this."

Ben rubbed his hands briskly over his face and sat up a little straighter, willing the auditor to believe the line of bor-der-truth he was about to deliver. "Well, we're nothing but colleagues. I thought we had been working towards being friends, but now I'm not so sure. I think perhaps she was simply taking pity on the new guy for a bit there."

"She's a girl. They all have their unreasonable moments. It is probably just *that time of the month.*" The auditor whispered the last to Ben.

Appalled at the man's lack of tact, Ben decided to just agree with him. It was easier than trying to point out where Reg had gone wrong in his entire philosophy of dealing with women. "Sure. Right. Whatever. Is there anything else?"

Reg laughed and leaned back in his folding chair, obviously uncomfortable but trying not to show it. "Of course, haven't even made it to your questions yet."

Ben made an expansive gesture and settled back into his desk chair, willing the little man to hurry up. "Well then, please, let's get this over with."

"Alright, why do you think you are qualified for this job?"

Ben snorted. "Besides the fact that I was hired?"

Reg didn't even bat an eye, just repeated the question. "Yes, why are you qualified?"

"I was a library science major, and I spent a long time working in an antique shop. It's given me a unique take on organization and research."

The auditor scribbled a few notes and then looked back up. "Sounds like a good enough set of reasons to me. And how do you run your days? What's a typical day like?"

The auditor asked question after question, all about the minute details of Ben's days, his methods for handling the property that came through his office. At one point, Sylvia returned with the sandwiches and handed them to Reg. The two men ate in relative silence before Reg picked his pen back up. "So, onwards and upwards, eh? You have access to all these powerful search programs. Are you ever tempted to misuse them?"

Ben crumpled his sandwich wrapper and tossed it in the trash before responding. "What do you mean by misuse?"

Reg leaned forward, eager. "For your own purposes. That sort of thing."

After a split-second hesitation, Ben responded, "No sir, I do not. I mean, not all of the searches so far have been strictly related to the items going up for auction and the like. I've been getting to know the system, trying random searches to see what comes up. So that as we move forward I know exactly how to best utilize my resources."

The man nodded, making more notes. "Well, that makes perfect sense, accounts for some of the things I was noticing. Nothing related, perhaps, to the search for your son?"

Ben went cold. He wanted this man and his chauvanistic antagonism as far from the search for his boy as possible. "What about my son?"

"I hear you've a bit of an obsession going."

"I wouldn't call it that. And no, I'm not using the programs in that fashion. If my preliminary searches trying to figure out the software have seemed related, it's in a strictly subconscious fashion, I assure you." This seemed to satisfy the auditor and they meandered around other subjects for a half hour before the auditor declared their interview was done.

"I think that's all for now. Could you be a gent and send your lady friend in? It's her turn for the grill next." Reg stood and stretched his back, waiting just long enough for Ben to get out of the more comfortable desk chair before commandeering it again.

Ben struggled not to comment on the man's lack of tact and started a new mantra reminding himself of the short time span the man would be sitting there. "Of course. I'll just go do her job in the meantime."

"That's the spirit!" Reg bent back over his notes, scribbling furiously.

Ben found Sylvia out in the shredding area, disconsolately staring at a piece of ivy stationary. "His highness is requesting your presence."

"Mmhm."

He waited a moment and tried again, unsure whether her noncommittal response was due to her lingering distaste for him or whether she was lost in her own world again. "What you got there?"

"Letter to Santa."

"In the middle of summer? Ambitious. What do they want?"

"A life-size Barbie and glow sticks." She dropped it in the shredder and clomped down the stairs, thrusting the partially emptied shredding box into his hands. "Care for a go?"

"Thanks, I'm sure."

He watched Sylvia trudge out of the sorting room and down the hallway, then took himself up the stairs to the top of the shredder. He shook the box out, watching the paper drift down and into the grinding plates that minced the paper. Strips were apparently not good enough; this shredder ground envelopes and letters into a fine confetti. He watched the spinning wheels for a moment, trying to shake off everything from the day; Sylvia's anger, his near-assassination attempt, Reg's interrogation. It seemed the old adage was right, bad things come in threes.

Leaving the machine running, he grabbed three more crates in a go, dropping them at the top of the stairs to pour them into the machine one at a time. As he watched, each one was rendered unreadable, having never been read or understood. The readers weren't supposed to read them, after all. The only person he'd ever seen actually read the letters was Sylvia.

There was a green envelope on top of the next crate, addressed in loopy script to *Poppi* from *Nina*. It was opened, and the letter stuffed haphazardly back inside after the cursory scanning of the readers. It was matching stationary with a small wren watermarked on the back.

Poppi,

> *When are you coming back? Mama says not any time*
> *soon, but we miss you. She cries a lot when she doesn't*
> *think we're watching, and that makes us sad. Please, Poppi,*
> *hurry up.*

> *Nina*

He tried to picture the family, broken, but gave up when all he could imagine was his son's empty bedroom. He threw the letter and envelope into the shredder, followed by the last bin of shredding and watched it all tear.

Now, when somebody actually takes responsibility and tracks down their wayward package, we are responsible for making sure it is then properly repackaged and addressed and sent to its rightful destination. It's such a pity that too few of our residents get claimed. Worse yet are the ones that people just give up on without even trying to find out what happened to them.

~ *Gertrude Biun,* Property Office Manual

The rest of the auditor's week went by in almost the same fashion. He kept the cubicle in the warehouse for himself, interviewing staff member after staff member: readers, sorters, and cleaning staff. He requested ancient files as well as reports and data from the previous few weeks.

Ben spent as little time at the Center as he felt he safely could. Since his office had been commandeered, there wasn't a lot he could do anyway. He transferred some items due for auction into the prep bay, but he couldn't do anything else as all of the spreadsheets and search engines were on the computer Reg was currently using. So he went home, reading and listening to all of the news about Leonard Moscovich he could get his hands on, papering his living room with this new face, a face either terrified by the mobs he was trying to push through or foolishly grinning at some school photographer's camera.

At the end of the week, all the staff members were called into the warehouse for a final review before the auditor filed his report. First, the sorters and support staff, then the readers, and lastly Sylvia and Ben.

Sylvia's review was at noon, right as most of the office workers were headed to their lunch break. She parked a cart from the bullpen beside Ben's makeshift desk and proceeded to the warehouse. Ben opened his mouth to say something encouraging, anything, but she didn't even look at him as she left.

She was gone for almost an hour. Ben had completed the cart full of entries and was eating a sandwich, waiting. He almost didn't notice her come in, she was so much quieter than usual. After placing the sandwich on the table, he stood, brushing off his hands.

"Well?"

Sylvia just shook her head, staring at the floor and went over to the coat rack, taking down her rain slicker.

"Sylvia?"

"It went alright." Her voice broke and she finally looked up, meeting his eyes for the first time in a week. Her mascara had run down her face and the tears were still standing in her eyes.

The anger that simmered against Reg started to boil in Ben's head, and he started towards Sylvia, reaching out a hand to touch her face, but she pulled back. "God, Sylvia, what did that asshole say?"

"Nothing, it's not important. I just—you won't be seeing me for a little bit. I've been given a two-week suspension without pay. I'll see you in a few days, I guess. Unless we run into each other at the market or something like that." She turned and bolted for the door.

He ached to go after her, but he just knew that Reg would take his abandonment of the warehouse as a reason to fire him, so he sat again, slowly, and picked up his empty coffee cup, putting it back down after trying to take a sip. After his review would be a much better time to go find her, and it would give her a little time to calm down.

Reg sent him an interoffice memo that afternoon—instead of walking the ten feet to the break room or handing it to him as he went in and out with the cart—that his review was going to be that evening at six, an hour after his shift technically ended. Ben scowled at the paper, wadded it up, and threw it in the trash. That bastard had another thing coming if he thought he could break Ben's insubordination at the last minute with tricks like that. Passive-aggressiveness only made him furious.

At six on the dot, Ben walked up to the door of the warehouse, paused, then without knocking, threw open the door.

"Mr. Grant, do you know why I've called you here?"

Ben stood at the front of the auditor's desk—his desk—resenting the old, lecherous Sean Connery look-alike in his chair.

"Well, Reggy," Ben started. Reg flinched. "I assume it has something to do with the audit and the reviews people have been getting all day."

"Well, yes." He shuffled his papers and cleared his throat. "Frankly, I'm surprised this place is still running. I'm certainly going to recommend an overhaul in the filing and tracking procedures."

Snorting, Ben sat in the chair and leaned back, arms crossed. Privately, he agreed with the man, but he would rather be damned than agree with him on anything at this point. Not after he put Sylvia through the wringer like that. "And I'm certain they won't go through. To reorg will cost money, and if I've learned anything this last month, it's that the postal service hates spending money. If it works, don't mess with it."

The paper shuffling was a bit more erratic now, and when Reg realized it had started to make him look foolish, he put them down. "But it doesn't work. Things are constantly going missing. There is a whole goddamn safe that is empty that should be full of things putting money in our coffers!"

"Just hold on there." Uncrossing his arms, Ben leaned forward to lean on the front of his desk. "That was before I even got here. I haven't lost an item since. We're pretty sure Mrs. Biun was the one who cleaned out that safe prior to leaving, too. Have you found her to ask yet?"

The auditor wrinkled his nose and looked down. "No, not as such. But we're looking."

Leaning back again, Ben muttered, "Try a tropical island off of France."

Reg frowned. "Say again?"

Ben raised his voice. "I was simply making a suggestion as to where you can put this audit."

The glare that the auditor directed at Ben was meant to be scathing but simply came off as constipated. "Well, if talking about organization and documentation isn't going to make any kind of difference, let's talk about you."

"Yeah, and what about me?"

"First, your attitude has been deplorable through this entire investigation." Reg gave a mighty sniff and gestured at Ben's crossed arms. "Prime example, right here. You've completely closed down, you're treating me like some kind of villain, and you are incapable of taking constructive criticism."

Ben leaned back in his chair and propped his feet on his desk. "Let's just call that a personality conflict. Something about you taking over my space, flinging accusations, and making my coworkers cry has just rubbed me the wrong way."

A flush of red started to work its way up Reg's face, and he struggled to retain his control. "You were *ordered* to offer this investigation your every cooperation."

Ben snorted. "This isn't the army; you can't order me to do anything."

The auditor was almost shouting now, struggling to control himself and leaning forward to brace himself on the desk. "We pay you to do as you're told."

Ben shrugged and smiled. "Well, I haven't hindered you in any way. I've given you access to all of my files and even tolerated working from a ten-year-old laptop. What more did you want?"

The grinding of Reg's teeth was audible from where Ben sat. It was music to Ben's ears, and if it was a precursor to him losing his job, he almost didn't care anymore. It was worth it to stick it to this pompous son-of-a-bitch. "A helpful attitude would have been nice. Your behavior has made it difficult to do my job here."

Ben stopped smiling and checked his watch. "Too bad, you didn't get it. Let's move on, because we're making no headway here, and it's after six."

"Fine. To the heart of the matter it is." The auditor pulled the last sheet of paper off of the stack. It was a claims form, one of the ones that went in the repackaged claims. He turned it over to show Benny's flyer on the back. The next piece of paper was an auction receipt. Again, it showed Benny's face on the reverse. The third sheet of paper was a return-to-sender form. And now there were three of Benny's faces staring up at the two men.

Ben felt himself start to go cold, his heart alternately thundering and whispering in his chest. He couldn't stand the thought of the slimy bastard having been anywhere near anything having to do with his son.

Reg was more settled now, fingers steepled, and he leveled his accusations one-by-one. "You have been making illicit copies, you have been illegally adding these flyers to government forms, you have been littering this office and the auction with these pleas for help, you have been coming in progressively later and later, and you were even reported drunk at the office one day."

Ben tried to speak but had to clear his throat and try again. "I have never been drunk on the job."

"Your coworkers beg to differ. Stop interrupting." The auditor knew he finally had the advantage, had finally found the weakness he had been searching for to try and take this new employee down a few notches. "You have hassled your coworkers, emotionally blackmailing them into participating in your schemes to defraud the U.S. Postal Service for your own ends. You have abused the databases at your disposal that are for the sole purpose of returning lost and insufficiently addressed mail."

There was a twitch in Ben's jaw and his hands were clenched at his sides. Everything the man said was true, but did he honestly think that Ben cared about any of that? That this list of offenses was anything new to him? He had known exactly what he was doing, what he was taking advantage of, and he had no intention of apologizing for it. "Are you finished?"

Reg smiled, satisfied to finally deliver what he considered the knock-out blow. "Almost. To sum it up, you are wasting this department's resources, and you are a menace in the workplace. My recommendation is that you be replaced as quickly as possible."

"Is that what you recommended for Sylvia, too?" Ben stood, leaning over his desk. "Replacement?"

The auditor actually leaned back a bit, for once taking into account that his prey outweighed him by a solid 60 pounds. "Her crimes are much smaller. No, I recommended counseling for her kleptomania actually. To stop her before her crimes escalated into stealing items that were actually valuable instead of mail destined for the shredder. She seemed to take it rather hard." Reg frowned and shuffled his papers.

"Counseling. Of course she took it hard. Do you have any idea of her history?" Ben slammed his hand down on the desk to cut the auditor's response short, causing the man to roll warily away from the desk. "Of course you don't. You never bothered to look into any of the people here, why they do what they do, you just came in and started tearing this place apart."

"If it makes you feel any better, I am also recommending Jillian for counseling. Her habit of talking to that urn of ashes in there is repulsive and a sign of deep imbalance. We can't have anyone here going, as it were, postal." Reg tried to give a grim chuckle and started to put his papers hastily into his briefcase.

Ben stepped back from the desk, aware that he was pushing this little man too hard and couldn't bring himself to care. The only thing holding him back from reaching across the desk to throttle him was the fact that he couldn't look for his son from jail. "So the question becomes, why replace me? Why not the others you deemed problematic?"

Reg stood, straightening his suit jacket over his beer belly. "Because you wasted governmental money in this pathetic attempt to find your boy, and you have been an active menace to other employees here."

"Pathetic?" What little thread of control Ben had managed to retain frayed to the snapping point. "The attempts to find my boy are not pathetic. What's pathetic is you coming in here trying to run everybody's life, thinking you know so much better. You are a prideful waste of humanity who revels in knifing people in their weaknesses." Ben's breath was coming in ragged hisses between his words now.

"Forgive me. What I meant to say is, the attempts to find your boy are not pathetic. Those are simply a waste of time and governmental resources. No," he grabbed his suitcase and started walking quickly to the door, seemingly desperate to put more space between himself and the now furious Ben. But he couldn't stop himself from shooting one last rejoinder over his shoulder. "Benny, my boy, it is you who are pathetic for thinking you can make any sort of difference in this slack-jawed fashion. We're done here. I'll be turning my recommendations in tomorrow. You will be hearing from us." The auditor made a hasty retreat as Ben lunged for the door and just missed having it slammed on his fingers.

Ben turned and stood staring blankly at the back of his monitor, left in the puddle of light from the lamp in his office, the warehouse in shadow around him. The desire to chase down Reg and break his face was slowly fading and he felt limp. Pathetic, that's how people saw him, saw his search. A waste of time and destined for failure. Maybe Reg was right, but what other options were left to him other than to keep going? Reaching over to turn off the light, he stood in the darkness for a couple of minutes before heading to the door.

His eyes ached and he had trouble focusing on Benny's face. His laugh, that wonderful sound that made his heart leap the first time he had heard it. What did it sound like? He couldn't bring it to mind, couldn't make it echo like he once could. He thought he could still remember what his son's hair smelled like right after Jeannie had given him his bath and he had come to beg Ben for one last story before he closed his eyes. Ben set the picture back on his desk and rested his head in his hands. *Please.*

He stood up in an abrupt motion, his chair slamming back hard enough to coast across the room, and he strode to his wall, scanning the pictures and notes, the map, and the twine strung between pins and scraps of paper. He reached up to finger the top right hand corner of the map, the small corner that stuck out from the blue tape holding it to the wall. Yanking on it, he tried to rip the map from its moorings. He only managed to tear a strip from the middle of the map, and so he scrabbled at the paper, pins sticking his fingers, twine connected to other papers pulling them along behind the fluttering roads and byways.

None of it had helped; it had only led him to darker places than he'd ever thought he would encounter in his life. None of his work had done anything to find Benny, he was still just as gone as he was on the first day, only more so because now he was being forgotten by the police and the news cycle. And by his father. Ben was silent as he tore paper after paper from the wall, tears just starting to run down his face.

Sweeping his arms across the walls, he started to keen. More and more of the results of his investigation ended up heaped on the carpet until the wall was bare. He knelt slowly, burying his hands in the paper, sorting through until he found the flyer with his son's face and turned to find the box with the pins in it.

Flipping it open, he sorted through to find a white pin and posted his son's face back in the middle of the bare wall. He stared at it, the hand holding the box falling to his side and the pins scattering across the floor. The patter of them cascading over the fallen paper drew his attention back down to the box in his hand. Twice broken, twice fixed, with brass hinges and chipped parquetry. He could almost see his son's fingers trace across the design, mimicking Star Wars sound effects and rocking on the stool in the store. Almost, but it was gone, along with his laugh and his scent, the sticky fingers pulling at his hair during piggy-back rides. All of it, gone.

A sob tore through him and he threw the box at the wall, watching it break once more. He regretted it immediately and scrabbled after the pieces. "I'm sorry, I'm sorry." Everything he touched, he broke. His marriage, his job, the search for his son, he couldn't even keep from breaking this box over and over again. He didn't even know what he was sorry about, but he couldn't stop saying it, *sorry, sorry* as he slumped against the wall, half buried in the drifts of paper, cradling the broken box.

It wasn't as badly damaged as the last time, the lid had held together where it had been glued before, but the bottom portion of the box was broken in two, and he didn't have any glue, none. He tried vainly to fit the pieces together, wishing he'd thought to pack even one of his travel tool kits for repair work. As it was, he had nothing with which to try and repair anything, let alone a box. But he thought he knew someone who might have glue. If she had paint, she probably had glue. Artsy people kept stuff like that around all the time.

He got up, tripping over the map and stumbled to the door, grabbing his keys, the box cradled to his chest. In ten minutes he was pulling up in front of Sylvia's house, the box still in his hand. He rested his head on the steering wheel for a long second before getting out of the car and weaving up to the door. He rang the bell and waited. He swayed from foot to foot although he'd only had the one drink, his knuckles white around the box. He couldn't tell anymore how much was the alcohol and how much was sleep deprivation and the numbness that had started to settle over his heart and head.

Just as he thought she wasn't going to answer, the door swung open and Sylvia was standing there, her hair straggling out of its pigtails, wiping paint from her hands onto the heavy canvas apron she wore. "Ben?" She reached out one blue-speckled hand and grabbed his arm as he listed in her doorway, pulling him inside. "What is it?" He held out his hand with the cracked box and she took it, uncomprehending. "Ben, I don't understand, you have to talk to me."

"Benny, that was the box I was going to give Benny for his next birthday. He thought it looked like something from Star Wars, remember, I told you? Now I can't, I can't give it to him, he's gone." Ben's voice broke over the last word and he started crying in earnest.

"Oh my god, he was one of them? One of the boys on the farm?"

He shook his head, the motion unbalancing him further. "No." He rubbed his hands over his face and whispered into them, "But I wanted him to be. God help me, I wanted for him to be dead." The numbness started to break apart and all that was left inside of him was pain. Not even any hope left, just a rushing, throbbing pain. A sob contorted his frame and he started to collapse into himself, but Sylvia caught him and guided him to a couch in the front room of the house.

"No, Ben, no. Don't say that. I'm sure you don't mean it." Sylvia hesitantly rubbed his back, her hands catching on the flannel and leaving little streaks of paint. When he didn't respond, simply sat there with his head in his hands, she moved a bunch of ratty art books off of the coffee table and sat in their place.

"Hey," she took his hands and lowered them, then tilted his face up. "Hey there. Why do you think you wanted him to be dead?"

"I asked Detective O'Connor—no I told him—please. Please tell me you found him. And I wanted him to be one of those eleven little boys. So badly. Jesus. What kind of father asks for his own son to be dead?" He wrenched out of her hands and stood facing an easel leaning against the wall. "I wanted him to be there, to be one of those boys tortured and suffocated. Who wants that?" He turned back to Sylvia, "Who?"

Sylvia sat a moment in silence, turning the bits of box over in her hands before answering. "Someone who is tired, Ben. Someone who needs to find closure. I know you, and I know you do not want Benny to be dead. You just need to know what happened. Some hint of a clue. You're driving yourself mad; you already drove Jeannie away. Very nearly lost your job this week because of it. That would have been the second job you lost to your search, remember. You need a reason to let go and move on." She walked up to him, laying her hand on the side of his face. "You are a wonderful father, a wonderful person, and you need to stop torturing yourself. Accept the fact that Benny is gone." Ben turned away and back to the wall. "*Gone*, Ben. But that doesn't mean you're a bad father." She watched him a moment as he stared through the easel, her lips pursed and hands on her hips.

"Ben, can I show you something?" When he didn't respond, she added, "Please?" He nodded slowly and she took him by the hand, leading him into what should have been the dining room of the house.

On each wall there were at least two canvases, sometimes three, with more leaning up against the walls beneath them.

Some were brilliantly colored, others were muted shades of gray and brown, some abstract, some portraits, some with other things on them, such as ribbons, lace, film negatives. But the common theme among them was the fact that each painting or collage was done overtop a layer of letters.

Hundreds and hundreds of letters, painstakingly gathered, Ben realized, as she slowly tipped bins of letters into the shredder. Love letters, letters to Santa, damaged junk mail, formal letters from businesses about overdrawn accounts. Pasted together and used as a canvas for a whole new impact.

Sylvia left his side and uncovered a canvas that was still sitting on the easel in the center of the room. "It was almost done. I was going to show you as soon as I finished, but now seems better."

This canvas had no letters on it. Instead it was papered in flyers. His flyers of his missing son that she had taken those long weeks ago. It felt more like years. He walked up to it, ran his hand over image after image of his son. They were resized, torn, puzzle-pieced together, finally all glued down with a decoupage finish. His son's face staring out at him from a hundred different images. And overtop of this collage there was a portrait.

At first he thought it was his son, but he realized the person in the picture was too old. It couldn't be himself either, it was too young, and the face was the wrong shape.

"Who?"

"It's Benny."

Ben traced the outline of the matured jaw. "Benny's six."

"It's what Benny should be. What he could be. When he's grown."

He picked up the canvas and sank to the floor with it, bracing himself against a wall. "When he's grown. If he's grown. I can't tell the difference anymore." Ben's eyes ached but he couldn't shed another tear. There wasn't any left. "Am I a bad father?" He was asking the canvas, willing the specter of his son to answer, but it was Sylvia who responded.

She slid down the wall next to him. "From what I have seen, I would be blessed to have a father like you. I can't tell you how much I have needed him over the years, needed any parent. What you have done for your son—nobody could do better."

"But I can't find him," Ben whispered, eyes still fixed to the painting.

Sylvia gently took the canvas from him. "It's time to let him find his own way back."

Ben thought about that while he looked at the picture. "But Benny is still just a baby. What if he can't find us? He needs us to find him."

"And if you kill yourself looking for him, what use are you? Your wife may have the right of it when it comes to trying to build a life for Benny to come back to. If you lose your job at the Recovery Center, how will you have the resources to print the flyers? Or even have the databases you need?" Sylvia stood and replaced the portrait on its easel and covered it again with the cloth. Ben made a protesting noise, but she shook her head. "It's not quite done. Come sit with me for a moment." She gently guided Ben back to his seat on the sofa, a wretched floral three-seater that had seen better, paint free days.

Slouching back far enough for his head to rest on the seat-back, Ben threw his arm over his eyes. "I know I'm pushing too hard, I know that. But no one else is looking at all anymore, and I have to make up the difference. I can't stop looking."

"I'm not saying you have to, you just have to realize what you're doing to yourself. You're destroying yourself one sleepless night after another." Sylvia curled up on the cushions beside him and started running her hand gently through his hair. "How long has it been since you slept, really slept?"

Ben shrugged. "That cold I got, I guess. That put me out."

Her hand continued its soothing path. "No, that was drugs and antibodies. When did you actually get a full nights rest and woke up feeling like yourself in the morning?"

"I don't remember. It has to be more than a year ago now. I can't sleep because of the nightmares, and the only thing that seems to help those is alcohol of one sort or another. But nobody is looking, not the cops, not the feds, they all gave up and went home. Just like Jeannie gave up. I can't give up, but I just want to…to rest. Sylvia.."

"Shhh." Sylvia kept up the soothing rhythm and watched as his breathing evened out and his arm slid slowly back down to his lap. Once she was sure he was actually asleep, she pulled the crocheted throw off the arm of the sofa and gently draped it over him. "Sweet dreams, Ben."

Ben woke the next morning to the soft sounds of a brush on canvas. Owney lay under the easel with his son's portrait on it while Sylvia worked on the texture of Benny's shirt. Pulling himself upright on the small sofa, he winced at the knots in his back and legs where he had curled up to fit on the tiny antique. His head throbbed and the sunlight was entirely too bright, but he felt more at peace than he had in a long while. Unwilling to disturb Sylvia as she worked on his son's portrait, he quietly stretched first one leg then the other while watching as she leaned in close, applied a deft stroke and then stepped away from the canvas. This was a different Sylvia than he was used to seeing at the warehouse, on the streets with him, or even last night. She was quiet and steady, her full attention on the work in front of her, and there was a softness to her eyes, a contentment he was loath to spoil.

The rustling blanket drew Sylvia's attention, and she put down her palette and came to stand in front of him, hands on hips. "And how do we feel this morning?" The painter was gone, and he was confronted with an entirely too perky young woman once again.

He couldn't help but notice that there was a small smudge of blue on her nose. "Better, I think. I can't believe I fell asleep here; that was so thoughtless of me."

"Yes, I'd say you'd stopped thinking about an hour before you got here. But that's neither here nor there as my grandmother'd say. Come on, I'll make us some tea." She bustled off, and Ben rubbed his hands over his face, trying to bring himself more fully awake. "What would you like?"

Hauling himself off the couch, he stretched a bit more as he made his way into the kitchen. The terrarium with the bearded dragon sat on her counter, and Ben stared absently through the glass. The lizard glared malevolently up at him and started to puff himself up, but decided to hide in a log instead. You and me both, buddy, he thought. Hiding after his behavior last night seemed like a much better idea than confronting it, but he felt like he was done with hiding from the problem. And what was burying yourself under mountains of useless paper if not hiding from the truth of the matter?

"Anything but chamomile."

Sylvia gave a short bark of laughter, which drew a glimmer of a smile from Ben. "See, a little humor is good for you." After she filled the electric kettle and set it to heating, Sylvia pulled down a delicate porcelain cup, changed her mind, and exchanged it for two enormous clay mugs. These went on the table along with cream and sugar. "You just needed to take a break, recharge. Or maybe have a break, one of the two." She came over and pulled out a chair for Ben

He sank into it slowly. "Still, I'm really sorry."

"Shush." Leaning against the table, she idly rearranged the tea things. "The only way I'm going to be mad about last night is if it didn't do anything good for you. Sometimes you just need to let go of everything and let it all out before you can see your way clear. Am I making any sense?"

"Yeah, mostly." She was right, he did feel empty, but not the same kind of empty that he had for most of the last year. That was a gaping wound, festering and malignant. While it wasn't entirely gone, it felt like the edges had been cauterized, the poison drained.

"Look at it this way, if you're this tired, you won't see something significant even if it reared back and slapped you in the face."

He needed to believe her. If he tried to go one more day like he had been, he knew he would fall to pieces—well, worse than he already had. Taking a deep breath, he admitted to himself, "I don't think I know how to take a break anymore."

The teakettle clicked off and Sylvia went to pour the tea. "I suggest a good starting point is getting rid of the stuff on your living room wall."

Ben thought back to his rampage and grimaced in pain. All those hundreds of hours of work laying in tatters on his carpet. "Done."

Sylvia paused after pouring the first mug. "Really? No fight? I was expecting that to be harder." Once both mugs were full, she put the teakettle back on its station.

"I was so mad, so horrified, I just...I tore them down. I

can't believe I did that, all that work, gone." He blew hard on the tea and was engulfed in a cloud of lemon and mint.

She sat in the chair next to him. "It's run your life for a year, I say good riddance."

Now that, that wasn't quite right. Yes, he could see now just how much his search had taken a toll on him and on his life, but it wouldn't be right to just get rid of it. "You know I can't stop looking. That really would make me a horrible father." He tried to take a sip and burnt his tongue.

She laughed as he hissed, trying to draw cold air over his tongue and she got him an ice cube from the freezer. "I know you can't. Frankly, it's part of your appeal, and if you did stop looking altogether, I would think less of you." The cube plunked into his mug and they both watched it melt in silence. When he tried again, the tea was cool enough to drink.

Ben frowned suddenly as he realized what she had said and tried to meet Sylvia's eyes. "My appeal? So that night, it wasn't just…"

She avoided looking at him and played with her mug. "Just what?"

Ben tried to think of a different way to put it, but couldn't. "Just a pity fuck."

"So *that's* why you got all weird on me. Why on earth would you think I would screw you out of pity?"

"You like lost causes." He gestured at the beardie's cage with his mug and nearly sloshed the hot tea over the edge.

She smiled and shook her head, blowing softly on her tea to cool it. "In animals, yes, it's endearing. In people it's annoying and time consuming."

It had been a long time since Ben had to have this kind of conversation, and he felt awkward and out of practice. "So why did you sleep with me if it wasn't because you felt sorry for me?"

"Because I like you, Ben. You seem to think that when people look at you and your search, all they see is something sorrowful and bad. I see a loving and devoted father with the strength to keep looking." She paused, then added. "That and I think you're super cute."

"Ha, right, thanks." The knot in his chest started to fade at her light banter, though it did nothing for the sorrow sweeping over him in waves.

He still couldn't believe that he'd begged for the detective to tell him his son was dead, but at least now, he somewhat understood why he did. Sylvia was right, he was exhausted, completely drained from trying to do everyone's job—his, the police's, the FBI's. He needed to slow down, as much as that would hurt, as hard as it would be to make the search anything but his first and foremost priority.

Sylvia was watching him quietly from over her tea, her damnably perceptive eyes reading each wave of emotion as it came. He finally got to the point in reliving the previous night where he had driven drunk through the city and crashed through her door a mess and his face burned with embarrassment. "God, Sylvia, I'm sorry I just barged in here like that last night. How are you being so nice about it?"

"We've already covered this: I like you and you needed someone to slap you in the face with your real motives since you couldn't seem to see them for yourself." She took a long sip of her tea before adding, "Plus I was tired of not talking to you. That was hard."

"Well, I owe you an apology for thinking terrible things about your sexual motives. And apologies for coming at you with all this terrible baggage." He paused berating himself over everything that he had dragged her into over the last couple months. "And for dragging you into everything at work." In the mess of the last 24 hours, he had almost forgotten work.

"Not terrible, just misguided. Though apology accepted for being an ass about the sex." She reached across the table and squeezed his hand. "But you shouldn't apologize for having emotions, Ben. They are what make us human. And if you think you got me in trouble at work, look around you, I should have gotten in trouble a long time ago." Ben smiled, looking more carefully at the canvasses that lined nearly every surface of the house. She must have collected hundreds, if not thousands, of pieces of mail, photos, and detritus from the bottoms of the bags over the years. He wondered idly when she had started and how she gotten everything to blend so seamlessly together.

After a moment, he let the mug drop heavily to the table and rounded on Sylvia. "How come when you say this stuff it makes so much more sense than when I was trying to talk to my wife about it?"

Sylvia laughed and used a napkin to wipe up his spilt tea. "Because I'm an outside observer, that's why. You trust my judgment because I wasn't involved in the trauma. Or that's what my shrinks told me. But let's change the subject for a while, let you calm down some more. What do you plan to do now? How was your review yesterday?"

The image of her running out of the office earlier came back with a snap. "Crap, here I am unloading on you, totally forgetting about what happened to you yesterday. Are *you* alright?"

"Uh-uh, you first. What are you going to do? With everything?"

He sighed, slouching in his chair. "I'm not sure yet. I think it's pretty obvious that I need to take a break from the search at least. Not long though. Just long enough to…rest up. I'm so tired I can't even think anymore. You're also right, I can't lose the job, so maybe I'll write a note of apology or something, offer to pay for the copies that went out, promise never to do it again. Maybe then they'll let me stay."

"Which you will."

Ben nodded at her. "Of course. I won't stop looking, nor will I ignore any resources at my fingertips. I think I'll just need to play things closer to the vest. And lay off for a while till I'm sure the Gestapo have stopped looking over my shoulder."

"Sounds like a plan. A good one, too." She dropped a spoonful of sugar into her tea and stirred gently.

"And you?" Ben prompted. "What happened?"

Sylvia waved her hand dismissively. "I've had worse. He hit those whole you're unstable buttons, and, yeah, I was in a snit, but I got over it. These things always blow over. I decided to take advantage of the enforced time off and cash in on a friend's offer to go participate in a show in New York. I met her in college, and she's working for this small gallery now and keeps pestering me to bring stuff up. I figure by then the audit will be forgotten, like it always is. If anyone asks, I'll just say I went on a mental health retreat."

"A show? In New York City? But that's huge, isn't it?"

Sylvia blushed and waved a hand. "Meh, not so big. It's a fairly small gallery, but it is cool. It'd be my first show ever."

"I thought you were in trouble for stealing things from the Recovery Center as is, won't you get in even more trouble if you display those collages?"

Sylvia laughed. "That's the best part about it. I only take things doomed to the shredder, which haven't really been read anyway, or cataloged. How could anyone prove they came from work? I'll just tell people it's all found material; that's real big right now."

Ben drained his mug. "Well, as long as you come back. I don't think I can do this without you."

"What, run the warehouse, find your son, or stay sane?"

Ben paused before answering, giving her question serious thought. "I think it's a little bit of each." He reached out towards her paint-spattered hand and she met him halfway, squeezing his hand briefly before resting comfortably in his grasp on the table.

Sylvia smiled, her eyes once more taking on the soft concentration he had seen while she was in front of her canvas. "Just try and keep me away."

LONG-TERM STORAGE

Things of a personal nature, an intimate or valuable sort, need to spend a bit more time with us. Lock them away for a long while, especially journals, until we can be sure that when we release them to the public, they have lost any potentially damaging power.

~ *Gertrude Biun,* Property Office Manual

Ben sat at his desk and stared at the computer screen, where his cursor blinked idly in the field for the sender's post office, but he couldn't remember what he was going to write. His fingers caressed the number pad on his keyboard, but he had to look at the claim tag four times to ensure the ID was correct. Sylvia was supposed to be back today, and he was too distracted to think straight. Sylvia had been gone for three weeks, overseeing the installation of her art at the friend's gallery and then had a fancy opening and stayed a week longer than she had planned due to the amount of investors who wanted to haggle with her personally over her paintings.

He had missed her more than he thought he would, her smile and laughter. The days at the warehouse went much more slowly and he found himself tempted by the liquor store and his piles of information without her strength beside him. But he had promised her that he would take a break while she was gone, so she wouldn't have to worry about him.

The door to his warehouse swung open unceremoniously and the cart's clatter preceded Sylvia into the room. As she swung into sight with an overly laden cart, Ben stood hastily from his desk and strode to the middle aisle. She glanced up at him and then away, shuffling her feet as she was forced to stop the cart.

"Well?" Ben stood with his arms crossed. He wanted to gather her up in those arms, smelling the sweet rosemary shampoo she had started using, feel her unnaturally strong arms squeezing back, but he wasn't sure how things were going to be between them now, and what exactly she wanted from him.

"Well, what?" She still didn't look up at him and he sighed.

"Well, you're back from New York, and all I get is a 'well, what?'"

She grinned sideways at him from under her newsboy cap. "It's good to be back, Ben, really. Good to see you." She pushed the cart aside and gave him a brisk, hard hug. She let go too quickly for him to return it and turned to her cart.

"I brought you something, anyway, thought you'd like it." She turned back around, and she had the canvas of his son in her arms. "I refused to let the gallery keep it, didn't want to sell it anyway. I think it belongs here, don't you?"

Ben's chest tightened briefly at the site of his son's grown face, but he wasn't swamped with the guilt and anguish he had been four weeks ago. "Absolutely." His hand brushed hers and lingered for a moment before letting her relinquish the collage. He turned back to his cubicle and pulled a stack of missing flyers off the top shelf of his industrial shelving unit and placed Benny there instead, nudging it this way and that to make sure it was centered.

"Perfect." Sylvia wormed under Ben's arm and stood, her arm around his waist.

Ben smiled, gratified at her touch. He rubbed Sylvia's arm, turned her back to her cart, and let her go, for now. The painting had told him all he needed to know. "So, what little treasures did you find for me today?"

Your purchase of this novel helps to support the National Center for Missing & Exploited Children® (NCMEC). The purpose of the Center is to help find missing children, end child sexual exploitation, educate children and communities about child safety and prevention, train law enforcement in dealing with these kinds of cases, and provide support to the victims and families of victims of these horrifying crimes.

The facts as of the last comprehensive survey:

- In 1999, approximately 800,000 children younger than 18 were reported missing.

- More than 200,000 children were abducted by family members and more than 58,000 children were abducted by nonfamily members. The rest of the missing children were either runaways or no one ever found out what happened to them.

- An estimated 115 children were the victims of "stereotypical" kidnapping. These "stereotypical" kidnappings involved someone the child did not know or was just an acquaintance. The child was either held overnight, transported 50 miles or more, killed, ransomed, or held with the intent to keep the child permanently.

- The NCMEC has assisted law enforcement in the recovery of more than 183,000 missing children since it was founded in 1984. Their recovery rate for missing children has grown from 62 percent in 1990 to 97 percent today.

- The AMBER Alert program was created in 1996 and is operated by the U.S. Department of Justice. As of April 17, 2013, a total of 642 children have been successfully recovered as a result of the program.

- As of December 2012, NCMEC's toll free, 24 hour call center has received more than 3,716,044 calls since it was created in 1984. Information about missing or exploited children can be reported to the call center by calling 1-800-THE-LOST (1-800-843-5678).

If you want to learn more or donate to help the Center's efforts, please visit http://www.missingkids.com/

ACKNOWLEDGMENTS

Writing is not near the solitary sport that society would lead you to believe. We rely on a lot of people to make our work the very best it can be before we hand it over to our readers, and I am no exception.

The first person I need to thank is Steve Yarbrough for guiding me through the first draft of *Undeliverable* as my MFA thesis at Emerson College and Pablo Medina for offering advice on where to take the second draft.

The design of the book wouldn't be nearly as awesome without Rebecca Saraceno's help during her Book Design course.

I owe many thanks to J.D. Panzer for tirelessly fielding rhetorical questions and reading more than a few drafts.

Michael Strelow, Scott Nadelson, Russell Rice, and Dave Hansen molded the young student I was into a woman who believed in herself as a writer.

My family is amazing and supportive, and I have to thank them for not telling me I was crazy when I told them I wanted to be a writer instead of doing something with a guaranteed salary.

I would have given up long ago on this manuscript without my readers, Sara DiBari, Karen Shaner, Amy Lewis, Kelly Kamp, Zac Bentley, Lesley Moussette, Erik Fogg, Peter Ireland, Claire Shulz Ivett, Jessica Colund, and Byron Hadley. Then there is Tom at my local post office and his endless patience for my enormous stacks of books to mail.

And, finally, many thanks to all the rest of my friends, too numerous to mention, who never once asked me to stop talking about my writing, and the Indiegogo supporters, named and unnamed, for taking a chance on me and helping to make this book a reality.

INDIEGOGO SUPPORTERS

Special thanks goes out to all my Indiegogo supporters that donated at the "Reader" level and above. You guys made this book possible.

Ester-Catherine Alexander
Anonymous
Joanna & Jonathan Demarest
Teresa Hernandez Gonzalez
Mark Stewart
Jody Wasend
Susan Wurzelbacher
Skip & Paige Yauger

Made in the USA
Charleston, SC
19 December 2013